PRAISE FOR VIVIAN AREND

"If you've never read a Vivian Arend book you are missing out on one of the best contemporary authors writing today."
~ *Book Reading Gals*

"A Rancher's Heart was a spectacular start to this new series and I am very excited to see what comes next for the rest of the Heart Falls crew."
~ *Guilty Pleasures Book Review*

"Brilliant, raw, imaginative, irresistible!!"
~ *Avon Romance*

"This story will keep you reading from the first page to the last one. There is never a dull moment..."
~ *Landy Jimenez*

"Arend became a favorite author of mine because not only does she write about sexy cowboys, she gives us families who love and take care of each other."
~ *SmexyBooks*

"This was my first Vivian Arend story, and I know I want more!"
~ *Red Hot Plus Blue Reads*

ALSO BY VIVIAN AREND

The Stones of Heart Falls

A Rancher's Heart

A Rancher's Song

A Rancher's Bride

A Rancher's Love

A Rancher's Vow

Holidays in Heart Falls

A Firefighter's Christmas Gift

A Soldier's Christmas Wish

A Hero's Christmas Hope

A Cowboy's Christmas List

A Rancher's Christmas Kiss

The Colemans of Heart Falls

The Cowgirl's Forever Love

The Cowgirl's Secret Love

The Cowgirl's Chosen Love

A full list of Vivian's print titles is available on her website:
www.vivianarend.com

A RANCHER'S LOVE

THE STONES OF HEART FALLS: BOOK 4

VIVIAN AREND

A Rancher's Love
Copyright © 2021 by Arend Publishing Inc.
ISBN: 9781989507520
Edited by Angie Ramey
Cover Design © Damonza
Proofed by Linda Levy

PROLOGUE

Twenty-two years ago, July, Silver Stone ranch

Tucker Stewart stood silently beside his uncle Ashton, hands shoved into his pockets to keep from wiggling as he waited to be dismissed. Every time he arrived for his annual summer visit, they went through this same ritual, and while it wasn't getting any easier, at twelve years old, at least now he expected it.

His uncle was talking with *his* bosses, Mr. Stone and Mr. Hayes. Since they were the ones in charge of approving whether or not Tucker got to spend the entire summer, Uncle Ashton always said it was important to make a good impression.

Of course, by now Tucker had realized that everything about his visit was pre-arranged, and he was good to go, but just in case, he didn't want to take any chances.

Not being able to live on the ranch, play with Luke Stone, and fish and ride and pick berries with the rest of the Stone kids would mean a summer that sucked. His best alternative would be tons of time at the local Winnipeg library, and while he liked reading, within reason, nothing *but* reading?

That was a fate worse than death.

"You ready for some more difficult chores this year?" Mr. Hayes folded his thick arms over his chest like a superhero. "I know Luke's been asking to help with the horses more, and he wants you around."

Tucker was tempted to try the pose himself, but his arms were nowhere near that size. No use drawing attention to anything that might make these important men realize that he wasn't very big. He hadn't hit his growth spurt yet, and that was another thing that sucked.

A head poked around the edge of a stall then vanished instantly. Dark brown eyes, a waving ponytail. Darilyn Hayes, which meant the *other* annoying girl who lived on the ranch was around. Because where Dare was, Ginny Stone was certain to be as well.

Another head popped briefly into view above the top of the nearest stall, like a gopher poking its head out of a hole. The mischievous expression on his summertime best friend made excitement tingle in Tucker's gut.

Luke. They'd go fishing and camp on the shore of Big Sky Lake. Maybe they could camp this year by Heart Falls, and go swimming and—

His uncle's hand on his shoulder brought Tucker's attention back to the gathering.

The other two men were examining him, faces twisted up like they were trying not to laugh.

"Sorry," he said quickly, deliberately straightening and meeting Mr. Hayes's gaze. "Yes, sir. I'd like that very much."

"You sure you want to work with the animals? I hear you're good with computers. Maybe there's another job out there for you. Something in research like your parents—"

"No, sir," Tucker interrupted before he could help himself, and the words came out high-pitched and slightly squeaky. He cleared his throat, then tried again, a little deeper. "I want to be a ranch foreman like Uncle Ashton."

Walter Stone grinned harder at Ashton, but he dipped his chin. "Well, if you're going to learn, learn from the very best."

"Yes, sir. That's my uncle."

Joseph Hayes rubbed at his mouth, his low comment directed with amusement toward his partner barely loud enough for Tucker to hear. "I've got no objections. Maybe his manners will wear off on your boys."

"Maybe they'll wear off on our girls," Walter suggested. "Heaven knows where Dare and Ginny learned those words they were skipping to the other day. By the way, Deb blamed me, so I blamed you."

"Having a surprise baby on the way is making you mean, Stone."

"Payback for the year your second was born, when I ended up with all the night calls for way too long," Walter returned. "Slacker."

"Jerk."

"Maybe before the insults veer into territory that will get us *all* into trouble, we could let my nephew go?" Ashton suggested, amusement in his tone.

All three of them snorted as Tucker shifted from side to side, his gang of friends, which now included Walker and Ginny, gesturing wildly from farther in the barn.

"Seems you're good, young man. Listen to your uncle, and get your chores done when he tells you to. Remember, it's a group effort that keeps this place running, yes? No riding without supervision, and no hanging around the new horses. Understood?" Walter Stone offered his hand as if Tucker were an adult.

Tucker solemnly shook it. "Understood."

"Now, get," his uncle said, calling louder as Tucker took off at a sprint. "Don't think we didn't know you were there. Varmints, the lot of you."

"We love you, Mr. Stewart." The sweet chorus rose from Ginny and Dare as Tucker raced past them, nearly bowling into Luke.

"Come on," his friend urged.

Like every year since Tucker could remember, they made their way up into the hay loft over the old, old barn. The musty scent slid from a memory into a brand-new reality, and he was grinning by the time they scrambled over the scratchy bales.

This might be where he lived every summer, but the feeling inside was so much more.

The ranch was the closest thing to heaven he could imagine.

"Over here," Luke whispered, gesturing for them to follow as he crawled on hands and knees through a tunnel nearly three bales long.

Darkness surrounded Tucker, random stalks poking into his arms and shoulders and then suddenly, sunshine. The tunnel emptied into a deep pit arranged right up against one of the windows in the loft wall.

"This is so cool." Tucker stared around him as Ginny, Dare, and Walker plopped out of the entrance one at a time to join them.

Dare reached into a small crack between the bales and pulled out a sturdy blanket, spreading it on the base beneath them. Then they all sat, Tucker leaning against one of the bales. He stretched his legs in front of him as he breathed deeply and peeked at his cohorts in summertime hijinks. "Hi."

"A new foal was born two days ago," Ginny announced. "And I found a batch of kittens that nobody else knows about."

"Dad said that we can camp at Heart Falls, as long as Caleb helps us pick the spot," Luke said at nearly the same time, ignoring his little sister. "Caleb helped build this hideout. Dad said Caleb's getting to be a real asset to the ranch, but he's still a super good big brother, so I know he'll help if we ask."

Walker poked at the golden-toned boards in the wall beside the window. He gave up his task and pressed his nose against the glass to stare into the yard. "I'm hungry."

"Ginny made cookies," Dare added helpfully. "Did you bring them?"

Ginny sniffed. "Of course."

She pulled the bag from her pocket, and for the next few minutes while they talked and caught up, they shared the slightly broken chocolate chip cookie pieces—she'd shoved the bag in her pocket, and crawling through the tunnel hadn't done them any good.

But every crumb tasted like sunshine to Tucker. He never got homemade cookies at home.

Which was why, as excited as he was about the camping, and how cool the hideout was, and everything else he was buzzing inside to experience, he turned to Ginny first.

"I want to see the kittens."

Her instant smile was also part of Silver Stone and memories and happiness. They all scrambled through the tunnel after Ginny, off on their first kitten search of the summer.

Everything was right in Tucker's world.

~

Sixteen years ago, July

THERE WAS nothing worse than being told you couldn't have a thing, Ginny Stone decided.

Her mother, Deb, eyed her hard and handed her another plate to wash. They stood side by side at the kitchen sink, cleaning up the lunch dishes. "Whatever mischief you're currently plotting, stop right now."

Ginny offered an innocent smile. "I have no idea what you're talking about, mother dear."

A loud burst of laughter was the instant response. "Oh, sweetie, you are a handful. But I am onto you." Deb Stone leaned closer. "I also love you more than you know. You're in a tough place, and I get that. But you need to let your older brothers have some space these days."

"So that Luke can go suck face with Courtney Masseny?" Ginny shrugged. "I suppose I don't want to witness that anyway."

Her mom blinked for a second. "Courtney? I didn't see that one coming."

"Please. She's been after him since third grade," Ginny complained.

"And you would know this how?" her mom asked with real curiosity.

"We take the bus every day, Mom. 'The ride to and from school is an education all in itself'," Ginny quipped. "That's what Caleb said the other day in his 'I'm older and wiser than you' voice."

"Caleb *is* older, and hopefully wiser, than you." Mom shook her head slowly. "Back to the matter at hand, your brother Luke...*sucking face*...notwithstanding, you need to remember there's a big age gap between you and Dare and the boys right now."

"Same four years that's always been there with Luke. And only two between us and Walker." Ginny grinned. "I know math isn't my strong suit, but I'm pretty sure I have that part figured out."

"Heaven help us if you ever have to do any real accounting," her mom teased. "Yes, it's the same four years it's always been. But four years works something like magic when it comes to being alive. When Dustin was born, Shayla was already three. They didn't do anything together back then. Now that they're older, they play together a bit more, but Shayla is still able to do more than he is."

"I assume this lecture will eventually have a point." Ginny dodged the snap of the towel her mom cracked at her butt. "Hey, that's not fair. I'm not armed."

"You've got a smart mind, girl, and a smart mouth to go with it. Learn when to use which," her mother admonished. "And the moral of the story is, once you're all grown up, four years won't mean a thing because time seems to compress the older you get. But right now, you're thirteen. Four years between you and Luke and Tucker means you're on this step, and they're over here. Let them be for a while."

Ginny did the math in her head. "You're saying I should leave them alone now, but once I'm grown up, I can bug them all I want?"

Her mother actually rolled her eyes before giving Ginny *the look.* "Go for it. Once you're an adult, you will hopefully have learned how to act and who to spend your time and energy on. They can tell you to go away if they want."

Which meant, if she'd done the figuring properly, Ginny had seven years to wait. "So when I'm twenty?"

"Try twenty-one," her mom said, pulling her in for a hug. "Don't try to grow up too quickly, sweetie. One step at a time. That's the best way to do anything."

Eight long years until she was a grown up. Ginny sighed.

Well, in the meantime, she had her best friend Dare, and

she had lots of time with her brothers, and Tucker, doing regular old fun stuff around the ranch.

But once she was grown, she would tell Tucker that *they* should go kissing behind the barn. If Courtney could wait six years for Luke—*ugh*—Ginny could wait a little longer for Tucker.

~

Thirteen years ago, February.

TUCKER HAD NEVER BEEN in the Silver Stone ranch house and felt such silence. It wasn't the quiet of a barn in the evening, with small animals moving comfortably. Not a peacefulness that spoke of life and potential and daily renewal.

It was the silence of death and loss and pain.

They'd buried them the day before. All five of those lost in the tragic car accident. Walter and Deb Stone. Joseph Hayes, his wife Jacquie, and their youngest daughter Shayna.

With one swoop, death had stolen away Dare's entire family. Tucker's heart ached at the sight of the sixteen-year-old currently wrapped in a blanket and curled up in Caleb's arms. Her tear-soaked lashes rested on her cheek as she breathed unsteadily. She looked lost. So very lost.

Caleb met Tucker's gaze across the room. Only four years separated them, but at twenty-four, Caleb had aged overnight as responsibility for the entire family landed squarely on his shoulders.

Because death had taken both of the Stone parents. Both of the Hayes, which meant everyone in charge of the ranch was gone.

Ashton was still there, and he'd do everything possible, but he was the foreman, not the owner. The ranch now belonged to Caleb, his siblings, and the broken-hearted girl in his arms.

The house seemed eerily quiet without Deb Stone laughing as she called out orders in the kitchen, or shouted from the office for someone to *please* bring her a cup of coffee before she passed out from accounting fatigue. It was strange to glance into the living room and not see Walter Stone in his favourite chair, speaking quietly to one of them in that no nonsense way he had that said firm and fair and yet absolutely loving.

Tucker had hurried to be there for his friends—the people who meant more to him than anyone else in the world. But now that he was at the ranch, he was powerless to do more than deal with chores and fight the tangle inside himself that he didn't understand.

Twenty years old, and this was the first time that death had intruded on even the edges of his world. He was gutted—

How much worse did his friends feel?

Luke sat at the table, back to the room, staring at the wall. Walker paced restlessly in the open space between the kitchen and the mudroom. Eight-year-old Dustin sat across from Luke, his face streaked with red as he stoically tried to stem his tears.

Ginny was...

Tucker glanced around quickly, wondering where she'd vanished to.

Pivoting, he discovered the not quite sixteen-year-old in the kitchen. She had the coffeemaker out and the kettle on. The contents of what looked like half the fridge were spread on the counter in front of her.

Their aunt was in the room, but instead of helping, the older woman sat beside her husband on the couch, the two of them eyeing each other as if urging the other to hurry up and speak.

Meanwhile, Ginny worked. Her face tight, lips pressed into a thin line that was night and day different from her usual happy grin. She had plates out, and sandwiches for lunch in progress.

There. Something he could help with. Tucker crossed the room and silently joined her.

She paused for barely a second before reaching into the cupboard and pulling down two enormous pitchers. She tilted her head toward the freezer. "Can you make juice? There are cans in there."

He squeezed her shoulder briefly, then got to work.

In the living room, Frank Stone cleared his throat. "This is tough, but it's not going to get any easier. Heather and I need to be going soon, so it's time. We're ready to help."

Caleb's voice seemed to have deepened in the past week. A gruff rasp that was chilly and borderline rude echoed in the silence. "So you told me. Thanks for the offer, but it's not necessary."

"You can't do it by yourself," Heather said sharply. "Be reasonable, Caleb. I know you're grieving, but you have to face facts. It's only logical, and it needs to happen now."

It wasn't as if Tucker could avoid overhearing what sounded like a private conversation. Not when Heather nearly shouted the words.

None of them could ignore it. Ginny paused in the middle of stacking sandwiches on a plate, her gaze riveted on her aunt.

"What's she talking about?" Walker stopped his pacing to face the room. A furrow settled between his brows as he tried to figure out what was being discussed.

Heather waved a hand, but Caleb cut her off. "We already had this conversation, and I told you no."

"Son, you're not thinking straight," Frank began.

"He's not your son," Dustin retorted. He abandoned his

chair and rushed across the room to stand beside Caleb as if ready to protect him. "He's my big brother."

"And he's a good big brother," Heather said, softer this time. "But you're young enough you need a mom and dad, and so does Ginny. Which is why both of you will come live with us."

Pandemonium struck. Shouts and questions and outright refusals.

"I'm not living with you." Dustin planted his fists on his hips in a position so reminiscent of Walter Stone, Tucker did a second take.

Frank Stone rose to his feet and jabbed his finger at Dustin. "You'll live where you're safe and cared for." The finger moved toward Dare who blinked hard, hands clenching the blanket as Caleb gently moved her aside so he could stand. "Once social services take that Hayes girl—"

"What?" Ginny bolted across the room like a wraith, sliding in front of her best friend to wrap her up in a protective hug. "Dare isn't leaving us." Her gaze darted to Caleb's face. "She's not. She *can't*."

Caleb pulled them both against his side and squeezed. "Hush. No one's going anywhere. We're a family, and we're staying together." He nodded at Dare to include her in the statement. "Dare as well. I've talked to social services, and to Dare. Luke agrees with me, which means no one needs to leave. Not Dare, not Ginny, not Dustin."

"Except them," Ginny snapped, glaring at her aunt and uncle. "You can leave. Right now, and don't ever come back."

Frank thrust out his hands as if Ginny's comment proved his point. "See what you'll have to deal with? You'll be asking us to take over before the summer hits, mark my words."

Caleb took a slow breath, his frown deepening. The girls and Dustin clung to him like a frayed rope on an old fence post.

Unsteady, wavering, yet knotted so tight they weren't going anywhere without someone expending a lot of time and energy to cut them loose.

Luke crossed to where Tucker stood behind Caleb. Walker joined on the other side. "We'll help take care of them," Luke said quietly but with absolute certainty.

"So, like Caleb said, thanks, but no thanks," Walker added.

That wasn't the end of the complaining or the threats, but Caleb got Luke and Walker to help, and in the end, the shouting and arguing moved outside while Tucker stayed where he was and helped the girls and Dustin get lunch ready.

Eventually, they were all seated at the big family table.

Caleb stared at the stack of plates and bowls resting in the usual spot in front of their father's chair. The chair Caleb now occupied.

He swallowed hard, dipped his chin, and then, like a man preparing for battle, picked up the soup ladle and began serving portions and passing them around.

Just the way Walter Stone had always served his family.

Tucker looked away and wiped his eyes to get control before he lost it.

Caleb carried on until they each had a bowl of soup and a sandwich. Then he sat back, speaking slowly. "This isn't what we wanted, but it's what we've got. And we *are* going to make it work. But I can't do this by myself, and not with just Luke's help, or Ashton's. We've *all* got to do what we can.

"We have to work together. We need to rely on each other, and that's what will make us strong."

"We're Stones," Ginny said firmly, even though her voice hitched a little. "We *are* strong."

Caleb's lips curled into the first smile Tucker had seen in the past few days. "We are Stones. But I don't want us to *just* be stones, rocks on a mountain. We still need to have fun, although I know that doesn't sound easy right now." His gaze skipped to Dustin. "Families have fun together, and I'll definitely need your help to remember that."

"Skipping stones," Luke suggested. "Stacking stones into alien creatures. Stone artwork."

Walker scowled. "What are you talking about?"

Luke shrugged. "Caleb said stones have fun. He's right. I can think of lots of things, when the time is right."

Before him, Tucker saw the family begin to pull together.

"Stone soup," Dare suggested. "That's one of my favourite books."

"There's a book about making soup from stones?" Dustin looked horrified, glancing at the remainder of the soup in the bowl in front of him.

Ginny and Dare exchanged glances then nodded firmly.

"I bet we can get that book from the library," Ginny told Dustin. "Once we do, you and I can make stone soup."

The youngest Stone sibling looked suspicious, but he nodded. "Okay."

Caleb laid a hand on Ginny's arm, squeezing gently as he gave her a nod of approval.

Transition had begun. Tucker took a deep breath and hoped things would continue the best way possible under the circumstances.

That night, he slipped out of his uncle's rooms and returned to the family homestead to grab a bag he'd forgotten. He stepped through the back door, and the barest of noises pulled his attention to the right.

Ginny stood in the laundry room, shoulders shaking. Huge, silent tears poured down her cheeks.

Tucker didn't hesitate. He closed the distance instantly and held her close. This was the semi-little-sister he'd run wild with for years. The one who'd messed with his tent pegs and broken his bike. Who'd resolutely fought to keep up with whatever harebrained stunt he and Luke were attempting, no matter that she was a foot and a half shorter and weighed half as much as they did. Fearless, stubborn to a fault...

Now crying with what sounded like a broken heart, and it was killing him because there was nothing he could do to make it better. No words to say, no reassurances.

She wiggled closer and pressed her teary face against his chest. "I hurt inside."

It came out so shaky they sounded like twelve words instead of three.

"I know," he whispered. "It's okay to hurt. It's okay to cry. Hell, it's okay to scream if you need to, but that one we won't do in the house because it might scare Dustin."

She hiccupped. A small laugh mixed in with the tears.

He patted her back and held her, standing in the clean-scented room, with reminders everywhere still of Deb, of Walter. Reminders of the past that was gone.

Tucker stood and held Ginny, and something inside him twisted with a brand-new understanding.

Silver Stone wasn't simply a place he came and visited every summer. These weren't just people he had in his life for a short time and then moved on. Losing Deb and Walter Stone meant seeing how much more important it was to not only treasure the things he had, but to treasure the things he wanted to have.

He wanted his friendships to stay strong.

He wanted people like the Stones in his life forever.

Down the road, he wanted a relationship like Walter and Deb had shared, not a cold and broken one like his parents had, based on unending unhappy compromises.

Ginny took another shuddering breath before loosening her

hug. Resting her forehead on his chest, she stared at the floor. "I'm sorry I lost it like that. I won't do it again."

"Damn it, Ginny." Tucker lifted her face to his, examining her carefully. Tears were there, but determination as well. As if she were preparing for whatever battle would come next. "You don't need to be strong all the time."

"I do," she insisted. "I won't let my family come apart. I won't let Mom and Dad down." Strong like her name. Ginny stepped back and wiped her eyes with the back of her hand. "I *will* do this. You'll see."

In that moment, Tucker knew that anyone who thought they could stand in her way would be proven very wrong.

He wouldn't bet against her for anything.

1

Current Day, Christmas Eve, Silver Stone ranch

After so long away from Heart Falls, the detour was impossible to resist. Instead of heading straight home, Ginny Stone took the turn off the highway that led to her favourite lookout. She parked her borrowed truck and stomped through the knee-high snow to the bench partially buried in a snowbank.

Staring to the west revealed the town's namesake in all its wintery glory. It was cold enough the mist escaping from the falls had frozen into beautiful lace-like structures. Under the ice, water still flowed swift enough to keep the lake open at the base of the falls. The rest glittered as fading sunlight reflected off the smooth, icy surface. A low rumble shook the air instead of the thunder that would be there in the summer, but it was familiar, and that made it sweet.

Sweet and strange all at the same time.

Ginny had been back a scarce half dozen times over the past three years. She'd taken breaks from her extended journeyman training in Europe to attend weddings, be home for a few key birthdays, and make sure her health insurance stayed valid.

Since July, she'd been back on Canadian soil full-time, but instead of coming home, she'd headed three hours to the north and stopped in Rocky Mountain House to help her foster sister, Dare, deal with newborn twins.

Ginny's gaze drifted to the east. To the large barns and arenas that made up Silver Stone proper. The massive ranch her parents had started that was the responsibility of all their children to make a go of it. The past six months she'd come for short visits, spending time with her nieces and nephew, and trying to get a feel for the changed ranch dynamics now that her older brothers had all married.

Short visits that had been equal parts joyful and discomforting. But now, she was *officially* back. She was home.

Home. What did that even mean anymore?

Like a grown child who'd returned to their elementary school, Ginny's world felt simultaneously a lot smaller and a lot bigger than it had been even a week ago.

Her watch went off, and she hauled herself back to her truck. It was nearly dinnertime on Christmas eve, and she had somewhere to be.

The ranch house looked the same as ever from the outside, except for the number of vehicles parked out front. Ginny hadn't expected so many—in fact, she had hoped to simply slip back without any fanfare.

The volume of noise inside the house was astonishing. But the place was warm and smelled like heaven, so Ginny pushed her way in and quietly slipped off her boots in the mudroom.

Then she stood and looked for a moment.

She recognized most of the faces. Even though she'd left, remaining a part of the family had been important. Between

Facetime calls and photos in texts, Ginny had kept up with the changes, or at least attempted to.

Still, it wasn't the same as being there.

Her gaze went first to try and locate her brothers. The four testosterone driven creatures who had made her growing years delightful and hellish. Typical siblings, really.

She didn't spot Walker, the brother closest to her in age, which made sense since his wife, Ivy, wasn't a big fan of crowds. But the other three were right there in the thick of things.

Caleb, the one who had taken over raising them so many years ago, actually cracked a smile as he set the massive family table. Second-oldest brother Luke and his wife, Kelli, were helping him.

Caleb's wife, Tamara, and her three sisters were all in the kitchen. *Their* husbands debated something enthusiastically from the living room, while Ginny's kid brother Dustin rolled at their feet, squawking with what sounded like death throes as their two nieces pinned him to the floor and tickled.

The tightness inside Ginny eased the slightest bit. Maybe she wasn't sure what she should do next, but she was absolutely certain this was where she was supposed to do it.

"Auntie G, you're here, you're here, you're *here*." Emma, the little blonde cherub who was Ginny's youngest niece, scrambled to her feet and raced across the room.

Dustin gasped as if he might have been stepped on a touch carelessly, but then Ginny couldn't see anything because Emma had jumped up to cling like a burr.

Huge sobs escaped the little girl, her face buried against Ginny's neck. "You *can't* go away again, not for a long, long time."

The sadness in the words were there, but the biggest thing to hit Ginny was joy at hearing her previously silent niece be so forcefully vocal. "Oh, baby. Yes, I'm home and I plan to stay."

Wet but slightly happier sniffles greeted her announcement. Ginny glanced over Emma's shoulder, even as she patted the little girl's back comfortingly.

Everyone in the room looked her way. Niece number two, Sasha, stood nearby. The preteen held out her arms for her hug and kiss and more teary hellos.

It was the best kind of chaos.

It wasn't until after supper that Ginny even attempted to make heads or tails of the crowded room. Tamara and Caleb pulled her aside as everyone else fell into a comfortable routine of clean up and preparation for evening activities.

"I didn't bother to text you an update that the horde would arrive before you," Caleb admitted. "Figured you needed to come home anyway, and a few extra people wouldn't scare you."

"A *few*?" Ginny counted heads as another couple arrived at the back door. A shout of happiness rose from Luke as he raced to greet them, Kelli hard on his heels.

"It's been a perfect storm," Tamara said. "That's Diane and Jack. They're staying with Luke and Kelli for the holidays. My sisters are here tonight, and my dad, because my brothers-in-law's families all made last minute plans—never mind the details. It's a tangled mess, but basically, we've got a full house."

"But we're glad you're back," Caleb insisted, rising to his feet in response to a call for help from one of the less familiar men in the room. "We'll talk tomorrow about your plans. Or the next day. But soon. We've got news to share."

He was gone before she could poke any further. Ginny eyed Tamara who had remained behind. "Are you pregnant?"

"Shut your mouth," Tamara said wryly. "I'm not masochistic enough to do *that* again. No, it's different good news, but you have to wait until we're down to immediate family."

"I am patience personified," Ginny drawled.

"Good, because I am so far behind on Christmas Day prep, it's not even funny. We need to get the kids to sleep before we can put up the tree, and with everyone storming the castle unexpectedly, that's going to take a Christmas miracle."

"Or a really fabulous elf who masquerades as an auntie." This Ginny could willingly do. "Let me take care of the girls. It'll be fun to get caught up, and I can keep them occupied until they pass out."

"If you're sure, I'd appreciate it. Sasha and Emma will be thrilled." Tamara eyed her eighteen-month-old son currently sitting in his grandpa's lap, blinking hard in a desperate attempt to stay awake. "Thank goodness that one will pass out on time."

For the next couple of hours, Ginny fell back into the still familiar, yet brand-new sensation of caring for her nieces.

"Uncle Walker called. He said Santa left some presents for us at his house," Emma informed her as they sat on her bed and worked on dressing dolls in holiday finery. "He and Auntie Ivy will bring them over tomorrow."

"That's good. I'm sure sometimes Santa's sled must get a little overloaded."

Sasha's face twisted through a series of strange contortions, her lips especially grinding together as if she were fighting to keep from speaking out of line.

Sure enough, as soon as Emma slipped away to the bathroom, Sasha scooted up against Ginny's side and dropped her voice to a mere whisper. "The whole Santa thing is old news to me. I mean, the bit about him being everyone, and not a real person. But I'm not sure Emma's figured it out yet, so *shhhh*. I don't want to spoil it for her. Okay?"

She pressed a finger over her lips and nodded decisively.

"I won't say a word," Ginny promised. "I'm a good secret keeper."

The conversation turned to the excitement of tomorrow, and that they'd have not only presents in the morning with Mama and Papa, but that their friend Talia was coming over for a birthday gift exchange—it was all very exciting, and Ginny loved the time to simply relax with the girls.

She'd spent oodles of time with them, from the time they were babies, but being away for three years meant she'd missed a lot of big recent changes. Finding out who they were now was wonderful and humbling.

So much to relearn. So much to figure out.

Lights finally out, goodnight kisses complete, Ginny rejoined the crew in the living room and helped set up the tree as the Stone tradition dictated. Laughter continued to flow around the room, but there were enough people, she easily stayed on the edges. Which meant she spent more time observing and less sharing her own plans.

Only, when she'd covered her third yawn in under five minutes, Ginny found her sister-in-law and quietly let her know she was headed to bed.

"Umm, about that." Tamara's smile looked a little frazzled. "I hate to tell you this, but there's no room at the inn."

Ginny paused. She'd slept in her old basement room the last couple times she'd visited, but there were a lot of guests still milling around. "Want me to stay with Dustin in the cottage?"

Her sister-in-law shook her head. "He's got a friend with him for the next two weeks. You do not need to hang out with a couple of twenty-two-year-olds. Also, Luke and Kelli have their friends staying over, the crew quarters are full. Bottom-line, would you mind crashing in one of the trailers? The one next to the south barn is clean, and there are bedsheets in there."

Tamara made a face. "I'm not sure if anyone got around to actually making the bed, though."

"I can handle that," Ginny promised. She laid a hand on her sister-in-law's arm. "It's okay. I'm *family*. You don't need to guest me up."

Tamara wrapped her in a big hug. "I'm very much looking forward to getting to know you better. I've always enjoyed the time we've had in the past."

"Me, too," Ginny said honestly. "Plus, we need to reminisce in Caleb's presence about how you were a total badass and took him to the ground the first time you two met."

The burst of laughter from Tamara was heartfelt, and Ginny's optimism returned. Maybe this coming back to the family fold would be easier than she'd hoped.

But she was glad to slip away a few minutes later. Away from the rumble of laughter and the sheer presence of people and back into the quiet of the winter night. Ginny grabbed her backpack from her truck and wandered slowly, taking in all the visible changes to the place she'd grown up but been away from for years.

The trailer Tamara had sent her to sleep in was a newer one, parked neatly beside the south barn. Maybe twenty-seven feet long, it looked sturdy yet cozy.

Three goats in their nearby pen watched with wild curiosity, and Ginny saluted as she passed. "As you were, fellow mischief-makers."

She opened and closed the trailer door as quietly as possible though. No use in warning the goats they had a neighbour, or the hellions would find a way to break out and come haunt her in the night.

The trailer smelled strangely good. She'd expected the air to be slightly stale, so the unusual scent was both a relief and a mystery. Bergamot? Coffee? Those two for sure, but something else familiar that she vaguely remembered...

Tired enough to simply want to crash, Ginny stopped in the small living space to get ready. She stripped off her pants, then slipped her bra from under her top, leaving only her oversized tank to sleep in.

"Be free," she mumbled softly, taking a deep breath to enjoy the lack of pressure on her shoulders from the bra straps. Big boobs were a pain at times, literally. "I crack me up."

Her eyes adjusted to the pale glow coming in the window from the yard light, so she didn't bother with turning on the overhead light. She shuffled toward the bedroom area, suddenly wary when a strange, out-of-place sound rumbled her direction.

Ginny cautiously peered around the corner.

Holy shit.

The bed indeed had sheets as Tamara had told her, but they were messed up, scrunched into semi-piles over the long, muscular form of a naked man. He lay face down, his butt on prime display. The edge of fear that had swept in vanished.

Ginny knew her mystery man.

Lying before her was Tucker Stewart, nephew to Silver Stone's long time foreman, her older brother Luke's companion in crime during the summers while they were growing up, and her own personal kryptonite.

What she should do was back away and find somewhere else to sleep.

What she did was stand motionless for far, far too long, simply staring.

Time had only made him more delicious. His face was mostly scrunched into the pillow, but his lips were visible. Strong and full, they parted slightly, a soft rumble an uncharitable person would describe as a snore escaping him.

She didn't need to see his eyes to remember the pale blue shade. Didn't need to see him awake to recall his all too brief smiles, always accompanied by a spark in his eyes, as if he were astonished that she'd pulled an expression from him other than his usual gruff visage.

Nope, memory painted plenty of pictures for the parts she couldn't see. The parts she could? *Holy mother.* Tucker had packed on muscle in the three years since she'd seen him last.

Triceps defined even in sleep, his visible forearm was dusted with a faint layer of light brown hair. His big hand pressed to the mattress where his strong fingers were splayed as if ready to cup her breast.

His big, *talented* hands. Ones Ginny had enjoyed feeling him run all over her. Broad shoulders that she'd dug her nails into as they'd shot together toward a sweaty, dirty, overwhelmingly pleasurable peak.

The curve of his hip teased her vision, one thigh pulled up to protect more delicate body parts. The hollow of shadow that hid his groin made her smile and lift her focus to the star of the show. His ass, the sheet shoved far enough aside to showcase every muscular dip and the straight row of dots scarring his right butt cheek.

Which was how she'd recognized him. *Ahem.*

She'd not only enjoyed seeing his naked ass up close and personal before, but she'd been there when her older brother Luke had given Tucker that scar. Twelve years old and pretending they were hosting a magical duel, Tucker had reacted to Luke's *spell* with determination, throwing himself backward only to unknowingly land full force on a rake.

Tucker was no longer that youngster. Nor the teenager she'd followed after like a love-struck puppy. Not even the serious young man she'd finally convinced she was grown up enough to know what she wanted—which included wild, vigorous sex with him.

Long lean lines, bare skin she wanted to touch…

She must have made a noise, because he woke. His body tightened, which did wonderful things to his ass.

He rolled. Ginny forced her gaze off the tempting bits —*parts*. *That was* not *a bit*—coming into prime display, shifting to meet his eyes.

Tucker blinked, then blinked again, as a dark smolder twisted into place.

"Ginny Stone. Well, well, *well*. Merry Christmas to me."

2

———

$\mathcal{W}$hat a tempting present to show up on his doorstep.

Tucker Stewart curled upright, taking his time to enjoy the vision standing motionless in the doorway of his trailer bedroom.

Luscious was the first word that struck, followed rapidly by *beautiful* and then *holy fucking hell*, because he was totally up shit creek without a paddle.

It had been three years since he'd seen her in person. From eight years old onward, he'd spent most of his summers at Silver Stone ranch, in theory to spend time with his uncle. The truth was probably a lot more tangled than that, but it had meant he had years to build friendships with the Stone children. Especially Luke and Walker, but also the four-years-younger-than-him Ginny and her best friend, Dare.

A few years in the not-so-distant past, something far more physical than simple friendship had developed with the woman before him.

Pictures of Ginny had shown up on his phone plenty over

the past couple of years, forwarded in notes from Luke or Walker as they tried to keep him up to date with where and what their little sister was doing. The messages had made him ache and made him happy. Except for the timeframe where she'd bleached her hair some godawful pink and white shade, and all he could think of was shaking her and telling her to stop messing with perfection.

Thankfully, her hair was now back to its natural deep brown tone, long and curling around her pale shoulders.

Natural, like the full, heavy breasts pressed against the thin material of her tank top. He kept going before he got hypnotized by her nipples tightening under the fabric.

The top stopped just past her hips, the icy blue of her underwear peeking from underneath like a tempting X *marks the spot.*

Long legs with ample curves and muscles all the way down to where the pale pink polish on her toes highlighted the delicacy of her feet.

Damn if he didn't want to eat her up one bite at a time. He'd start at the bottom, get lost in the middle for a long while, then gorge himself on her full lips when he finally made it that far.

A mouth that twisted at the corners more and more the longer he stared.

She folded her arms over that gorgeous chest and met his gaze. "I'm pretty sure my sister-in-law didn't mean for me to find a naked man in my bed. Either that, or she's now my favourite person in the whole wide world."

"Which sister-in-law?"

"Tamara."

"She probably doesn't know I'm here," Tucker admitted. Being amused was dangerous, but the sensation was pretty unavoidable around Ginny. The damn woman had a way of making him lose all mental clarity. "You mind if I get dressed, or do you plan on joining me?"

He'd meant it as a joke, but from the way her eyes lit up —*fuck.*

Nope. Cutting this one off at the pass...

"Back up, Ginny, and let me get some clothes on," Tucker ordered.

Instead, she stepped closer, gaze dropping to dangerous territory. "But I'm ready for bed."

The husky words stroked his cock as firmly as if she'd used her hands.

Screw this. Ignoring the fact he was naked as a jaybird, he moved decisively. Tossed back the covers and slid toward her. A second later he was on his feet, the fronts of their torsos in full contact. Which meant his instantly hard dick pressed to the softness of her belly, and he flashed back to times and places that should never have happened.

But damn if he didn't relive them far, far too often.

Control. Get your goddamned self under control.

He caught her shoulders and kept her right there, skin to skin, heat to heat. It was torture of the most delectable kind. Especially when she stared with that hint of challenge and bravado that pushed his every damn button.

"Having you under me would make for one hell of a perfect evening. Just say the word, and I'll make it happen." Tucker trailed his knuckles over her cheek slowly, then traced her lush mouth with a fingertip. "Only you'd better hope no one in your family gets it into their heads to stop in, because I'm not about to lie to their faces if we get caught burning up the sheets. No more keeping this thing between us quiet."

The sigh that escaped rocked her entire body, but she stepped back and let him pass. "You play mean," she complained.

"You're the one who rightly insisted anything we did was our business and no one else's," he reminded her. "But secrets don't stay secret if we're caught *in flagrante delicto*."

"You're right. Also, stop showing off your damn intellect." But she snickered, gaze still firmly on him as he pulled on a pair of old sweatpants that would have to double as pyjama bottoms. "Looking good, Tucker."

He snorted. "Stop objectifying my brain."

"Ha. It's the least of your *assets*, and you know it."

"Enjoy the Full Monty?"

She let out a forlorn sigh. "Every damn time."

They grinned at each other, and when he opened his arms wide, she dove into them, this time squealing like a little girl. The contact wasn't sexual but back on track with *friends* and *family* and exactly where they needed to be.

Exactly where Tucker hated that they needed to be.

The only good part about being here was being closer than ever before to fixing the travesty of him and Ginny being a no-go for more than clandestine fun. He needed a little more time to update his master plan before he said anything.

No use in rushing before he had everything lined up properly.

Ginny laid her head on his chest. "I missed you. *Jerk.* You're shitty at keeping in touch."

"Me? You were the one on the other side of the world. I wasn't messing with time zones and all that bullshit."

She squeezed him again then sat in the chair against the wall. "What are you doing here? And I don't mean the trailer, but at the ranch?"

"Technological screw up." He settled kitty corner, reaching into his gym bag and pulling out a sweatshirt. He spoke as he dragged it over his head. "Uncle Ashton sent a text at three a.m. that said I needed to get my butt out here as quickly as I could."

Ginny blinked in surprise, her expression immediately sliding to worry. "Is he okay? I didn't see him in the house, but that wasn't out of the ordinary. He's usually around on Christmas Day, not the evening before."

"He's fine," Tucker assured her. "Well, a little less fine after I shouted at him."

It had been the weirdest thing. Tucker's phone shut off between midnight and five except for emergency contacts, and his uncle was one of the few who could get a hold of him no matter what.

Ginny was another, but he wasn't going to tell her that now.

"I tried to get in touch with him, but no answer. After half an hour of fucking around, I figured I may as well get on the road. I waited until six o'clock here to contact Luke, which meant I'd gotten nearly four hours of driving behind me."

"You drove all the way from Winnipeg since this morning?" Ginny shook her head. "Damn, I'm sorry I woke you. I hate anything longer than three hours, and you did over thirteen."

"Roads were good, so I made it a little faster than that." He kept a straight face. "We don't need to tell my uncle about that part."

"Where is Ashton?"

"He's fine. Luke couldn't find him at first, and he wasn't answering his phone. Finally showed up after lunch, and Luke said he was completely surprised to hear I was on the way. He swears he never sent any text."

Ginny pulled a sweater from her backpack and tugged it over her shoulders. "Well, I'm glad he's okay, but that's odd."

"Very. But since I was already mostly here, Ashton told me to come for the holidays."

"I hope you don't need to turn around and drive back in a couple of days."

He'd done it before, but getting to enjoy an extended stay was good for many reasons. "I contacted my boss while I was driving. J&R Stables gave me two weeks off. Said they'd decided to run with a limited staff anyway since the place needs some upgrades done before customers can return. They were having some electrical problems, so it's probably a good thing."

"Well, that is good news." She covered her mouth, but the yawn still escaped. "I'm sorry. I'd complain it's been a long day, but mine wasn't anywhere near as bad as yours."

"It's not a contest," Tucker drawled.

"Ha. Tell that to Luke."

Which made something inside him happy. After many summers spent together, Luke was a good, good friend, but they did tend to bring out the competitive nature in each other.

Her eyes lit up. "I'm glad you're here. It's like a summer reunion, only in the middle of winter. Without sunscreen."

He gestured to the bedroom. "You need sleep. You're less coherent than usual."

Ginny paused. "I thought you didn't want to get caught in the same bed."

"We won't. You'll take the bed, and I'll sleep out here."

"Bullshit." Ginny rose, reaching for her coat. "I'll go find a different trailer to sleep in."

"Bullshit," he echoed back. "This one is all warmed up, which took half of forever, by the way. It's damn cold out there, and it's a waste of time. You get the bed, I'm out here. Then it's all good when someone sneaks around in the morning to surprise you."

Ginny pooh-poohed that idea. "They'll be too busy staring at the Christmas tree and stuffing their faces with Tamara's cinnamon buns to wonder where I am."

She tried to stifle another yawn.

Exasperated, and closing in on his own limits, Tucker caught her by the shoulders and marched her back into the bedroom. "Sleep. There will be plenty of time to torment me in the coming days."

"You should have the bed," she said, but when he glared at her, she tossed aside her sweater and crawled onto the mattress.

Tucker watched her ass. There was no earthly way to resist.

Her head hit the pillow and she tugged ineffectively at the covers. He gave up and helped, tucking her in. Avoiding accidental contact with any hotspots—he was up for fucking sainthood after this.

Ginny's eyes opened to half-mast as she licked her lips. "You're sweet. You know, you like to act all gruff and stern, but really, you're a total pushover."

"Shut up," he said with a laugh, kneeling on the bed beside her so he could lean close and press a kiss to her forehead. "No spilling secrets, remember?"

"Okay." She watched him with those big eyes. "Tucker?"

"Yeah?" He wouldn't bother to make a bed. Just crash on the floor.

"While you're here, can we have sex?"

He swore softly, instantly aroused.

A laugh drifted upward as she stretched lazily, breasts pressing the blanket into dangerous curves. "I won't tell. That will also stay our little secret."

"Go to sleep, you evil woman."

"That wasn't a no," she pointed out, the words fading on a soft exhale.

Tucker firmly closed the door between them. He tossed the quilt on the floor and collapsed onto it. Between the drive and the demon woman sound asleep less than ten feet from him, he was more than exhausted.

He was also done for, because she was right. He hadn't told

her no. In fact, the first chance he got, every wicked thing they could dream up was totally on the menu.

Keeping secrets might eventually kick his ass, but he would walk through hell for another taste of Ginny Stone.

~

ON THE EDGE of waking up, Ginny snuggled deeper into the cozy warmth around her when the trailer door opened. The faint metallic screech of hinges protesting the cold loud enough to carry through the thin panel door of the bedroom.

Her brother Luke's voice rang out a moment later. "Tucker? What the hell are you doing on the floor? Is something wrong with the bed?"

A low groan rose from Tucker. "Close the door. You're letting out all the heat."

"You must have been wrecked last night." Luke chuckled softly. "You forget what a bed looks like?"

Ginny hurriedly crawled off the mattress and made her way to the door. She swung it open before Tucker could answer.

Luke's gaze shot to her, his eyes widening for a second before he slammed a hand in front of his face as if blocking a dangerous sight. "Dammit, Ginny, you're indecent. Put some clothes on before I go blind."

She folded her arms over her chest. "Grow up. I'm more than adequately covered. Besides, they're just boobs."

"They're my *sister's* boobs, which means I don't want to see them." Luke waved a hand at Tucker. "*He* doesn't want to see them."

Oh, how Ginny wanted to say something blunt right then.

Fortunately, before she could put her foot in her mouth, Luke woke up enough to clue into the real issue.

He glanced between the two of them then gave Ginny hell. "What are you doing in here? This is Tucker's trailer."

Tucker was on his feet, deliciously bare-chested with his low-riding sweats barely clinging to his trim hips. "Tamara never got the word I was here, so Ginny got sent out as well. It's okay."

"Damn, sorry you had to crash on the floor." Luke eyed Ginny who had relented and was pulling on a sweater and sweatpants to ease his mortification. "I can't believe you didn't let him sleep in the bed after the drive he'd made."

"I offered," Ginny said dryly, totally amused. "He turned me down."

Tucker's eyes flashed a warning, but his lips twitched at the absolute truth she'd shared.

Luke seemed oblivious to the fact his best friend and his little sister were adults, because he blithely carried on, every bit of sexual innuendo ignored. "If you're awake enough to want food, we're doing brunch at our place at eleven. Come over when you're ready and I'll give you coffee first."

Tucker stretched, muscles rippling dangerously. Ginny couldn't tear her gaze away.

"Coffee is good. Coffee I don't have to make, even better," Tucker offered with a solemn nod. "Give me a few minutes, and I'll be there."

Luke glanced cautiously toward Ginny as if worried that she'd taken off a layer or something. "You too, I guess. Or you could go to the main house and visit with Caleb and the girls. A little like old times."

That was one area Ginny had given a lot of thought and talked over with her foster sister and best friend, Dare. The past six months had given her time to consider the right way to go forward. "Nope. They're building new family traditions, and while I look forward to spending more time with them, I'm not messing with that. You and Kelli are stuck with me crashing your place."

Luke looked thoughtful for a moment then dipped his chin. "Yeah, you're probably right. Come on over, then, and I'll introduce you to Diane and Jack. I don't think you've met them yet."

"Not in person," Ginny said as cheerfully as she could without edging into obviously fake.

"You're in for a treat. They're good people." Luke gave Tucker a slap on the shoulder then headed off through the door, whistling brightly.

Ginny let out a slow sigh before noticing Tucker's gaze on her. His expression was far from her favourite, the one full of smoldering heat. No, this one reminded her far more of some super sleuth determined to get the bottom of all her secrets.

"What?" she demanded.

He stood silently for a moment then shrugged. "Just hit me how strange this must feel for you. Coming back, and wondering how you fit in."

Her jaw must be hanging open. "That was a pretty nail-on-the-head comment."

A wry smile twisted his lips. "I've been in your shoes. It's the same sensation I faced every year, coming to stay for the summer. I'd spend the entire year daydreaming about all the fun we'd have, Luke, and Walker as well." His lips twitched. "You and Dare, when you weren't being annoying little brats."

Ginny held up a hand. "Guilty."

He nodded slowly. "Truth is, I always came back and expected things to change. That Luke would have a new best friend, or that I wouldn't feel welcome in the same way." He stepped toward her, tucked his fingers under her chin, and lifted her face to his. "Know, what?"

She shook her head, the heat of his fingers caressing her skin far too enticingly.

"Never happened. Not once in all the years did I ever feel rejected or left out." He leaned closer, and for one second, she thought he might kiss her.

Instead, he offered her one of his rare true smiles. "You'll be okay, darling. Trust me. Trust *them*. They're your family, and everything will work out fine."

Which is what she'd been hoping and dreaming the entire time she was gone.

She laid a hand on Tucker's chest because being this close and not touching was impossible. The steady beat of his heart under her palm offered balance and strength. "I hope so."

"I know so." He tilted his head toward the bedroom. "Now get your ass in gear and get dressed. I need coffee, plus we're raiding Luke's fridge. Bullshit on this brunch at eleven nonsense. I'm a growing boy."

It wasn't an answer to all her worries, but it was the reassurance she needed, at least for here and now.

Her mother's voice rang in her head, even after all these years. *Do the next thing, sweetie. Sometime the path won't make sense until you do the next thing.*

Ginny grabbed her backpack and went into the bedroom to get dressed. When she came out, Tucker was waiting, his hair damp and freshly combed into place.

"Bathroom's yours." He turned his back and began rearranging things in his gym bag.

She washed up quickly, which meant it was only a couple of minutes later and they were outside on the wintry Christmas Day.

The walk to Luke's house from where the trailer sat on the far side of the barns took them in a wide sweep around the main arena. The morning was cold and clear, and Ginny took a deep breath, enjoying the crisp wintry air settling in her lungs.

"There are a few more changes this time," Tucker noted. He lifted a hand to a brand-new barn with a training yard attached. "Sweet."

Ginny agreed. It was good to see Silver Stone continue to make strides forward. The horses were a huge part of that, but raising them or training them wasn't an area where she had ever contributed much.

She glanced toward the oversized greenhouse tucked to the west of the main ranch home and promised herself she'd take a thorough look later that day. For now, there was so much else she wanted to hear about.

"What about you?" she asked. "What about your changes? Last I heard you were working with the thoroughbred auction house in Winnipeg."

He clicked his tongue. "Ginny, that's at least three updates ago. Now I'm working at one of the stables on the outskirts of town. Gives me some different experience, and they're a very reputable operation."

"You're helping take care of horses for people who stable them there?"

"And I give lessons. A few times we've gotten to do some serious training with animals who need a little extra attention before they make good rides." He kept staring around as they walked. "Every place I've worked is like a tiny jigsaw piece of this place."

"You really should work here," Ginny said. "I don't know why you never applied."

His expression grew solemn. He shook his head. "Timing doesn't always work the way we want." They walked in silence for the final distance, then Tucker gestured her ahead of him up the steps onto the wooden porch outside Luke's house. "Ladies first."

"You just want to watch my ass," she murmured softly as she passed him.

The sputter that escaped him was a reward all in itself.

3

---

ucker was in dangerous territory and hated it with everything in him. Not only did he need to be careful because Ginny seemed primed and ready for mischief, but he had to admit, he was worried.

Like he'd confessed to Ginny earlier, part of him was twelve years old again. uncertain of how he fit in at Silver Stone. The sensation was made worse because he knew exactly how he *wanted* reality to be.

Entering into the warm comfort of the sprawling ranch house gave him another of those *torn between the past and the future* sensations. The scent of coffee and something sweet and spicy drifted on the air.

He automatically helped Ginny take off her coat, hanging it on one of the hooks by the door.

Then he paused because she was staring, her expression somewhere between amusement and an all-out smirk. "What?"

She gave a quick little curtsy. "Thank you for being a gentleman."

It would've made her happy if he'd rolled his eyes, so

instead he caught her by the shoulders and pushed her into the main part of the house. "Coffee first. You're too hard to interpret when I'm low on caffeine."

"Poor baby," she crooned. "Tell you what. I'll get the coffee, you raid the fridge. Luke won't get as cranky if you're the one rooting around in there."

"Deal."

Their entrance into the house had finally been noted. Luke and his wife Kelli were seated on an oversized but ancient looking couch. Across from them on a slightly newer, but equally enormous couch, was a smartly dressed and very attractive couple.

"Tucker." Luke rose to his feet and gestured him over. "Come meet everyone."

The dark-skinned man on the couch rose as well, extending a hand. "Merry Christmas. I'm Jack Emment. This is my wife, Diane Jakarta."

"Merry Christmas to you both. I've heard good things," Tucker said, shaking Jack's hand then reaching over to do the same with Diane. The beautiful Black woman had a mass of tight curls that were braided in an intricate pattern then gathered in a huge cascade over her right shoulder. "You must have an extraordinary sense of humour if you've been hanging out with this guy for any length of time and still like him." He jerked a thumb toward Luke.

"Darlin', Luke and Kelli are two of our favourite people," Diane said, her voice sweet southern honey. "And from the way he's been talking about you, you're one of *his* favourite people."

"That's because he's currently ahead of me in our annual summer *who's better than who* score," Tucker said conspiratorially. "But I aim to change that up pretty quick."

"You also beat me up the last time we fought," Luke reminded him, "But I'm not holding any grudges. Much."

"Not what I heard..." Tucker said before clearing his throat and glancing toward the tree. "Oh, look. Decorations."

They were still laughing as he turned toward Kelli who had leapt to her feet and was now approaching with a grin. He knew her from way back as well. One of the Silver Stone ranch hands, and if he remembered correctly, she'd been around since the summer he turned nineteen. Now no longer a ranch hand, but married to the man Tucker still considered his best friend, her changed situation gave him a kick. "Kelli James—excuse me, Kelli *Stone*. Congratulations and hot damn. You always knew how to pick the best."

She squeezed him tight, patting his back with enthusiasm. "We missed you," she complained as she pulled away and offered an uncharacteristic glare. "The first summer you didn't show up, I got stuck with most of your shitty chores."

"Sorry about that. As much as I loved coming out here, the reality of a full-time job finally reared its ugly head." There'd been more at play than that, but the answer sufficed for now. He glanced to the side, looking for Ginny.

The damn woman was in the kitchen.

"Hey. Ginny. Come and say hi to our friends," Luke ordered.

"Coming. Just have to get some wake-me-up happening." She grabbed two mugs and walked boldly toward them, handing one to Tucker before placing her own on the side counter and going through the whole greeting routine. "It is really nice to finally meet you," she told Jack and Diane sincerely.

"And you." Jack settled back on the couch, arm curled around Diane's shoulders.

Kelli all but vibrated with excitement. "I know I got to hug you last night, but it wasn't enough. Plus, I kind of want to repeat what Emma said and declare you're not allowed to ever go away again. I missed you, girlfriend."

"Missed you, too," Ginny agreed, hugging the other woman tightly.

Tucker was the only one in the room who could see Ginny's face, and the slow breath in she took, and the way her eyes squeezed up tight. Her expression was laced with so much sadness—which seemed odd in conjunction with what the women had both said was a happy event.

He pushed aside his curiosity, waiting until Ginny was free to gesture her toward the only other chair in the U-shaped seating arrangement. "Sit. I'll grab us some food."

"I can wait," Ginny countered. "You sit."

Nothing was ever straightforward with this woman. Still, he wasn't about to start arguing in front of Luke's very classy friends. Tucker planted his ass in the oversize easy chair.

Then he barely held onto his coffee when Ginny settled on the oversized arm rest, hip against his torso.

"How long are you visiting?" Ginny asked Diane.

"Two weeks." Diane glanced out the window and shivered visibly. "Which goes to show how much I love you guys, because there is *snow* on the ground."

"Right? What's up with that?" Jack asked, deadpan serious. "Snow in Alberta in December. Who would have guessed?"

Diane snickered, but she tapped her fingers on his shoulder. "Stop it."

Ginny crossed her legs, which pressed her hip a little tighter against Tucker's side. He could not get over how oblivious Luke and Kelli were to the fact that Ginny was inches away from sitting in his lap.

He focused on keeping his drinking arm steady as he took a sip.

"That's a very shiny looking ring," Ginny commented. "I

seem to recall Luke telling me that you two weren't married, so the *Mr. and Mrs.* must be a recent addition."

"It is. Shiny and brand-new." Jack tightened his embrace around Diane's shoulders, and pointed a finger across at Luke and Kelli. "Took a page from their book and finally managed to sweet-talk my woman into getting hitched without any pomp and circumstance."

Diane curled against him, and pressed her hand with the ring against his chest. Diamonds flashed bright enough to blind. "He surprised me on the way here. We stopped in this cute little chapel before we even hit the airport. The next thing I knew, we'd said I do, and the deed was done."

Kelli snickered lightly. "So to speak."

Diane shook a finger. "You're such a naughty girl."

Beside Kelli on the couch, Luke grinned hugely. "I'm glad it turned out well for you. You have no idea how much trouble we got into with our impulsive *let's hold a wedding right now* moment."

"Really?" Ginny frowned. "Who gave you trouble? I thought it was super romantic that you guys called in Mr. Fields and said your vows down by Heart Falls. Heck, you even had wild horses as witnesses."

"That was part of the problem." Kelli wrinkled her nose. "None of them offered their signatures. We ended up doing a bit of a repeat, just to make everything solid and legal."

"Okay, that makes sense. The government always causes problems." Ginny folded her arms over her chest, coffee cup cradled in her free hand. "I thought maybe someone in the extended family had given you grief, which, hell no."

"It worked out okay in the end," Kelli assured her. "I still count the vows by the waterfall as our real ones."

"Remember, we didn't have you here to defend us," Luke teased. "That means we had to follow the rules."

If Ginny hadn't been sitting on the arm of his chair, Tucker never would've even noticed. But with her body in contact with his, the very slight stiffening of her spine was as loud as a shout.

Jack turned his attention fully on Tucker. "Luke told us about your wild drive to get here. We've always enjoyed our time with Ashton when we've visited. Is your uncle okay?"

That he could answer easily. "Other than being confused why there's a message on my phone that's not on his, he's fine. We spent yesterday afternoon getting caught up. I don't know where he gets his energy from, but I sure hope it runs in the family. I want to be hightailing it around everywhere when I'm sixty. Mysterious text messages in the middle of the night, notwithstanding."

"He's lucky to have you," Diane said softly. "It's good to know you got family willing to come and back you up at the drop of a hat."

"Yes, ma'am. That's the best type of family," Tucker agreed.

It wasn't his imagination. Ginny kept getting more and more uncomfortable perched on the arm of his chair. While he answered questions about his job at the stables and listened to their plans for the next couple of weeks, he wondered what was going on.

It had to be a part of that thing that they talked about before. The whole figuring out where they fit in. They'd both been gone for a long time, but while this had been an important place to him while growing up, it was Ginny's home.

He let the talk swirl around him until his stomach protested loudly enough that they all heard it, and with laughter following him, he made his way to the kitchen to grab a bite to eat.

He had time. Two weeks—although it seemed he wouldn't get to spend as much of it with Luke as he'd hoped, not with his friend and Kelli needing to entertain their guests.

Still, Tucker was at Silver Stone. Somehow that made things better. When Ginny snuck beside him, stealing a muffin off his plate, he decided enjoying the time with whoever he could would not suck.

~

GINNY EXCUSED herself as soon as the brunch dishes were cleaned up. "I'm heading over to the main house."

"We'll be there for supper," Kelli promised. She gave Diane a shake of her head. "It feels strange to plan to leave you here by yourself."

"Girlfriend, Jack and I having a simple Christmas dinner by ourselves? That's one of the best gifts you could give us," Diane insisted. Then she looked slightly sheepish. "And by simple, I mean we bought everything prepackaged and prepared, so before you go, show me how to use your oven."

Laughter continued behind her as Ginny made her way outside, striding quickly down the path to the edge of Big Sky Lake.

She'd walked for under a minute before she realized the snow crunching underfoot seemed exceptionally loud, which made her glance over her shoulder.

"What are you doing?" she asked Tucker, following in her footsteps.

He shrugged and caught up with her. "Not sure. Just wanted to give them some time together."

They walked silently for a moment. The itch at the back of her neck kept getting bigger. Ginny absolutely hated feeling this way.

Screw this. She needed a mental reset.

The truth was she'd spent the past three years facing her fears and getting the next thing done. Simple things like dealing with language issues, or tougher ones like showing up at remote farms for jobs that weren't what they were supposed to be.

Being uncomfortable and uncertain had been part and parcel of her life for a long time. She needed to use that to her advantage. Yeah, the ranch might be her home, but it was as good as a foreign country right now.

She knew how to deal with new places better than the current tangle in her gut would declare.

The other matter making her blood boil could be shoved aside for a little longer.

Impulsively, she bumped against Tucker. "Want to do something fun?"

His stern expression was back in place, but a hint of interest was there. "Dare I ask?"

Oh, she hadn't even thought about *that* kind of fun. Which really was quite a travesty considering she'd meant the question when she'd asked him the night before. At some point, she hoped sex was back on the table. "Nothing dirty."

His face relaxed slightly.

"Yet," she added.

His exasperated sigh was delicious. "Ginny."

"Let's go see Dustin. If he's not there, let's go see your uncle."

"And if he's not there?"

She threw her hands in the air. "You and your damn agendas. If we can't find either of them, we'll go see the kittens in the barn. Because there's *always* kittens in the barn."

He stood, hands jammed into his pockets and a thoughtful expression on his solemn face. "Let's skip Dustin for now. He's got a friend visiting. I know you want to touch base with my uncle, but I spent four hours with him yesterday."

"So, kittens?" she asked brightly.

He dipped his chin. "Kittens."

Climbing into the hayloft, the well-worn ladder smooth under her fingers, Ginny took her time. Savoured the sensation, because this was one of her earliest memories. The sweet scent of hay, a touch of an itch at the back of her nose from the ever-present dust.

The sharp poke through her jeans as she crawled on hands and knees toward one of the favourite nesting places from years gone by.

"Bingo." Tucker's deep rumble sounded nearly in her ear, his strong body inches away as he leaned close to peer into the gap between bales. "Oh, that's a pretty batch."

Ginny ignored the urge to roll under him and instead peeked into the space filled with squeaky baby *meows*. "Whoa. Brown with little white paws, the entire litter. They look like they're wearing snow boots."

The mama cat watched them warily, kittens lined up along her belly in an assembly line as they nursed greedily.

"Let's not touch," Ginny said softly. "This mama looks extra protective."

Tucker didn't say anything. Just lay on his belly with his arms folded so he could rest his chin on his hands and stare at the little furry creatures.

Okay. Ginny copied him, stretched out at his side. Their breath slowed, and the magic of the barn stole over her.

She'd been home less than twenty-four hours. It would take time to feel comfortable again. She couldn't pretend that she'd never left—and wouldn't want to, because she *had* learned a bunch of fascinating things while she'd been away. Too many lessons she eventually wanted to share with the people who were important to her.

But she also couldn't pretend that the world hadn't changed while she'd been away. She needed to get okay with that.

Voices sounded, and she rocked to her feet. She was at the railing looking down in time to see Caleb's family pour into the barn. Followed by—

"Walker. And Ivy. Oh my God. Brace yourselves," she called in warning.

Tempting as it was to use Kelli's old method of throwing herself out of the loft to reach the ground sooner, Ginny was more comfortable keeping her feet under her. It was still only seconds later when she threw herself into Walker's arms.

His hat flew off as he twirled her in a circle, squeezing tight. "Brat. Missed you."

"That seems to be the theme of the day," Ginny said as brightly as possible. "I'm glad to be home."

He caught her unspoken message because he gave her an additional pat on the back before setting her free.

"Come visit us this week?" Ivy asked.

Ginny had plenty of teenage memories of the quiet woman who was now her sister-in-law. Ivy still looked fragile, with her silver-white hair and fine bone structure, yet somehow appeared far stronger than before.

"I would love it," Ginny said honestly before giving Ivy a slightly less exuberant hug than she gave Walker in an attempt to not break the woman in two.

"We're going riding," Emma said as she tugged on Ginny's sleeve. "You too?"

"Sure. We're not going very far, are we?" Ginny checked her watch. "Don't you have a friend coming over?"

Emma's eyes went wide, and she nodded vigorously. "Papa said we'll ride in the arena until after Talia visits."

"Wow, that's a good idea."

Caleb wandered past, chuckling softly, saddle hefted over his shoulder. "You don't have to say that as if it's an utter surprise. I do have them at times, you know."

"Hush," Ginny mock whispered. "Girl bonding. Don't interrupt."

Emma put her hands over her mouth and snickered softly.

A moment later, Sasha was there as well. Only she had her fists on her hips and eyed Ginny with suspicion. "Mom said girls' night out is for bonding, but we're too little to go. Kelli says you gotta put in the work before you get to play."

Some things would never change. Sasha's Kelli-isms were still a thing and still hysterical. "You're right, and Kelli's right. But girl bonding is not *just* for grown-ups. It's also about spending special time with your people, and that means any age counts."

Sasha considered for a moment. "Then today is special because Talia is coming to visit."

"Yep." But an inkling of another idea snuck in.

Ginny stored away the thought for another time, because between the visits from a birthday friend and Christmas presents, the girls probably had enough excitement to keep them bouncing for the next forty-eight hours.

Not too much later, most of the family were up on horseback, easy conversations happening while the horses paced slowly along the edge of the fence line. Two by two, mixing and matching every few minutes.

When Emma's friend showed up with her father, and her father's good friend, Ginny slipped aside to observe a little more closely.

Her gaze went unerringly to Tucker. He wasn't riding but standing near the barn with one foot up on the bottom railing, his arms along the top as he chatted with Ivy.

Another memory slipped in. Tucker knew the entire Fields family, and Ivy, from way back. He really was mixed up in a whole lot of history.

Seeing him there just felt natural. Felt right.

Made things inside of her crave his heat and talented hands.

As if thinking of him somehow tapped him on the shoulder, his gaze swung to the right and their eyes made contact. No one was watching, which meant Ginny didn't worry about hiding the things bubbling inside her.

Two weeks. If that was all she got, then she would do her best to convince him they needed to take advantage of every opportunity.

Shrieks of laughter rose from the left, and Ginny hurried to see what her nieces and their friend were doing.

All of them were in the goat pen, each one cornered by their own personal goat bodyguard.

The rest of the afternoon and dinner passed in a violent rush, until the Stone family once again gathered in the main ranch house. Presents under the tree, new toys and scraps of wrapping paper from the morning's event already in evidence.

But now was for the whole family, and while Ashton played his fiddle and Dustin danced a jig with Sasha, Ginny found herself with eighteen-month-old Tyler in her arms.

The little tyke seemed fascinated by the necklace she wore. Leaning down, he sniffed the ceramic surface like a puppy after her scent. He babbled between times, patting his hand against her cheek and catching hold of the ends of her hair. But mostly it was the ceramic pendant she wore that held him fascinated.

"Whatever you've got in there, I need a bucketful," Tamara said dryly. "I swear it's Tyler catnip. He's usually grumbling by now, but you're working some sort of magic."

"I'll get you one," Ginny promised. "Herbal-based and safe for both kids and pets—I double checked."

Tamara mouthed *thank you*, then headed to beside the tree where Caleb had risen to his feet.

Ginny's oldest brother made a slow perusal around the

room, noting everyone was present. Emma and Sasha had been sent to the basement with a new movie, so only the adults in the family were present. Along with Ashton and Tucker, of course.

Caleb cleared his throat. "Seems as if I made an announcement like this only yesterday, but Tamara reminded me it's been at least a couple years. I've got an update on the state of Silver Stone's finances, and I want you all to listen close."

4

———

*T*alk about being in the wrong place at the wrong time. Tucker lifted a hand to nab Caleb's attention, then gestured toward the door. "I'll let myself out."

Caleb waved him down. "Stay. This affects Ashton, which means he'll need you to bounce ideas off." Caleb's expression kicked up half a notch to a half smile. "I seem to remember you being around a couple of other times that were pretty momentous for us Stones. You deserve to enjoy this one."

Tucker settled back beside his uncle, hands raised in acceptance.

The oldest Stone brother took a deep breath, meeting each of his siblings' eyes in turn. "A few years ago we met like this, trying to come up with a laundry list of ways to save the ranch. Maybe we weren't all here in body, but together, we shared ideas, every single one of us. Because that's how we said we would do things. Ever since that first family meeting after Mom and Dad died, when I promised we'd stay together as a family. It's been a hell of a trip, but between hard work and a bit of luck, we're in a brand-new place now."

Dustin frowned. "I thought the finances had been doing well ever since the breeding program took off."

"That was a turning point, yes. But I've got more news for you." Damn if he didn't outright grin as he caught Tamara's hand. "Oil and gas rights just delivered. Tamara's brother-in-law owns the company that will be utilizing the claim, and he's generously set us up with a more than typical share of dividends."

A chorus of questions and excitement raced around the room.

"We struck oil?" Kelli asked. "I haven't seen them drilling anywhere."

"Because we chose areas that are less accessible, thus less visible. With the new technology Finn's team is using, it works to our advantage."

"So we have...*oil* on Silver Stone?" Ivy was tucked in the corner as usual, but her eyes were bright. "Isn't the price of oil down, and the cost of production up?"

"Everything that goes around comes around, but part of those pricing issues come from corporations wanting the lions' share." Caleb nodded, but his grin remained solid. "It's a good question, but the bottom line is that we were doing well without the discovery, but now we have a buffer. This gives us a solid financial base that means dreaming a little."

"And we'll never have to sell?" Dustin looked on the verge of tears, emotion obviously getting the better of him.

Caleb dipped his chin firmly. "We may still have ups and downs, because this is ranching, and we never know what weather and life will throw at us. But we're good at dealing with those emergencies. I wanted you all to know that we've now got the opportunity to think about a different future."

Luke nodded, happiness shining bright as he considered what that meant. "We had the breeding program on slow mode, but if there's more money in the budget, we could increase pace a little."

"Major repairs that we've been holding off on or making do —those should get tackled first," Tamara suggested. She gestured toward Ashton. "I bet you've got a list."

"Not that big," the man said pointedly. Tucker's uncle leaned back in his chair and folded his arms over his chest, but his expression was one of outright pride. "It'll be good to loosen the purse strings a little, but I haven't felt hard done by. You've run this place well, Caleb." He glanced and included the rest of them in his praise. "You've all done well, and I'm proud to have been a part of it."

"We've been lucky to have had your expertise all these years," Walker returned steadily. "This is really good news, Caleb. But it's a little unreal."

"It's not going to change anything overnight," Tamara said firmly. "We wanted you to know now so you can get into that dreaming part we mentioned. Are there things you've been holding off on that you'd like to do? Not just for Silver Stone, but farther. In Heart Falls, or beyond."

"You want to go to school for a while, figure out where, and we'll make it happen," Caleb said to Dustin. "Think on it."

Kelli waved a hand from where she sat next to Luke. "What if there's nothing to change? As in, we already have all the money we need and are pretty happy with how things are?"

Luke chuckled, picking up her hand and kissing her knuckles. "Asks Miss Heiress, who repeatedly turns down every gift her grandfather offers."

"Money doesn't buy happiness," Kelli insisted.

"You're right," Caleb said with a nod. "We don't plan on changing things up massively or trying to hit the lifestyles of the rich and famous. But we can breathe and enjoy life more. Enjoy each other as family. That's something to celebrate."

"Agreed." Walker stepped forward and pulled Caleb into an embrace, patting his back firmly. "Thanks for everything you've done over the years."

The entire room turned into a series of hugs and brotherly shoulder pounding. Tucker was proud to celebrate with them.

Something inside was building, though. His deep need to be a part of this family more than just on the periphery. He wanted so much.

It was time he pushed past the dreaming to action as well.

Fortunately, Ashton decided they should leave the Stone family to spend the rest of the evening by themselves. He nudged Tucker's arm. "Come with me. Wouldn't mind some time to talk."

Which probably meant his uncle wanted to toss around ideas on ways to improve the ranch.

Tucker said his goodbyes, stopping to shake Caleb's hand. "Sometimes luck does come to good people."

Caleb shrugged. "If it hadn't happened, like Kelli said, we would've been perfectly happy." His lips curled upward. "But I'm not turning it down. Not the chance to give Tamara and my kids a future with a bit more ease."

"Like I said, good people." Tucker dipped his chin to Tamara and headed after his uncle.

GINNY'S EARS WERE RINGING. She wasn't sure if it was because blood pounded through her hard enough to echo inside, or because the house had finally quieted down.

After Caleb's momentous announcement, the family continued to chat for a little longer, but then Luke and Kelli left to rejoin their guests. Walker and Ivy slipped away, her brother pausing to kiss Ginny's cheek and give her a squeeze along with a reminder of her promise to visit that coming week.

Tyler was asleep, and the girls were still watching their movie.

Ginny remained behind because, truth was, the whirling emotions inside her ran the gamut from joy to full-on anger, and she needed to deal with that last one before it became something bitter and sharp.

Confession was the only honest thing to do with people she loved so much.

Tamara settled in what had obviously become her corner of the couch, close to her husband's easy chair. Caleb brought her a cup of tea, and she blew him a kiss. "Thanks, hon."

"You're welcome." Caleb turned to Ginny. "Here's yours. It's not as good an herbal blend as you used to make, but it's close."

She took it carefully before sitting on the couch opposite the two of them. "Can we talk?"

"Of course." Caleb lifted the footrest on his chair and leaned back with a contented sigh. "You've got to have all sorts of ideas. I'm excited to hear them once you've had a chance to make a list."

Ginny felt like shit for not following that trail. Her big brother was so obviously thrilled at the good news he'd shared that evening. She was as well, and yet...

Should she put this conversation off for a while longer? What right did she have to dump her anger on him now?

They can't fix it if they don't know it's broken.

Her mother's voice arrived, as always, right when she needed it. Guardian angel or just a really well-balanced psyche that knew when enough was enough?

Ginny sighed.

Tamara's gaze sharpened, and she spoke before Ginny

could. "What's wrong? I know we haven't had that much time together, but it's clear something's bothering you."

Ginny nodded then met Caleb's gaze straight on. "Why didn't you tell me when things got bad with the ranch?"

Caleb blinked. "We did. We called and got your ideas about ways to—"

"That was at the eleventh hour, when the options were a miracle or selling out." Ginny spoke slowly, but her usual firm optimism had changed to a nearly quivering whisper. "I wasn't here, and I should have been."

"You were taking part in a once-in-a-lifetime opportunity—"

"—that would have meant nothing if we'd lost Silver Stone." Her throat was closing up, but she had to get this out. "In some ways, it feels as if my work means nothing anyway, because I wasn't *here*, wasn't part of the family to deal with the worry and the day-to-day struggles."

"I didn't want you to have to face that. None of us did." Caleb leaned forward on his elbows, every bit of attention focused intently on her. "You were a part of us, though. Your calls and visits were highlights for everyone."

"I'm glad to hear that, really. But still, there was a solid year and a half where things could have gone badly, and you never told me. I was even home for a month in the middle of that time, and no one said a word." She shook her head. "Maybe you didn't want me to face that worry, but by not telling me, you left me out, Caleb. You didn't give me the chance to be a part of the solution. To be here to help make things easier to face."

"You would have had to give up your apprenticeship."

"And I would have done it in a heartbeat. Because I'm a part of this family, and I want to be here for you. You've always been there for us. Finding out later that I wasn't a part of it doesn't make me feel protected. It makes me angry. I should have been told."

Tamara had sat quietly throughout the entire conversation up to now, her grip on her cup growing tight enough that her knuckles turned white.

She put the cup down and faced Caleb. "I never knew this."

This time he turned his confused glance on his wife. "Knew what?"

Tamara gestured at Ginny. "That your sister wasn't fully aware of the challenges we were facing. We talked about her all the time—about the things she could do to help when she got home, with the gardens and other areas. But it sounds as if you never passed on any of those thoughts."

"They were plans for down the road." Caleb's confusion grew deeper. "I'm lost." He shook his head as he looked at Ginny. "I've been trained a little better since you left in the fine art of listening when someone is telling me a thing, so I'll start again. Ginny, we never made you aware of how bad things were —for reasons that made sense to me at the time. You're saying that was the wrong decision."

He paused and gave her a chance to respond.

"It was." Ginny swallowed around the knot in her throat. "I am so happy to be home. I am so happy to have a home to return to, and I know that's meant a lot of work and sacrifice on all your parts." She included Tamara in her comment as well. "Please don't think I'm ungrateful. This isn't about that at all. And your good news is incredible, and I feel as if sharing this is a childish rant, stomping all over the beautiful cake you've presented me. But it's been burning up inside me for the longest time, and I don't want it to taint anything we do going forward."

"Hell, kiddo. I'm sorry." Caleb got to his feet and opened his arms. "Come here."

She was in his embrace a moment later, tears falling freely. The safe, secure place in her brother's arms felt right—

But she wasn't a child anymore.

"I didn't leave to go traipsing across the countryside on a holiday. I know gallivanting across Europe sounds exciting in concept, but in reality, it wasn't always. It was damn hard work, and at times I was scared. Or I'd finish up the day dirty and exhausted, same as if I'd been at home. But I *wasn't* at home, and I would've been if I'd known." This time she said it clearly. No quaver in her voice, just complete honesty. Then she didn't shout, didn't demand, just calmly finished. "Please don't leave me out again. I need to know *I'm* valuable to you. And protecting me by keeping me ignorant isn't the way to show that."

"I promise," Caleb said, his voice a low rumble against her temple. "Of course, I can't promise I won't screw up at all, because making mistakes is what big brothers do best."

"Ha." She let out a long breath. "I'm sorry for dumping on you tonight."

"Trust me. I'm far happier we've dealt with it now before you've got a full supply of herbs at your disposal." Caleb snorted as she dug her fingers under his ribs. "Your magic elixirs are dangerous, witchy woman."

Tamara raised a brow.

Ginny smiled sweetly. "Laxative tea. I don't even remember what he did, but he deserved it."

Two little girls zipped into the room, running full tilt into Caleb as he released Ginny from the hug.

"Dad, the movie was so funny," Sasha shared.

"Sasha giggled so hard, water came out her nose," Emma said softly, hands pressed to her mouth.

It was impossible not to feel the joy radiating from these two. Ginny dropped to a squat and examined Sasha closely. "Doesn't look as if there's permanent damage."

Sasha made a face so reminiscent of Caleb it was eerie. "It was water, not glue."

Behind them, Tamara snorted. "That's a very specific observation that I don't think I want any more details about. You two go with your daddy and get ready for bed. I'll be in to say good night in a minute."

"Good night, Auntie Ginny," Emma said, turning her face up for a kiss. "You'll be here tomorrow, yes?"

"For a whole lot of tomorrows," Ginny promised.

One more hug from Sasha, and an impulsive additional hug from her big brother. Caleb pressed a kiss to her forehead. "I'm glad you'll be here tomorrow, too."

The girls swirled away, bright happy leaves dancing around the tall sturdy figure of her brother.

Tamara laid a hand on Ginny's arm. "Here's where I apologize. I screwed up big time."

Ginny shook her head. "You said you didn't know. I don't hold you responsible for a mistake Caleb made. Plus, I get that it *was* a mistake, and he meant well. This is done, and we can put it behind us."

"You're right, and we will move past this, but I still need to apologize because I should've known better." Tamara looked sheepish. "You've heard the saying *assume* means making an *ass* of *u* and *me*?"

Ginny nodded.

"You and I have talked plenty over the past couple of years. Technology can leave something to be desired in terms of dealing with nuance. But I never brought up anything regarding financial or work plans because I assumed you would when you were ready. I thought Caleb had you up-to-date, and you were dealing with other priorities."

Hell. "You thought I chose to stay away rather than come help?"

Interestingly, Tamara paused, her expression pensive. "You know, I can honestly say I didn't jump to any conclusions as to why you weren't coming home. I haven't spent the past couple of years thinking ill of you, if that's what you're worried about. You'd made a commitment and you were sticking to it, and I—honestly—admired you for your bravery and the risk you'd taken to go somewhere so far away."

Ginny took a shaky inhale before confessing, "It was damn far away at times."

It seemed sister-in-law hugs were just as soothing as big brother hugs, although a lot squishier. Tamara wrapped Ginny up tight and squeezed, holding on for dear life. "You're home now. This *is* your home, and I'm sorry that I did something that made you feel even the least bit unwanted or unnecessary."

"You're pretty easy to love," Ginny admitted. "Adding in all the other wonderful things about you, such as you're in love with my brother and my nieces, and you made a really cute baby. Plus, you can cook like hot damn."

Tamara laughed even as she grabbed a box of tissue and held it out. "There's something special about sisters. I can always use another in my life."

Ginny mopped up her face then sat, finally taking a drink of the tea Caleb had made her, letting it soothe the tension in her throat.

"Next thing," Tamara said, "before I have to go tuck in the munchkins. I suggest you keep living in the trailer for now."

Astounded, Ginny lost her words.

"Because I was thinking," Tamara continued. "I know you used to have the room in the basement here, but I don't think that's a good long-term solution. Dustin is in the cottage where I understand Dare used to live. Dustin's got a friend staying with him for the holidays, so we can't kick them out yet, but there's no reason why he can't move to crew quarters eventually."

"If Dustin doesn't mind, I would love the cottage," Ginny admitted. "Dare and I have been best friends since forever, so I spent just as much time there as I did in this house."

"I don't think Dustin would mind. I have a feeling he might be off on the road himself sometime in the near future," Tamara said. She dipped her chin. "Okay. That gives you a little more grown-up living space for the next couple of weeks. You're free to stop in any time, though, plus come use the washer and dryer whenever you want. But I'll tell the girls the trailer is off-limits. That's your space."

Ginny opened her mouth to say something about the Tucker situation when Tamara held up a hand.

"Before I forget."

She reached under the couch and pulled out a narrow briefcase-shaped object and offered it to Ginny.

The package was wrapped in parchment paper that looked age-bleached and faded in spots. The card on top featured Ginny's name in a handwriting she hadn't seen for over thirteen years.

"Oh my God." Ginny traced a finger over the letters.

"I found it while cleaning out boxes that had obviously been packed since the accident. There were a few others all wrapped up, with names on each of them. Your mom was a really good advance planner, so this is from her. To you."

The weight of it in Ginny's lap was like an anvil. She looked up and saw compassion on Tamara's face.

"I don't think I can open this right now," Ginny admitted.

Tamara nodded. "Take it with you. Let it sit for a while if

you need, and if you want some company when you do unwrap it, let me know. Or Caleb—he would do absolutely anything for you."

Ginny was getting choked up again. "I know. He's the best, he really is."

Tamara smiled, blinking away her own tears. "Kind of partial to him myself."

"We need to stop this," Ginny said with mock complaint. "I am the fun sister, and you are the get-it-done head chickie. We are *not* the weepy girls."

"Head chickie?" Tamara snickered. "I will take that over many other nicknames you could've come up with. Give me a hug before I go rescue Caleb from getting begged into reading *just one more chapter* for the seventh time.

A final hug, and Tamara disappeared into the back of the house. Ginny picked up the three abandoned tea mugs, washed them and left them in the drainer. She pulled on her boots and coat then carefully loaded the present from her mother into a reusable grocery bag to protect it from the snow falling lightly outside.

She headed back to the trailer, where, because neither of them had done anything about it as far as she knew, she would eventually find Tucker.

One part of the tangled knot regarding coming home had been handily dealt with and completely solved. Thank God. Ginny had hoped it would be that simple. But it had taken a lot of mental and emotional energy to up and confess how she felt, and now she felt drained and so, so tired.

Only with the shock of adrenaline from the ghost from the past present she carried? It didn't matter how tired she was, energy vibrated through her.

Wired. To. The. Hilt.

She actually snorted in amusement as she climbed the

stairs to the trailer. Poor Tucker. He wasn't going to know what hit him when he got home.

~

ASHTON'S PLACE WAS COMPACT, only a little bigger than the crew quarters for the hired hands. Tucker looked around the two-bedroom, motel-like space with interest.

Ashton's bedroom sat to the left, the second bedroom set up as an office space on the right. Between them was the bathroom. In front of all of it was an open living space with a small kitchen on one wall and a kitchen table big enough to seat four card players. Clean and tidy with minimal clutter, it was Ashton to a tee...except for one thing.

Nearly every single bit of space on the wall with the bathroom door had a colourful macramé hanging pinned on it. They were pretty, and well-constructed. It wasn't that they were gaudy...

Okay, with that many, it was no longer charming, but slightly ridiculous.

Tucker hadn't said anything the day before, but now it was impossible to resist. "You've taken up arts and crafts in your spare time?"

Ashton put the kettle on, pulled out a pack of beef jerky and threw it on the table. "They're gifts. How the hell do you tell someone to stop giving you things?"

Tucker sat himself at the table. "You tell them *thank you, but stop*?"

"Sure. Tell me you'd say that to Emma. 'Please stop drawing pictures to put on my fridge.'"

"Emma did not make the macramé," Tucker drawled.

"Annoying woman," Ashton grumbled.

Which answered the next question Tucker would've asked.

There was only one female Ashton described in that tone of voice. Ivy's grandmother, Sonora Fallen. Matriarch of the local Fields family and perpetual pain in Ashton's side.

"You should just admit you like Sonora," Tucker said.

"I'll confess if you do the same," Ashton shot back instantly.

Oh, hell. His uncle was not talking about Tucker confessing to an admiration for Sonora.

Tucker attempted to play innocent. "Don't know what you're talking about."

His uncle glared. "Don't waste my time pretending you haven't been mooning over Ginny Stone since she grew up. Plus, I'm damn sure that sometime in the past years that mooning became more than just wishful thinking."

Not the comment Tucker had expected. Not from his uncle, at least.

At some point he figured Kelli, or maybe Tamara, would ask some pointed questions, because too many times that day alone he'd caught himself gazing obsessively at Ginny whenever she was around.

But his uncle? *Hell.*

Tucker leaned back and stretched out his legs. "Surprised you're not warning me off."

"So you admit it?"

Tucker nodded. He held up a hand quickly. "But nothing happened between us until she was old enough. I wouldn't do anything improper. I swear it."

A very unexpected snort escaped Ashton. "Son, that's the last thing you need to reassure me on. I'm pretty damn sure she seduced you."

Well, fuck. "What?" Tucker shook his head. "No. Don't answer that. I don't want to know."

His uncle looked far too amused. "If you don't have it on your calendar in triplicate, it doesn't happen. And that girl is a pile of trouble— Correction. That *woman* is a pile of trouble, and she's always known her own mind. I'm not about to read you the riot act when you're both grown adults who can make your own decisions."

Thank goodness for small mercies. May as well straight up admit to one part then—not the sex, though.

Tucker shrugged. "Yes, I like her. More than like her. If it were possible, I'd be doing what I could to make things between us a reality."

A confession he had never expected to make to this man. Ashton had always been a good uncle, but this wasn't the type of conversation they usually indulged in.

"That's what I figured. So as a part of that dreaming Caleb just talked about, I have a proposal for you."

Curious. Tucker leaned his elbows on the table. "Go on."

"Since I know you like to have things plotted out well in advance, an annoying habit you got from your parents that has persisted in spite of all my attempts to break you of it, bust out your spreadsheets and get working on this." Ashton folded his arms over his chest. "You're right. I am interested in Sonora" — he stuck a finger in Tucker's face— "and you are not to repeat that to *anyone*. But that means at some point I want to be ready to do the next thing."

"Makes sense. What does that have to do with me? Or Ginny? Or spreadsheets?"

His uncle offered a sly grin. "I want you ready to take over as foreman when the time comes."

5

———————

I want you to take over.

The words echoed in Tucker's head, damn near rattling his brain. "You want to retire?"

"Eventually. I don't want to stop completely, but I'm getting up there," Ashton admitted. "I like what I do, kid, but I like it less at five a.m. after being up until three a.m. dealing with one disaster or another. That's a young man's task, and I left young a bunch of years ago."

Tucker sat and let this new information roll over him. He mixed the idea of what Ashton was saying up with the goals he'd had on his own books for a long time and came up with a brand-new reality.

Seems they were going for blunt. So be it.

"I had planned to ask to be brought on full-time as your apprentice the summer I turned twenty." Tucker watched his uncle do the mental math and his expression grow sad. "Yeah, that's the year we lost the Stones and the Hayeses. They'd mentored me a lot to that point, along with you, and Walter had pretty much told me that was the next step. But with the accident, Caleb ended up raising not only his family but Darilyn Hayes as well, and no way could they afford to take me on. So I bowed out of that idea."

"That accident turned so many people's lives upside down. Damn drunk drivers. Damn them to hell." Ashton shook his head then met Tucker's gaze. "Truth is, that would've been perfect timing."

"We can't change the past. But I haven't sat idle since then," Tucker assured him. His comment to Ginny earlier that day came to mind, about how all of his past job experiences had been a slice of Silver Stone. That had been deliberate on his part. "Since I couldn't be here, I did what I could to learn elsewhere. I'm not ready to jump in and take over today, but I've got a good base."

"Damn right, you do." This time Ashton's expression was full on approval. "I wondered why you weren't staying on at one place for longer than a year or two. Had me worried for a while that you had restless feet like Ginny."

Tucker had seen Ginny's face as she stared up at the loft ceiling and all but melted, sinking into the comfort of the familiar old barn. He wasn't sure that she'd really had wanderlust either, but that wasn't the topic right now.

"Let me pull together an official resume," Tucker offered. "If you think this is something Caleb would approve of, we need to set a start date so I can talk to my current boss and give my notice."

"Caleb told me years ago to hire someone and start training them at my discretion. Since all that time I put in over the years ensured that you didn't grow up to be an asshole, I think I can work with you." Ashton raised a brow. "You're more like me than my brother."

"I'll take that as a compliment," Tucker said dryly. His relationship with his parents was pretty much nonexistent.

His uncle looked him over, hard. "You have much to do with your folks recently?"

"No." Tucker raised a brow. "When was the last time you touched base with your brother?"

"A month ago," Ashton returned before making a face. "Like talking to a brick wall. An unhappy brick wall."

"Because they *are* unhappy. Nothing can be done unless they both agree with every decision, which means they keep compromising their way into bullshit that makes both of them miserable."

It had been a struggle for Tucker to figure out even part of what made his parents tick—their priorities weren't even remotely logical to him. As if he'd been switched at birth with a far more down-to-earth couple's offspring. Knowing the truth, though, had made it easier to deliberately step even farther from his parent's sphere of influence on his life.

After a quick mental check to see if he found even the slightest bit of *give a damn* lingering—which he didn't—Tucker shrugged. "They made their choices, which clearly don't include me."

"I know they're bad, but—"

"They don't care," Tucker interrupted, stating the truth plainly. "I made a last-ditch effort last October and suggested I'd drop in over Thanksgiving. They told me they already had plans, and if I showed up, there would be an odd number at the table."

His uncle cursed softly.

Tucker had enough other people in his life who did care to make up for his parents, including the man now before him. "I've made my choices as well. I lean toward simple and honest manual labour. You taught me the value in that—you, Walter, and Joseph, before they passed on. You've done more for me over the years than my parents ever did. Let me be there for you now. I'd love to work for Silver Stone, but I'd also love to make your life better going forward. So, thanks for the opportunity."

Ashton dipped his chin, leaning forward and slapping a hand on the table. "Then it's decided. Get your paperwork together so we can make it official, but as soon as you're done with your work out east, we'll get you started. I won't say anything to anyone but Caleb. We'll let the rest of the crew and family know once you've got a date."

He held out his hand, and like in the old days, Tucker shook it firmly, looking the man in the eye. "I won't let you down."

"I know you won't, son." Ashton sighed heavily, leaning back in his chair and closing his eyes. "Now, get."

Tucker chuckled. "Getting."

He stepped outside into the snow and cold, mind spinning with the change of plans and the possibilities that lay ahead of him.

Son.

It was true. Walter, Joseph, and Ashton had all been more father-like than the man who'd sired him. Both his parents were cold, bitter people. The less impact they had on his life going forward, the better.

He was halfway to the trailer when he realized that after the initial comment about Tucker and Ginny, his uncle had never mentioned the woman again. He was three quarters of the way to the trailer when Tucker realized not once that day had he mentioned to anyone about the double booking of their quarters.

He was on the steps of the trailer and walking into the warmth before he acknowledged this was exactly where he wanted to be. Coming home to Silver Stone.

Coming home to Ginny.

The furnace was running, the air around him warm. He slipped off his boots and glanced around for a sign of the woman. "Ginny? You awake?"

"In here."

He paced to the door of the bedroom and peered in.

She sat on the bed, pillows propped up behind her back. Pale pink pyjama pants covered her long legs, paired with a colour-coordinated tank top. She had fuzzy slippers on her feet and a blanket loosely draped around her shoulders.

Her gaze was fixed on the faded yellow envelope in her hands.

"What's up?" he asked quietly, making his way closer so he could settle at the foot of the bed.

All concerns about their sleeping arrangements were ignored, because he'd rarely seen that expression. It was the lost and tired and scared expression that Tucker knew Ginny Stone hated to the core of her being. The one that said she didn't have enough energy to deal with something.

The breath she took was so big it made every bit of her body rise slightly. "Tamara found a present. It's been hidden away for years." Ginny met his gaze, moisture in her eyes. "It's from my mom."

"Holy shit," Tucker whispered even as he moved closer, sliding in beside her and slipping an arm around her shoulders. It was instinctual to offer comfort even as she continued to hold the envelope in the air.

Her hand shook and the paper trembled.

Ginny curled against his chest. "I have to admit it. I have never quite understood what the word discombobulated meant until now. Dis-com-*bob*-ulated. Sounds like uncomfortable fellatio."

He snickered. "Ginny."

"If I don't joke, I'll cry," she admitted. "And I'm only partly kidding because, holy hell. I did not expect this on top of the rest of the day."

He tugged the envelope from her fingers, amazement and wonder meshing as he spotted the still-familiar handwriting on the envelope. "Are you sitting here trying to brace up enough energy to open it?"

She waved a hand toward the side of the room. "The rest of it is over there. An entire box from the past, and no. I do not want to open it right now. I kind of want it to not be there. Not be in my brain, not be a possibility. Because I want to open it so badly, but I'm scared."

Tucker cradled her closer, the warmth of her torso contrasting with the cold in her fingers and arms. "Dammit, Ginny. How long have you been sitting here?"

"Don't know."

Screw this. He adjusted position until she was damn near in his lap. He pulled the throw blanket over them both. "Did you call Dare?"

The two of them had been thick as thieves for years and years. If anyone could talk Ginny through this, it would be her sister.

Ginny rubbed her cheek on his chest. Slowly, almost like one of the kittens in the barn. "Thought about it. It's Christmas day, Tucker. I already messed up Christmas for one of my siblings. I didn't want to add to anyone else's stress."

"Who'd you mess up Christmas for?" he asked in surprise.

Ginny sighed again. An enormous sound as if she were a hot air balloon releasing all its steam. "I gave Caleb shit for not ever telling me that the ranch was in financial trouble."

Utter shock slipped in. "You're fucking kidding me." She tightened in his arms, and he hurried to reassure her. "That wasn't directed at you. You never knew things got tight? No one told you?"

"Nope." She patted his chest. "You big strong types feel the need to protect delicate little creatures like me." She tilted her head back. "It's okay. He apologized, and it's done, so no more indignation required on anybody's part. I shouldn't have even told you. I'm *not* telling anyone else. It's over and forgotten. I mean it."

She sat up and pressed a hand against his cheek.

"I won't say a word," Tucker promised without being prompted. "But I'm glad you told me. That's an awful lot of emotional crap dumped on your plate all at once."

While he understood far too intimately the need to protect Ginny, he still retained that image of her from that long-ago day. So stubbornly proud to be able to give to others. So insistent that she *would* be strong.

Discovering she'd been left out of family details would have been like sticking a fillet knife in her. Heck, he'd been pissed when his uncle hadn't said anything until Tucker had browbeat him into spilling the beans about what bothered him so much.

Oh.

Oh.

The teasing comments from Luke about Ginny not having been there must have cut deep. That was the frustration he'd seen on her face earlier.

Now she turned those big emotion-filled eyes on him again, but it wasn't frustration, and it wasn't sadness. The depths sparkled with the mischievous sexual creature who had him tangled up so tight he didn't have a chance to resist.

"What's that look for?" he asked cautiously.

She wiggled until she straddled his thighs. Her perfect ass rested on him, the heat of her sex very close to where his cock rose behind his jeans. "We need to talk."

Crap. His hands were on her hips, and his far too eager

fingers had found their way under her pyjama top. Bare skin blazed hot against his palms as he slid them to her waist.

Involuntary, really. He wasn't doing this on purpose.

"I forgot to tell anyone about the mixed-up sleeping arrangements," he confessed. "Slipped my mind."

Ginny slid her hands off his shoulders and down to his chest, fingertips swirling tiny circles over his pecs as she all but petted him. "One of us should have written it on a to-do note, because it slipped my mind, too. In fact, Tamara informed me this trailer is all mine for the next two weeks. A no-kids-allowed zone."

Wasn't that a tidy bit of temptation?

Tucker wanted to shake his head to get things to line up properly, but he was rapidly losing the desire to be smart. What he wanted was to focus on here and now. In losing himself in pleasure and making Ginny happy as well—at least two or three times.

Only, was that the right decision? Because while he was fully on board with taking this wherever it needed to go tonight, he had a bigger picture to plan.

He was moving to the ranch. He was finally able to work at the one place where he wanted to remain full time. All of which created the perfect opportunity to make a play for Ginny, long-term and forever.

He was pretty sure that wasn't the kind of thing that should be started with another episode of their ongoing fling.

Ginny stroked her fingers through his hair, easing in closer and meeting his gaze straight on. "Two weeks. Let's give in and enjoy the hell out of each other for the next two weeks. Be honest, you know you want to."

Crap. This wasn't just temptation, this was temptation on a silver platter.

Ashton had said not to tell anyone about the potential

change in job situation until Caleb had been informed. And Tucker *was* here for the next two weeks, no matter what he arranged with his job back in Winnipeg.

A soft chuckle escaped Ginny's perfect lips. "You're thinking too hard."

"The devil's in the details," he warned her even as he slid his hands around her torso to massage the tight muscles in her lower back. Screw it. She liked the truth? He'd give it to her. "I like sex with you. I like fooling around with you, and I am fully on board with sleeping with you."

AFTER THE EVENING with all its tension and pent-up emotions, Ginny savoured the bubble of amusement that struck. "I really adore how your list started at sex then progressed down to sleeping together."

His lips twitched as if fighting against a smile. "I'm honest. When I picture you in my bed, neither of us is getting any shut-eye."

"You've pictured me in your bed?" Dear God, where had that sex kitten voice come from?

He stared at her lips. "Don't ask questions you know the answer to, darlin'."

Shocking how good that made her feel. "Are you on board with the sexing idea?"

Heat radiated off him as he slid his big, talented hands back to her hips and then, oh hell *yes*, dragged her closer until the thin layer of her pyjamas rode over his jean-clad crotch. "Yes, except we have one slight problem."

Which Ginny guessed was the fact he wasn't kissing her yet. Or that neither of them had stripped off their clothing, or that the bed wasn't shaking as he enthusiastically pumped into her.

"Only one?"

He tucked his fingers under her chin and lifted until they were face to face. Lips inches from touching. "Got any condoms?"

Ginny swore in at least five languages, which caused Tucker to laugh, far too much amusement in his tone.

"I take it that's a no." A second later, she was under him, flat on the bed. Bulging biceps braced on either side of her, Tucker rested his hips between her thighs and settled enough to set her heart pounding. "I guess that means I need to get creative."

Yes, please, with sugar on top.

Only Ginny had ideas as well. "Take off your clothes," she ordered, tugging ineffectively at his T-shirt.

Tucker gave her a little more of his weight, effectively pinning her in place. "I'm in charge," he informed her.

"Ha," she barked. "Right up until I wrap my lips around your cock. Then we'll see who's in charge."

Glory, hallelujah, an actual smile slammed onto his handsome face. "Even with your lips around my cock, it'll still be me."

He all but growled the words, and goose bumps rose. Tucker Stewart large and in charge was a magnificent thing.

Only, if she'd bet that he'd turn things down-right dirty in a hurry, she'd have lost.

What she got instead was her face cupped gently between his palms, his gaze sliding over her features. Lingering on the corners of her eyes before dropping to her mouth.

Did she look as if she'd been crying? With emotions running on high, she must be a—

Tucker kissed her, and all the tangled, battered thoughts fled, leaving behind nothing but sweet, rising passion. A slow, intimate entanglement, his mouth nuzzled hers followed by tiny nips with his teeth before the pressure increased and he stole his way between her lips. Controlling her instant response, easing her with him at what was a far more restrained pace than she would have set.

The finish line was in a different place this time. So be it—

Ginny let go.

Maybe not for good, but for now, she pushed aside her worries and fears. Shoved back the sadness she'd carried from being gone for so long and feeling on the edge of her tightknit family. An outsider looking in, welcome but not really a cherished member.

Strong fingers grasped her chin, opening space between them. Tucker's all too astute gaze back on her. "You with me, goddess?"

Instant happiness leapt in. He was the only one who used that nickname. "I am. Just dumping some baggage."

Seriousness flickered in his eyes. "I can help you dump it faster."

He stripped her top over her head and pulled off her pyjama pants, leaving her naked.

Cool air traced over her skin, but his gaze—nothing but scalding heat. He pressed his palms to her waist again, but this time, the smooth caress continued all the way up until his hands were on her breasts.

A happy sigh escaped him. "I missed you. And you."

He flicked a thumb over one nipple and then the other as he spoke, and Ginny outright snickered. "For a second there I thought you were talking to me. Did you name them yet?

"Mine, and Also Mine."

She was still laughing when pleasure rippled through her and twisted the sound into a moan. Tucker lifted her breasts, pressing them together. He placed his mouth unerringly over one tight nipple and danced his tongue over and around, alternating sides until tingles spread over her torso like a starry net.

He closed his lips and sucked, and a sharp line of need rushed directly between her legs.

"I missed you, too." The soft confession came out unbidden. She didn't want him to stop, though, so Ginny stroked her fingers through his hair and encouraged him to keep nibbling on her breasts.

Only he pulled away, his serious expression back in place. "I missed you as well. For real."

He had their lips together again before she could worry that she'd killed their momentum. Instead, the heat between them continued to grow, but so did another pocket of contentment and wonder.

Her old friend was here. Her sometime lover, yes, but a friend first and foremost. That was the part she didn't want to miss out on.

A friend she planned to make feel very good tonight.

"Take off your clothes." She whispered it this time instead of demanding.

Tucker sat back, reached over his head, and stripped off his shirt.

So much warm skin to caress. So much muscle to shape under her fingers as she scrambled up and reached for him again. "You've gotten pretty pumped, dude. It looks good on you."

"Started training with the local bronco crew. I bulk up too much to be any good on the circuit, though."

Ginny skimmed her fingertips over his right pec and shoulder, cupping a wide-open hand down his biceps and triceps. "You went out on rodeo?"

He scratched his fingernails over her skin lightly, the corners of his mouth turned up again. "You really want to talk about this now?"

"Just making conversation," she teased.

"Need to give your mouth something else to do," he countered.

She went for the button on his jeans. "I'm game."

He pushed her hands away but took care of the details himself. Inch after inch of smooth skin exposed as the jeans fell away.

Inch after inch of his erection revealed as well. Hard and jutting toward his belly as he tossed his clothes aside.

But when Ginny reached forward, intent on claiming her prize, she was once again crowded back against the mattress. Tucker loomed over her, all stern and sexy. "Stay put."

Slowly, so slowly, he lowered. Heated skin met heated kisses, and all her worries truly fell away.

This was what she'd missed the most. Not the sex, but the intimacy of it all. His tongue teasing hers before stealing away to torment the spot under her ear, the top of her collarbone, the swoop of her breast up to her nipple.

The entire time Tucker kissed and nipped, he rubbed against her, his hard body hot and possessive and perfect.

He slid a hand ahead of his lips, cupping her sex firmly. More heat, rubbing his palm slowly against the sensitive spot at the apex. As he suckled one nipple into his mouth, a finger pressed through her curls and into her wet core.

Tucker's forehead met her torso and he breathed shakily. "You are so fucking wet."

"You get me excited," Ginny admitted. "You're pretty much a wet dream machine."

That got the snort of amusement that she'd hoped for.

It also got more than she bargained for, because in a heartbeat, slow vanished.

Tucker dropped between her legs, put his mouth over her sex and went to town. He pressed long hard strokes with his tongue over her labia and between. Then sharp, quick flickers at the peak, and her clit all but buzzed a warning of the rapidly approaching storm.

He slid his finger back inside, still teasing, and the tingles expanded even farther.

Tucker added another finger, stroking slowly, then faster, rubbing in exactly the right spot until her hips were all but vibrating.

"That's it, beautiful. Come all over my fingers. Show me how you're going to squeeze my cock the next time we fool around. Because I'm going to take you hard. Bend you over and push into you until I'm buried deep and then I'll fuck you until you're boneless."

His fingers—so deep inside. So full. Teasing and stroking and—

Ginny broke. Her orgasm rushed, swirling for a second before becoming a million stars escaping in a cosmic explosion.

Tucker swore, adjusting position to kneel up on the bed beside her. He had his cock in his hand, pumping furiously as he stared down. Gaze jumping from her breasts to her mouth, to between her legs where she lazily stroked herself to keep the rumble of pleasure going.

"*Fuck.*" The thick head of his cock peeked out from his hand over and over. His abs tightened even more as Tucker's head fell back, semen flying over her hips and stomach in pale white lines as he pumped his release free.

Perfectly dirty. Dirty and perfect.

Tucker sank back on his heels, chest rocking with each sharp inhale as he worked to catch his breath. "Damn, woman."

"I know, right?" Ginny stretched her arms overhead, pulling them back as her knuckles banged into the trailer wall.

He smirked. "Tight quarters."

"That's what he said."

Which triggered another of his rare smiles. "I like that you're a dirty girl," he admitted, "only I was more focused on the fact there's not enough room to take you in the shower and clean you up."

"Ravish me against the wall, more likely," she teased. "You did that the one year, remember? When we met in Banff."

"Trust me." Tucker leaned over and grabbed his T-shirt, sliding it over her belly in a careful clean-up caress. "Every single one of our escapades is burned into both my brain and my retinas. You are one sexy woman, Ginny. I have zero problems remembering every wicked moment we've shared."

She waited until he was done, then tugged back the covers and gestured him in. "After you."

Tucker paused to pull on his boxer briefs.

Ginny curled up on an elbow and watched with gut-happy satisfaction. "Feeling shy? Want me to pull on my pjs?"

"Hell, no," he said quickly, joining her on the mattress. He arranged them until she was wrapped up in a Tucker burrito, naked back to his front, the long length of his cock under the fabric pressed to her backside. "Just making sure there's at least one barrier in the way so I don't start thinking I'm having the dream of the century and discover we've gone somewhere we don't want to go without a condom involved."

"Good idea." Ginny relaxed into him. "Tucker?"

His answer came slower. Softer. "Yeah?"

"I'm glad you're here. In Silver Stone, but also, that you're in bed with me." She'd never been one to hold back. Why start now?

"Me too. Now shut up and go to sleep before I get cranky."

"How can you get cranky after you just—"

He covered her mouth with his hand, nuzzling her neck as he whispered gently, "Shut the fuck up, goddess."

She snickered, then licked his palm.

Tucker was still chuckling softly as she nestled in and fell asleep.

6

***

An insistent buzzing tickled in Ginny's ears. She was so cozy and warm it was hard to pull herself awake and even harder after she realized the reason *why* she was so comfortable was the sleek muscular form of Tucker against her side.

They had both rolled to their backs, but their legs were connected, heat cocooning in the space around their bodies.

Buzz, buzz, buzz.

When another second set of alarms went off, this time across the room and accompanied by a strange rattling noise, understanding kicked in. She had messages, and Tucker's phone, on the other side of the room, was also going off.

She slid from under the covers and grabbed hers first, peering at a series of messages lighting up her screen from Dare.

She ignored them for a moment and headed across to where Tucker's jeans lay abandoned on the floor. His phone buzzed again, rattling against the linoleum. She stole the phone out of his pocket and caught a glimpse of her brother Luke's name.

Ginny glanced at the bed.

Tucker stretched lazily, pale blue eyes looking her over with rising heat. "Put the phone down, and I'll find a better way to wake you up," he promised.

Ginny resisted the urge to flip the device at him. Instead, she reached into his duffle bag and pulled out one of his T-shirts, slipping it over her head as she grinned. "I think you should answer your messages. Just so my brother doesn't get it in his head to come over here for the second morning in a row with a wake-up call."

Tucker shot upright, thrusting his hand forward. "Yeah, good idea."

Ginny bounced onto the bed and across his lap first, diving in for a morning kiss before she could think better of it.

He didn't seem to have clued into the concept that morning breath was bad, and just the pressure of his arms around her as he hugged tight—not a thing wrong with that scenario.

She scooted back quickly though, just in case. "My sister's messaging me. Let me see what she wants."

The two of them must have looked a sight. Rearranging pillows so they were propped up sitting comfortably in the bed to check their phones.

"I swear to God we must look like one of those social media disaster ads. *No one communicates anymore...,*" Tucker muttered softly, but he still thumbed open his messages.

Ginny snickered then glanced down to see what Dare had spewed at her.

Dare: *It's seven o'clock, wake up, wake up.*
Dare: *Boxing Day, and I've got a million things I need to do, but I want to talk to youuuuuuuuuu.*

Dare: *Wake up, sleepyhead. I can't imagine you've got anything happening over there that should've exhausted you so much that you're still sleeping.*
Dare: *Ping*
Dare: *Ping*
Dare: *Okay, I'll stop now, just in case you actually are still sleeping. Lazy butt. Message me!*

Ginny chuckled as she messaged back.

Ginny: *Motherhood has not increased your patience any.*
Dare: *I'll have you know I'm extraordinarily patient in some areas. You are not one of them. The Coleman gathering today is at Whiskey Creek ranch for Boxing Day shenanigans, as Lisa would say. What mischief are you up to?*

Ginny glanced over at Tucker who was making funny faces as his thumbs moved over the screen. Oh, there were a few things that she wanted to *do*. Speaking of which—

Ginny: *One. I told Caleb what I was upset about, just like you suggested, and everything's cool and over and forgotten.*
Two. Tamara gave me a present from my mom that's been packaged up for nearly fourteen years.
Three. I'm currently in bed with Tucker.

She hit *send* with gleeful delight.

Tucker elbowed her in the side. "The expression on your face right now is downright evil."

"Talk to my brother and ignore me. I'm having fun with my sister." Ginny ordered. She leaned closer, though, peeking at his screen. "Are you telling him about us?"

He sighed. "I guess that means you just told Dare where

you are, yes?"

Before Ginny could answer, her phone went off with three rapid pings in a row.

"I'll get back to you on that," Ginny told Tucker.

On her phone, Dare was blowing things up.

Dare: *Holy shit*
Dare: *That's for all three of your bombs*
Dare: *Did you have fun? Did you stay safe?*

Of course Dare would focus on the Tucker part of the occasion.

Ginny: *Yes, mom. Safer than a certain* other *person I know.*
Dare: *Stop it. We used condoms. Anyway, was it good?*
Ginny: *As always. Tell you more about that, later. Right now I'm a little more focused on the present from Mom.*

This time the message took a little longer to arrive, and Ginny feared her sister was probably writing some huge missive. She glanced over and examined Tucker again.

He had put his phone away and was watching her.

May as well stick to the truth. "Yes, I told Dare you and I are in bed together. She knows about all the other times. I told you that, and you said it was okay."

He shrugged. "Just getting everything straight so there's no misunderstanding later."

That didn't sound like a *hey, ho, everything's kosher.* "What does that mean?"

He leaned forward. "It means once you're done talking with your sister, we're having another conversation about the sexing business, capisce?"

Ping.

Ginny waved a hand in the air. "I'll get back to you on that as well. I'll have my people call your people."

She got a lip twitch out of him. It was stupid how good that made her feel.

Dare truly had written a mini novel.

Dare: *First, I'm glad you talked to Caleb. I'm glad it's behind you.*
I need to say—you are so freaking good at that telling the truth thing, and I'm glad. I would have stewed over it for three years and ended up hating everybody, including myself. But like you said, you've talked about it, it's over, it's done. I love you.
Dare: *Next part. The present from your mom. I read that, and I swear a freaking load of butterflies took flight in my gut. That is the most* Oh My God *thing I've heard in a long time.*
How are you doing? Do you want me to come down and be there when you open it? Do you want to—I don't even know what to offer. Tell me what you need, and I'm there for you.
I love you so much, and I'm equal parts excited and terrified for you right now.

Yup. Her sister understood completely.

Her own answer took a bit of time to compose.

Ginny: *I love you too. Right now the present is sitting on the dresser top, looming ominously. Thank you so much for offering to be there when I open it, and I would totally take you up on the offer other than that's not a good idea, because you're the one with the babies, and you're going to come to me? If I need you to hold my hand, I will admit it and haul my carcass up to you.*
Ginny: *But it's already feeling a little less gut-numbing. I think I might open the envelope first and see how emotionally devastating Mom decided to be. It could be a card with a farting*

dog on it, and there's not a lot of backlash from that. Know what I mean?

Dare: *I could see your mom doing that.*

Ginny: *So can I.*

Dare: *My babies are calling, and my man is waving frantically. I've got to go. Call me if you need me.*

Ginny: *I will.*

Dare: *I love you, Truth.*

Ginny: *I love you, Dare.*

Ginny stared at her phone for a minute, the familiar phrasing such a part of her past.

Tucker stroked his fingers up and down her arm in a gentle caress. "You okay?"

It was good to answer, once again, truthfully. "I think I am."

She had good people around her. So many people willing to support her and help her, and that's what she wanted to be for them. Supportive.

A seed of an idea began to grow.

BARELY PAST SEVEN and already the day was lining up to be a doozy. Tucker curled himself into an upright position so that he and Ginny were face-to-face.

"How's Dare?"

A true smile of contentment crossed Ginny's face. "She's good. Her three kiddos are adorable, and her husband's so freaking head over heels for her that it's kind of obnoxious to be in the same room as them. Plus, she's got hordes of Coleman family at her beck and call."

"Yeah, but she doesn't have you anymore," Tucker pointed out.

Ginny dipped her chin slowly. "I was glad I finished my journeyman program in time to be there when Dare had her twins. And while I have now had way too many sleepless nights for a nonparental human, I adored being there with the babies. But now it's time to do the next thing. For both of us."

"Which means you here at the ranch?" Tucker asked.

He really needed to know the answer to this. It had been hinted at yesterday, but never straight up said. All of his plans were for nothing if she wasn't sticking around. Because as much as he wanted to help his uncle, as much as he loved Silver Stone...

Ginny was the deciding factor.

She straightened, her breasts pressed to the front of his T-shirt. He ripped his gaze back up to her eyes, and she smirked. "You are so easy to distract."

"Answer the question, woman."

"Yes." She nodded firmly. "I'm *home*, and I plan on being the best...*something*. I have no idea how to finish that statement right now, because there's a lot of things up in the air, it seems."

She had no freaking idea.

Tucker shook his phone. "Luke told me there's a hockey game starting at eleven a.m."

Ginny frowned. "Which teams have games on Boxing Day?"

A laugh escaped before he could stop it. "*Ginny*. Pond hockey. Your brothers, me. The poor Southern gentleman who's probably never been on skates in his life."

"Oh, that kind of hockey." Mischief danced over her face. "I wonder if my old skates are still in the basement."

"You can be goalie for my team," Tucker offered.

Her jaw dropped with an exaggerated gasp. "Number one, no way am I standing defenseless while my brothers flick rock-solid pucks at me."

When she didn't continue, he frowned. "What's number two?"

"There is no number two. Number one pretty much says it all. I like my teeth in my mouth, thank you."

He curled his arms around her and rolled until she was on top. "I like the way you're put together, too. Teeth, lips, spectacular breasts."

She folded her hands over his chest and rested her chin on them. "Really? This is an interesting conversation twist."

"Just continuing the one I mentioned before. Regarding sexing."

She didn't stiffen, but Tucker knew enough about Ginny's body language to read she was in wait-and-see mode. A little cautious in case he threw something unexpected at her.

He wasn't ready to lob the true grenade yet, but at some point, it was happening. Until Caleb gave them the go-ahead, Tucker couldn't assume his place was a shoe-in. Which meant not changing his and Ginny's relationship.

Yet.

Only one thing was non-negotiable. "We've had good reasons to keep our adventures discreet. Until there's a need to change that, I'm okay with Dare being the only one who knows."

Okay, so Ashton had also implied he had his suspicions...

Tucker met Ginny's gaze steadily. It was mere days at the most before he'd be able to confess to that part.

Ginny twisted her head slightly. "You didn't say the *but* yet, did you?"

"Smart woman. The *but* is... if anyone finds out, we agree to tell the truth and don't scramble like we're living in some awkward sitcom. We tell them that we're adults, and our decision didn't involve them. Keeping something from my friends because it's none of their business is completely different from lying to their faces."

Ginny raised a hand in the air. "I am the most truthful person in the entire Stone family. Plus, I agree with you, but please, can we avoid spilling the beans, if possible? I really don't want anybody to beat you up. It's bad enough when you and Luke go off and pound on each other—I still do not approve, by the way."

Tucker raised his brows, ignoring her comment about fighting because that was a confrontation just waiting to happen, and he didn't want it now. "I'm sure Luke would claim it was your fault. Which it totally was if we're being honest."

"You wanted me just as much as I wanted you," Ginny said.

He had, after the shock of her coming onto him had faded. "I never suspected a thing, but I'm damn glad you made a move when you did. At least, looking back."

She grinned hugely. "Yeah, once you got over trying to be heroic. And then once you got over being scandalized at the idea of doing Luke's sister. And once you got past the..."

"You done anytime soon?" he drawled.

She smacked a hand down on his ribs then turned it into a tickle.

She knew all his hot spots and took merciless advantage. By the time he had caught her wrists and tugged until she was spooned against him, they were both once again relaxed and content, comfortable with each other in a way that made Tucker drift back to some very specific thoughts.

It was good to have some things be straight forward and simple. Everything else was tangled these days. Even one of the messages from Luke had been a little off. In the middle of hockey talk and a plot that involved skidoos, Tucker's friend had dropped a *what the hell.*

Sometime today we need to talk.

Um, yeah? Tucker was all for that, but the mysterious comment made him wonder if Luke had an inkling about Ginny and Tucker's real relationship.

Current relationship, which Tucker couldn't wait to move to the next level.

Ginny squeezed the arm he had tucked around her. "Let me up. I need to know."

She crawled out of bed as he sat, curious what she was up to.

Before they'd started fooling around, she'd placed the envelope on the present balanced on top of the dresser. Now she returned with the envelope in her hand, staring at it as if it was a snake about to strike.

"You going to open your present?" he asked quietly.

One long, slow inhale later, she shook her head. "Just this."

Then damn if she didn't crawl right into his lap. She arranged his arms to her liking, curling them around her torso until he anchored her in place.

She slipped the envelope open and pulled out a card.

"Merde," Ginny whispered.

Tucker pressed a quick kiss to her cheek. "Stop when you need to."

"I want to do this." She twisted the card upright and held it so he could see as well. It was a store-bought one with an idyllic pastoral scene on the front. Horses grazed in the foreground with huge mountains rising behind them.

She cracked the edge open, and a folded piece of paper and a silver chain slid into her lap. Ginny ignored them both and finished opening the card.

The inside was blank except for two separate bits of writing.

*Happy sweet sixteen to my little girl who's not so little now.
This coming year will be full of adventure, and all the years after
that. I know that whatever you choose to do, you will be brilliant
at it, because you're my live-wire. Always full of energy, always
brightening up wherever you go. Happy birthday, sweetie.
From your daddy.*

*Happy birthday to my wild outdoor girl. Watching you grow has
been a joy and delight. Sixteen is a special birthday, so here's to a
lot of candles and a lot of fun. Love you.
Mom.*

Ginny leaned back into Tucker, resting her cheek against his. She stroked her fingers over his and stared at the card for a moment. "Is it silly to say I can hear their voices reading those words?"

"Not silly at all." Tucker gave her a squeeze. "I'm glad. They were good people, and your dad was right. You do brighten up every place you go."

Her eyes sparkled. "Thanks. That's a really sweet thing to say."

She dipped her hand down and lifted the chain.

"That is the strangest necklace I have ever seen," Tucker said.

"Me too." Ginny lifted the pendant in her palm. Not quite a square, not quite a triangle, the wood was polished golden, but nothing super fancy. "I mean, it's pretty, but it is a chunk of wood. An old chunk of wood."

Tucker lifted the folded paper. "You up to do this right now?"

"Hell, why not?"

She slowly unfolded the page and they both went motionless.

7

______

The page in front of them made no sense. Mostly pictures, crudely drawn and inexplicable.

"My dad," Ginny said as dryly as possible, because disappointment had swept in. "I'm pretty sure he thought he was being cute, but his drawing skills were terrible. Is that a horse, or an elephant?"

"Hippo," Tucker guessed. "Although, the fact you live on a ranch is probably a clue that it's a horse. Or a cow."

"Probably, but not definitely." Oh, no. She met Tucker's gaze straight on. "Here's where I need to curse a little at sixteen-year-old me. You know the number one thing I was obsessed with during that timeframe?"

Tucker grimaced. "Am I supposed to say the name of a boy band right now? Oh, I know. Kenney Chesney. He's been around forever, right?"

As guesses went, that was pretty good. "That year was my puzzle and geekery phase. I wrote an entire English essay in Klingon. When the teacher complained, I resubmitted it, only this time in high Elvish. I sent notes to Dare in class using

Playfair ciphers and then deliberately dropped them on the floor so other kids would pick them up and be confused."

He raised his brow. "You think your parents gave you a puzzle for your birthday?"

She wiggled the paper in the air. "This part of it, anyway."

It wasn't the kick to the heart she'd feared, and in some ways, that was good.

She glanced for a moment at the box then shook her head. "Okay, the card turned out less shocking than I expected, but I'm not prepared to roll the dice anymore. The rest of the package has to wait until later."

Tucker agreed. "If that's what you want, then let's get on with our day. Want me to make you a coffee while you grab a shower?"

He was a good, good man. "Since the magical condom fairies haven't appeared, I'll take being spoiled as a very close-ranked second option."

He had on his stony face, but she could tell he was amused. "I'll have to remind you how good the sex is. I don't mind coffee being second, but it shouldn't be a close-ranked second."

"Coffee and *shower*, remember that part," Ginny said. She threw herself at him and stole another hug. Breathed in the scent of him and wondered how much damage a nervous system could take from being thrown up and down and up and down in rapid succession for a lot of days in a row.

Coffee was ready as promised when she came out of the bathroom. And miracle of miracles, there was food in the fridge, so while Tucker showered, she made breakfast. First breakfast, like hobbits, because whichever house they went to next, somebody was sure to feed them.

But when Tucker demolished three of the egg sandwiches she'd made without pausing to breathe, she knew cooking had been the right decision.

He finally sat back, nodding his approval. "Thanks. I know fried eggs aren't your favourite, but that helped lay down a base so I don't starve before the morning's out."

Before they left, bundled up against the cold, Tucker shocked the hell out of her and dragged her tight into his arms, kissing her fiercely.

She enjoyed every second of it, including the stars floating in front of her eyes when he finally let her go. "Wow. Thanks?"

He winked. "Since we want to keep this under our hats, I needed a top up before we went out in public."

They were out the door and into the blinding white snow field. "I think I'd like to go say hi to the girls. AKA, the cutie patooties at my brother's house."

"I'm going to see what leftovers Luke has. He asked me to join him." Tucker waved and headed in the opposite direction.

It was too tempting. Ginny scooped up some snow and quickly packed it into a nice firm ball. Cocked her arm back and aimed...

Tucker didn't look back, just called over his shoulder. "If you throw anything at me, I will get revenge."

Well, damn. "When did you get eyeballs installed in the back of your head?" she demanded.

"I see all. I know all." She held the ball higher, threatening, but he laughed and pointed at the side mirror of the truck he was passing. "Just kidding."

Ginny was still giggling as she made her way to the back door of the house where she'd grown up. Stepping without looking to deal with the small out-of-kilter turn to reach the porch. Nearly banging her knees on a bench that hadn't been there the last time she visited.

Familiar. Brand-new. She bounced between those two sensations every time she turned around.

As she entered the house, the scent in the room was perfection, though.

"Please tell me you didn't eat all the bacon," Ginny announced loudly.

Six heads pivoted toward her from where Caleb's family plus Dusty and his friend were seated at the massive round kitchen table. Seven, as she spotted Tyler in his highchair.

Tamara gestured her forward. "Join us. There's plenty."

"I only need the bacon," Ginny admitted. "And need is probably too strong a word because I already ate. Only, bacon— anytime, anywhere, am I right?"

"You're so right." The lanky dark-skinned young man beside Dustin was on his feet, wiping his mouth with a napkin before reaching out a hand. "I'm Shim. Here. There's an extra chair for you."

When he pulled out the sturdy straight-back beside his own chair, Ginny bit her lip to keep from making a joke.

Instead she pulled on her manners. "Thanks."

She sat, staring across at Tamara. Her sister-in-law's amusement was clear for a split second before she nabbed the plate with the remaining bacon and passed it around the table to Ginny. "You ate? That means you found the groceries then."

"I did. Thanks. It was nice to cook something simple when I wanted it."

"I figured you might have missed that lately."

Tyler banged on his tray and made a complaining noise.

Tamara offered Tyler another piece of bread slathered in peanut butter. "Stop growling like a bear, please. Or growl softer so we can hear each other."

"Grrr." This from Sasha, who smirked mightily and elbowed her little sister. "*Grrrrrrr.*"

Emma giggled and joined in briefly before telling Tamara seriously, "We're the three bears, Mama."

Caleb lifted his coffee, hiding a grin behind his cup. The entire family was so comfortable and real, and Ginny was glad to be back in the thick of it.

Dustin leaned around Shim to get Ginny's attention. "Hey. You coming out to the lake to cheer us on? Shim and I are clearing the ice after breakfast."

"I thought I'd look in the basement for my old skates," Ginny confessed. "It's been a while, but I think I still remember how."

"Want to be on our team?" Shim asked.

Dustin groaned. "Oh, please. Don't."

A snort escaped Ginny, but she covered it up the best she could. "Was that *don't* for me or Shim?"

"Shim," Dustin said instantly. "*And* you. There'll be way too many guys on the ice. You should skate somewhere safer."

Sasha had been listening intently and now leapt into the conversation. "What does that mean? It won't be safe to skate?"

"Uh," Shim's head swung back and forth as he tried to keep up with the conversation. "I just thought—"

"Papa, we want to skate, too," Emma interrupted, sadness dripping from her little voice.

"We do. We will." Sasha glanced at her little brother. "I need to teach Tyler how to skate."

"Of course you do, pumpkin. That's why Dustin will clear a second rink space for you and Emma and your friends to use. Right?" Caleb lifted his gaze to his youngest brother.

"Sure." Dustin leaned forward again. "You can skate on that one, Gin."

"Gee, thanks, *Dus*."

He glared. "That's not funny."

"It's hysterical," she returned before ignoring him and carefully piling three pieces of bacon on top of each other. She held it up and made eye contact with Emma. "Know what this is?"

"Stop playing with your food," Caleb grumbled, but he was clearly amused.

"You're not playing hockey with us," Dustin growled, sounding remarkably like Tyler.

"A bacon...." Emma frowned. "I don't know."

Sasha tilted her head as she announced, "A triple-decker bread-less sandwich?"

"Too much to put in your mouth at one time?" Tamara said at nearly the same moment.

The longer the rambunctious and chaotic conversation continued, the bigger Shim's eyes got, his grin growing as well.

This time Ginny was the one who leaned on the table, easing around Shim as she waggled the bacon in the air at Dustin. "This is a super-skater vitamin, which means in a minute, I'll be unstoppable."

She crunched down with vigour. The bacon shattered into teeny delicious pieces in her mouth, and Sasha and Emma crowed with delight.

Unfortunately, the bit still in her fingers also shattered, spraying poor Shim with a fine coating of crispy fat.

He laughed even as he brushed off crumbs and glanced around the table. "You guys are awesome."

"You're an only child, aren't you?" Caleb said dryly.

"Yes, sir." Shim coughed as Dustin hit him in the chest. "*Ouch*, what was that for?"

"He's not a *sir*, he's my brother," Dustin drawled then met Caleb's eyes. "I mean, you are awesome and everything, bro, but jeez."

Caleb's lips twitched, but he ignored Dustin and looked his friend over. "You can call me Caleb if you want, but whatever makes you comfortable. I don't mind."

The young man nodded. "Thanks."

Ginny didn't remember Caleb ever smiling this much before. Now he all but smirked as he waved Dustin and Shim off. "If you've had enough to eat, get working on clearing the rinks. The rest of the crowd will be here before you know it."

They shot to their feet, thanked Tamara for the meal and headed for the door.

"Well, that was the quietest and most peaceful meal we've had in ages," Tamara said as Tyler started to complain. She hauled him out of the highchair and handed him to Caleb. "Here, sir. A child for your entertainment. Leave the dishes. I'll take care of them in a bit. Right now, Ginny and I need to go find some skates, because she's got a game to get ready for."

"Damn right," Ginny said, followed immediately by, "Oops. I mean, darn tooting."

Emma giggled, and Sasha laughed. Caleb shook his head, but he kissed Ginny's cheek then rounded up his children. "Come on. Your mama deserves a break. You can be my clean-up crew."

"Which means you and I have treasure to find," Tamara told Ginny firmly as they headed down the stairs.

Treasure. A reminder of the mysterious present and the puzzle Ginny needed to solve. But right now, this was more important. Time with family, with her nieces and brothers.

Time to whup her younger brother's ass. She could hardly wait.

TUCKER DIDN'T BOTHER to knock upon reaching Luke's house. He did, however, peek around the corner before marching into the kitchen, just in case. No use scaring the daylights out of anyone.

Well, except maybe Luke. Scaring him would be priceless.

The coffeemaker was on, but no one was in the room. Tucker strode forward and made himself at home, filling a cup to the brim and fixing it up just right.

He turned around and nearly jumped out of his skin. Luke stood inches behind him, grinning like a feral beast.

"Fucker," Tucker grumbled as hot coffee sloshed over his fingers. He changed his cup to the other hand and forcibly jammed his palm against Luke's shoulder to spin him out of the way. "Good morning, you jerk."

"Good morning, sunshine." Luke grabbed his own cup of coffee. "Did you find the food I put in the fridge? I saw you had some stuff in there already, but I figured what the hell. May as well leave it."

"Yeah, thanks." No need to expand on that comment.

Luke gestured him toward the two easy chairs in front of the fireplace. They were positioned to one side of the general living room, a cozy place for two people to spend a morning.

"Sit for a minute," his friend ordered.

"This is a nice spot." Tucker looked around in appreciation. Nothing too over the top. The house construction was solid, but all the furnishings looked as if they'd been picked up at a secondhand store. "I bet this is where you and Kelli sit in the mornings when you get a chance."

"You got it," Luke agreed. Then he made a face. "Of course, both of us having the morning off happens only a couple of times a week. Ashton does his best, but it's nearly impossible to keep from scheduling one or the other of us for a morning shift."

"Maybe that's something that can change." In fact, if Tucker had anything to say about it, it was something he would make damn sure happened.

Yeah, his uncle had years of experience, but if things were

going to change for the better, this was something that needed to happen.

Luke looked confused. "You know some way to cut chore time in half? Or some way to add hours to the day?"

"I know a perfectly simple way to cut your work hours," Tucker said dryly. He paused, took a sip of his coffee and made an appreciative noise. "Damn. That's good."

Luke leaned back in his chair and laughed. "Stop being an ass. Tell me."

Tucker shrugged. "Seems Caleb's announcement means there's a little more money in the coffers. Hire some more hands. You're the best person for some jobs. Kelli is amazing at what she does—and neither of you need to do the grunt labour anymore."

His friend blinked hard. "Holy shit."

A soft chuckle escaped Tucker. "Seriously? The idea never once crossed your mind?"

Luke shook his head. "My first thought was all the money I plan to spend on stock and training equipment."

"You'll have to make decisions about priorities, but seems to me getting more time to spend with Kelli is valuable enough to figure a way for it to happen."

Appreciation spread as his friend nodded slowly. "Good to know you're not just a pretty-faced hick."

"Jerk," Tucker said dryly.

Luke leaned forward, coffee cup put aside as he met Tucker's gaze intently. "Here's the thing. I felt bad yesterday. I didn't mean to rush you off or make you feel as if I didn't want you around."

It was Tucker's turn to be surprised. "No idea what you're talking about."

"With Jack and Diane here, it didn't register that I should've sat down with you and made some plans." Luke spread his hands for a moment. "I didn't pivot very well, but I want you to know I am glad you're here. And while I'm going to enjoy Jack's company, I also want time with you. It's been way too long."

Getting to spend time with Luke was also on the *hell, yes* list of great reasons to move to the ranch. But since Tucker couldn't say anything yet...

He propped one foot on his knee and leaned back. "Yeah, I missed you too, sweetheart."

Luke snorted. "So. Hockey game today. Some of the guys from the fire hall and local ranches are also coming. Should be a good time."

"Looking forward to it," Tucker admitted. "Of course, you know I will score more goals than you."

"Bullshit. I bet I score at least two more than you," Luke snapped back.

"Oooh, look who's cocky now. You think you'll score at least twice?"

"You're such an ass," Luke said, but he laughed. "Come on. Let's get cooking. Jack and Diane will be up soon, and Kelli will be back from the barn. We may as well get some food ready so we can spend the rest of the time finding equipment for you so I can kick your ass."

"Does this mean we're going to be on different teams?" Tucker thought about Ginny. It had been ages since she'd been on the ice.

"Of course not," Luke said. "I'll still score more goals than you, but have you seen the size of our fire chief? The man's built like a yeti. I need you on my team to balance the odds."

The weather cooperated in a big way, bluebird bright sky with the barest hint of a wind. Just shy of ten o'clock, Tucker sat on the bench beside the cleared area on Big Sky Lake and took deep breaths of the crisp air until his lungs tingled.

Ginny dropped onto the bench beside him and grinned. "Hey, cowboy."

"You found some skates."

She pulled off her boots and went to work sliding on a pair of battered black men's skates. "Looks as if they got you outfitted up as well."

Tucker stood, checking his balance and glancing around at the crowd growing out on the ice. "They're a little tight, but doable."

"You do well in tight places," she teased.

The places his mind went—

"Minx."

Ginny glanced up from where she was looping the long strings around the top of the skate, double knotting the bow. "Hey, head over to the recreational ice for a minute. Caleb said he wants to talk to you."

Well, shit. He had not expected a summons this quickly. Tucker dipped his chin even as he grabbed his hockey stick. "See you in a bit."

He made his way across the ice, testing the blades and working out a few of the kinks. Jack flashed by, offering a thumbs-up as he passed, twirled, and carried on with some fancy crossover foot work.

Well. Who knew? Luke had brought in a ringer.

Tucker slowed as he skated down the narrow, singlewide tractor path between the hockey rink and the second circle-shaped one that was crowded with a lot of younger people. Diane skated beside Kelli, slow and careful. Caleb's daughters were there, and a lot of their friends. More benches lined the snowy side, and some of the younger skaters pushed chairs over the ice to help with their balance.

Caleb stood in the center of it all like a tall tree surrounded by dancing pixies.

Tucker approached cautiously, making sure to not interrupt the singing girls.

But Caleb motioned him forward. "Not the most professional setting, but I figured you'd want to know sooner than later. Ashton told me his plans. Said he's going to train you up for when he wants to retire."

"I've got a lot of the skills already—"

Caleb waved a hand. "I approve. You don't need to sell me on the idea. In fact, it's pretty much exactly what I wanted to happen. Ashton's a good man, but he deserves to work a little less."

"Which means I can work more," Tucker promised. He held out a hand and Caleb shook it firmly. "Thank you. I really appreciate the opportunity."

"We'll do up the paperwork as soon as possible. And talk about finding you a more permanent place to live. You okay where you are now?"

Tucker kept an absolutely straight face. "I'm comfortable."

Emma's feet slipped from under her and she landed on the ice with a *plop*. Caleb reached for her, glancing over his shoulder. "Carry on with your day. I've got people to skate with."

Back on the other side of the ice, Tucker wondered if the blades of his skates were actually touching the ground. That was the simplest job interview he'd ever had in his life. Damn, did he ever appreciate a straightforward man like Caleb. Tomorrow he'd get things straightened away with his work at the stables.

Today was time to play.

A loud whistle sounded from the far side of the open rink. All the hockey players meandered over, standing in a loose semicircle around the silver-haired black man who looked them over with amused satisfaction.

"I'm Malachi Fields. I'm the man who'll decide whether a goal is legal or not—"

"Seriously? Pond hockey with a referee?" This from one of the volunteer firefighters.

"You've obviously never played with us before," Luke drawled. "Consider this only half a notch below the Stanley Cup."

"We take our hockey seriously," Dustin said.

"I hope you skate better than you dance," another man shouted.

Dustin had just taken part in a community fundraiser, and now he twirled on the ice then threw his arms out in a good-natured gesture. "Enough jabbering. Pick the teams."

Luke and one of the lead hands, Alex Thorne, were named captains. Tucker tried to store away the names being called out, but it went fast and furious. In the end, he was on the same team as Luke, Dustin and Dustin's friend, Shim.

Somehow, Ginny ended up on the opposing team.

Action was fast from the first moment, the puck flying down the ice and only occasionally disappearing out of bounds past the snowdrifts piled up as a boundary of the cleared ice.

Tucker got a breakaway and sprinted down the rink, ready to flick the puck at the man in the net when something the size of a Mack truck barreled into him from the side.

Tucker slid all the way across the cleared ice and into the hardpacked snow on the edge.

Bradley Ford, the fire chief he'd been warned about, skated over and held out a hand. "Sorry about that."

Tucker grinned as he grabbed the other man's wrist and used it to get vertical. "No problem. Keep your stick on the ice."

Yeah. One step below the Stanley Cup? Nowhere near as technically fine, but their enthusiasm and determination were definitely up there. The puck moved so rapidly at times, it seemed there might be more than one on the ice.

"Hey. Who threw the extra pucks on the ice?" Dustin roared, which made Tucker laugh for all the wrong reasons.

Especially when Ginny went zipping past, stealing the puck from under her brother's stick and heading straight for the net. Only Shim got in her way, and the two of them went down in a heap.

She laughed as she got to her feet, but Shim definitely lingered in her area a little too long for Tucker's liking.

The next time the puck started moving and Dustin and Shim made a pincher move on Ginny, Tucker decided it was time to change tactics. Ignoring the net completely, he skated after his own teammates, casually elbowing Dustin toward the rough bit of ice at the very edge of the rink.

"Hey. We're on the same team," Dustin complained, frantically working to keep vertical.

Tucker turned and skated backwards, raising his hands in mock apology. "Sorry."

He glanced over his shoulder, planning his trajectory.

Ginny slapped her stick against Shim's. "Don't make me get mean," she warned.

"Give me your best shot," the kid said with far too much innuendo. "I can take it."

The puck headed straight toward the three of them, Luke shouting Tucker's name.

With a breezy air of competence, Tucker shifted his stick at the last second so that the puck slid off, straight to Ginny. In the next instant, he plowed into Shim, mass and momentum sending them both flying until they toppled into the snow at the side of the rink.

Tucker spoke softly as he glared into the young man's

surprised face. "Mind your manners around Ginny," he warned.

Then Tucker got to his feet and headed back to where Ginny had both arms raised in the air after having scored a goal against his team.

Luke skated past, disgust on his face. "Jeez. I had no idea it had been so long since you've been on skates that you've lost all sense of coordination."

Tucker stared across at Ginny, who grinned, totally aware he'd given her the assist. "Yeah. Guess I need to work on that."

8

Ginny was unlacing her skates when her brother Walker dropped into a squat in front of her. "Want to come home with us? We can visit for the afternoon then I'll bring you back."

She was game, but she also desperately needed to get into town while the shops were open, and this was a great excuse. "Let me drive myself. I want to have a shower, and I need to stop in town for a few things. Want me to bring anything?"

He shook his head, rising to his feet. "We'll feed you a late lunch. Look forward to catching up."

"Me too," she said honestly.

Tucker was nowhere in sight when she hit the trailer to change and grab her purse, not even by the time she crawled into her borrowed truck and headed into Heart Falls.

She would've liked to do the condom purchase somewhere a little further afield, but not buying protection wasn't an option. If all they had was two weeks, she needed to make sure no opportunities were missed.

Her purchase of chocolate bars, condoms, and a package of

fresh mint got the expected raised brows, but at least the unfamiliar kid running the first till was young enough to not come out and say anything.

She was happy to avoid the other checkout where Mrs. Wilson, her retired fourth grade teacher, was chatting full blast with her current customer. Mrs. Wilson would have given her the third degree then informed everyone in town that Ginny Stone was home and planned to have sex.

Both of which were true, but it really didn't need to become a local meme or anything.

Ginny stuffed her purchases into her reusable shopping bag and left them on the truck seat.

Ivy and Walker's house was situated beside the cemetery on the very edge of Heart Falls. They'd done some work on the cottage, fixing the porch and repainting, but it was a far cry from the newer homes popping up on acreages all around Heart Falls.

Ginny's gaze snagged on the cemetery. Dare's parents and her little sister Shayla were buried there.

Impulsively, Ginny crossed the short distance to the wrought-iron entrance. Others had visited since the last snowfall, and walking paths were trod down in a gentle loop through the quiet stillness.

Joseph and Jacquie's tombstones were neat and tidy. Brand-new plastic flowers stuck up from the holder at the base.

Sadness welled in Ginny's heart. So many opportunities had been lost because these special people weren't in the world anymore. But they had left something good that went forward.

"I talked to Dare this morning." Ginny said it conversationally, the same way she would've after sprinting the distance between the ranch house and the Hayes cottage, so many years ago. "She's doing great. Her babies are all adorable, with chubby cheeks and squirming jiggles. Joey is a wonderful big brother to them, and Dare's having so much fun chasing them all. She's still doing her blog. It's changed over the years, and she's not quite as long-winded as before. You'd be proud of her."

It was a sign of how hard she was working to not cry that she hadn't even noticed she wasn't alone until somebody stepped beside her and carefully put an arm around her shoulders. The motion was so familiar she knew in an instant who it was.

She leaned against Walker's side. "Hey, big bro."

"Hey, brat." He squeezed and held on.

They stayed there for another minute before Ginny caught his fingers and tugged him back the way they'd come. "So. How was skating on the baby rink?"

Walker chuckled. "Not nearly as dangerous as what you were up to."

"I live for danger," Ginny quipped.

"This isn't news."

She kicked snow his way, darting ahead until she could turn and look up at him. She jammed her hands into her pockets. "You good?"

"Very good," he said far more seriously. "Come in, and we'll get comfy before we start catching up."

The inside of the house was picture perfect and yet comfortable. Ginny had zero qualms about planning to put her feet up on the couch. First though, she was enveloped in a hug, the porcelain-skinned Ivy holding on with surprising strength.

"I'm glad you're back," Ivy said in her soft tones.

"That seems the general consensus. I'm still surprised, though, every time I hear it," Ginny teased. "I mean, I'm not an ogre, but I'm pretty sure it was a lot quieter around here without me."

"You can say that again." Walker poked his head out from

around the corner where delicious smells were coming from the kitchen. "Cup of tea?"

"Yes, please. With a little honey."

"Got it."

Ivy curled up in a cushy-looking rocking chair, gesturing for Ginny to sit where she wanted. "You want to tell us about your time away, or are you looking to brainstorm about what's going to happen now? Or both?"

"Wow. That's a tough choice." Ginny accepted the mug from Walker. "Thanks."

What a difference a day made. Yesterday an older brother had handed her a cup of tea, and she'd been all but vibrating with anxiety and anger. Today she was sweetness and light with so much to look forward to.

Had to be the orgasm Tucker gave her last night. There was no getting around it. She caught herself smiling as she took a sip of the tea.

"It's not as good as yours," Walker said as he settled in the chair next to Ivy's. "I want you to do what makes you happy, but is it terrible if I mention I hope you decide you absolutely have to get back to making herbal concoctions? Even if it's a hobby."

"I haven't even peeked in the greenhouse," Ginny confessed.

"You've officially been home for just over twenty-four hours," Ivy said with amusement. "Plus, it's the holidays. I think you're allowed to leave it for a while longer."

Which was true, but now everything that she had been ignoring suddenly stacked up in one massive to-do list. "I think we should talk about what our goals are for the future," Ginny said decisively. "I like brainstorming with Walker. He was usually pretty good at it."

"Because I didn't tell you which one of your ideas you should do?" Walker offered.

"What? You weren't bossy? How is that even possible?" Ivy teased.

"Only bossy when I need to be," Walker said with a smile.

"Ooh, icky. Stop with the lovey-dovey stuff." Happiness rushed in even as she taunted. "Nah, don't stop. You two have always been so gosh-darn cute together."

"So, brainstorming," Ivy said with a smile, obviously attempting to get control of the situation. "The greenhouse didn't sit empty the entire time you were gone."

Ginny shook her head. "I leased out the contracts for my Community Supported Agriculture boxes to a local family for two years, which is how long I was supposed to be gone in the first place. When I had to stay a little longer to finish the journeyman commitment, we extended the CSA agreement for a year. Tamara had talked about doing some of it on her own, but it was easier to let someone else manage the whole thing."

"So you could start up again this spring?" Walker asked. "Plant seeds, get things growing. Get in touch with your contacts for the things you don't want to grow?"

"I could," Ginny agreed. Only this was where Caleb's announcement had shaken up her original idea. She'd learned a lot during her travels and was excited to put new skills into play. But she'd also learned there were certain parts of working with others that she absolutely did not want anymore.

She met Ivy's soft gaze. "Here's part of what I did the past few years—lots of grunt labour. Which was good at times, but also frustrating. There were some of the growers who didn't honour the 'teach your journeyman new skills' idea very well."

Walker growled in disapproval. "I'm sorry to hear that. I hope you reported it."

"I did, when appropriate," Ginny said quietly. "Sometimes

I might have been to blame for not understanding what I signed on for because of language issues. And sometimes the biggest lessons came from when I buckled down and did the job in spite of it being a bit of a stretch. But I can learn from my mistakes, and I know this—I don't want to simply garden anymore. It's valuable, but it's not my forever job."

Ivy nodded. "Knowing what you don't want is important. But I'm also sorry to hear you felt frustrated."

"Thanks." Ginny sniffed her tea and made a mental note to check the mint garden at the ranch when she got home. "I need to make a pro and con list. Figure out what's the most beneficial use of my time and energy."

Walker leaned forward. "Remember, you don't need to make a ton of money from whatever you do. So that list should involve a lot of things that really make you happy."

Absolute truth. "Yeah, you're right. And that's going to take some thinking, but I'm pretty sure I'll be making something herbal at some point. That's one of the things I know for certain." She curled her arms around her legs, glancing between the two of them. "And I'm happy to be here. It's good to know that as the next things progress with the family, I can be a part of it."

"An important part," Ivy said firmly.

"I like you," Ginny responded, watching as Ivy's smile brightened. "So what about you guys? What new thing have you been dreaming about?"

Walker and Ivy exchanged glances. Happiness bloomed between them so hard and strong it would've been annoying if it weren't so amazing.

"We've been talking about something for a while, and it looks as if we're ready to move ahead," Walker said steadily.

Ginny glanced around the house. "Renovations? Additions?"

A gentle snort escaped Ivy. "Definitely additions. We want to adopt."

"Oh my *God*." Ginny shot to her feet and scooted over to give Ivy another hug. "That is so exciting. Really? When, who?"

"No timeline yet," Walker said before accepting a hug of his own. He waited until Ginny resumed her seat to continue. "We've spent the past while researching and really talking out what we can handle. The next part will be the legal steps. A lot of social work visits. Getting everything into place."

"You know Alex Thorne? Ranch hand at Silver Stone?" Ivy asked. When Ginny nodded, she continued. "He grew up in the foster system, and he has a sister who is actively fostering, so we talked to him about what he thought."

"Fostering always sounds really difficult," Ginny said, a little nervous because while Ivy was physically delicate, Walker had the gentlest heart of anyone Ginny knew. "I don't think I could do it."

"After talking to Alex, we think it would be too hard for us," Walker said slowly. "The people who can offer that kind of support are wonderful, but we need something different."

Ginny put it all together and made a guess. "You're not adopting a baby, are you?"

Ivy shook her head. "We want to take older kids. Siblings, if possible."

"Part of what we're doing with that dreaming Caleb offered is to get things rolling. When it happens, I'll come home full-time until I can move back up to part-time hours," Walker said. "Ivy can't get out of her teaching and principal job at the drop of a hat, but I can easily be replaced at the ranch."

That was absolutely not true. "You are irreplaceable, but I do agree you guys will make a great mom and dad," Ginny assured them.

"We're excited," Ivy said. "And having a blended family doesn't worry me—it's all I ever knew."

That's right. Ivy and her three sisters had all been adopted.

"Well, remember Auntie Ginny is always available to help." She shook a finger at Walker, who looked as if he was about to turn down her offer. "I spent six months helping Dare take care of her kids. Loved every minute of it—no, that's a lie. I didn't like the poopie diapers. But since you will have older kids, and poopie diapers should not be a part of it, I am very much looking forward to helping you as well. I love you. Both of you, *and* your future kids."

Ivy's eyes were a little watery. "You're a wonderful little sister."

Sisters. Ginny nearly gasped. "Your sisters must be over the moon. And your parents. And your *grandma*."

Walker and Ivy laughed. "Yes, there are a whole lot of people who will be very excited. We've just begun the journey though. In the meantime, we dream."

It seemed an appropriate moment for a change in focus. Ginny swung her legs to the floor so she could lean forward. "So. Living arrangements. What's the master plan? Renovations on this place, or are you moving?"

The conversation shifted into Walker and Ivy's more immediate needs for upgraded space to accommodate a bigger family. As the afternoon passed, Ginny offered suggestions and gloried in the reflected happiness of her brother and his wife.

Coming home to this new future was important. Ginny was so glad to be a part of the excitement and hope filling their home.

Tucker enjoyed a late lunch with his uncle, getting caught up on recent changes at the ranch. It was late afternoon when he excused himself to head back to the trailer to deal with everything involved in switching jobs.

Contacting his current boss offered another surprise.

"You just saved me from breaking bad news," the older man shared. "Inspector went through the buildings and threw us for a loop. To meet code, we've got to rewire the entire system, which means the only thing we can legally board are a dozen horses in the one new barn. Which means, we don't need any workers for the next while."

"You mean you were about to fire me?" Tucker asked with a laugh.

"You've got every positive reference I can offer," Raymond promised. "The only thing I can't give you is a job. I'm glad you got something new lined up. I've appreciated having you around."

Forward motion was always great. "I will need to come back for my stuff. Any timeline on that?"

"The sooner the better," his now ex-boss said quickly. "When I said the entire system, that also means the lodging. I could use help getting all the animals moved into the temporary quarters or shifted to new boarding situations."

Well, damn. Tucker need to take a road trip. "Let me check the weather for the next couple of days. If there's an open window, I'll come back and get started on that right away."

"That would be a hell of a lot of help. While you're here, we can finish up your final paperwork."

After hanging up, Tucker sat at the table and took a deep breath. Seems he was now officially unemployed. Temporarily, but still. Nothing official had been signed yet with Silver Stone.

How unlike him to just roll forward without stopping to get

everything lined up first. Ginny's impulsive ways were finally wearing off on him.

Her mischievous expression flashed to mind.

Shit. Tucker glanced at his watch. Four thirty, on Boxing Day. What were the chances that he could still make it to a store in time to buy condoms?

He had to try. He scrambled to his feet and pulled on his coat, shoving open the door and nearly knocking Ginny off the steps.

"Whoa there, cowboy. You chasin' down some doggies?"

He automatically accepted the bag she handed him, backing out of the way as she crowded forward. "I would say I needed to hit the store, except you've probably been brilliant, haven't you?"

By the time she peeled off her coat, he'd peeked in the bag, sighing happily as he pulled out the extra-large box of condoms.

She stole it from his fingers. "Those are mine."

Dear God. This woman. "Okay. I want to see you put them on."

The heat that flashed in her eyes scalded him. "Oh, you can totally watch."

This conversation just went five hundred degrees hotter and a completely different direction than it needed to. "Hold that thought."

She hesitated. "Really?"

"Trust me, we will put your purchase to good use soon enough, but there's something I need to tell you."

By now she had her boots off. She grabbed him by his belt buckle and hauled him into the living space. "Something serious enough you're putting a pause on sex, even though it's been years? Okay, I'm all yours."

Which was pretty much everything that he'd ever hoped for. Now to start working on making it true.

"You said you wanted to fool around for the two weeks I'm here on vacation." When she nodded but didn't say anything, Tucker went for it. "Other than going back to Winnipeg to pack, I'll be staying at Silver Stone for longer. In fact, I'm pretty much staying for good."

He could all but see the gears turning in her quick brain as she put two and two together. "If you're not going home, that means you have a job here, yes?" Her eyes got big. "I bet it's Ashton. Holy crap, is he actually retiring?"

"I'm really kind of complimented that you jumped to me taking over for him that fast," Tucker admitted.

Ginny waved a hand. "Hell, yes. I mean, yeah, there'll be things you need to learn, but you've spent more time at our ranch than most of the workers on the current payroll. Is Ashton sticking around to mentor you?"

"That's the plan." The fact she wasn't freaking out about him staying in the area—that was a hopeful sign, wasn't it?

She collapsed back on the couch, totally relaxed. "Congratulations. That's gotta be really exciting."

He linked his fingers through hers. Jumping in a little farther. "Thanks. Now I need to prove that I can actually do it."

He rubbed his thumb against the back of her wrist. Her eyes widened slightly as she lifted her gaze to his. But instead of something about extending their two-week sexing relationship, something totally different came out of her mouth. "Me too. The *prove it* thing."

It was such a change of direction from being about to ask her to date him that Tucker stalled. He pulled it together fast enough he hadn't sat there silent for too long.

"What do you want to prove?" he asked.

She stared into space. "The whole time I was away I kept picturing what I would do when I got home that would make a difference. From stuff to grow to make money, to making sure everybody had the fresh fruits and vegetables they wanted—and now Caleb says some of that's not needed anymore."

"But some of it is still hugely valuable," Tucker pointed out. "There's a reason why people go to the farmers market. There's a reason why people buy organic. If that's something that you want to do, that's valuable."

"It is." Ginny nodded slowly. "I'm still wrapping my brain around this. I'm not sitting here thinking *oh, woe is me, there's nothing I can do.* I'm more sitting here thinking about *what should I do.*"

Which was far better. "That's a very good thing to pick what you want to work at."

"And that's what I want," Ginny insisted. "Work. I don't want the good fortune the ranch received to be an excuse to get lazy or complacent."

He squeezed her fingers until she met his gaze again. "Goddess, get real. The last thing you've ever been is lazy."

"Good, so there's no reason to start now," she said brightly. "I think we should make a pact to work together."

Now they were getting somewhere. "I agree."

"If I do one thing, it would be to somehow show my family how important they are to me. Every one of them." She stared off into space again, thinking hard.

"I think they know," Tucker said softly. "Truly."

She smiled. "Thanks."

A moment later she'd closed the distance between them. The familiar position of her ass resting on his thighs as she straddled him woke every anticipatory nerve in his body.

Ginny stroked her fingers through his hair. "Operation *Prove It* is now in place. You will spend the next however long it takes showing your uncle, my brothers, and the ranch hands how brilliant you are."

"Jesus, I wasn't scared to death until you put it that way," he complained.

She chuckled evilly. "I will spend the same however long it takes coming up with some new ideas of how to make a difference. How to make Silver Stone an even better place for my family, and my community. *Gah*." She contorted her face into a terrifying visage. "Simple, really. Starting from scratch with nothing and no directions, not even IKEA ones written in Swedish, with mislabeled bags of nuts and bolts."

Tucker decided he was more amused than alarmed. "And how do we keep track of Operation *Prove It*?"

She considered even while she began to drive him wild, teasing her fingers up and down the placket of his shirt. Unbuttoning one, two, three buttons...

"Once a week we will check in. We will report on our biggest failure, but also celebrate our biggest success. That will let us bitch about the things that didn't go well and still keep things in perspective, because any forward motion is good motion, right?"

"Right," he agreed, leaning so she could push his shirt off his shoulders. He was more than willing to help her strip him naked.

"Is it a deal?" She stuck her hand into the narrow space between their bodies.

He wrapped one hand around her nape, the other pressed to her lower back so he could pull her closer. "It's absolutely a deal."

She sighed into his mouth, melting against him as their tongues connected. A deep, slow kiss that ignited the banked fire inside him far too quickly. He still needed to clarify their relationship, but hell if he could resist doing this first.

Satisfying a hunger that had been left unchecked for far too long.

9

———————

atching Ginny strip away her top shirt was a visual feast, made even better when she tugged at his T-shirt until it escaped his jeans. Together, they worked until they were both naked from the waist up and Tucker had access to those glorious breasts once again.

Goddess, indeed. A wanton earth mother with tits that made his mouth water. Tucker filled his hands as he kept their lips together for a little longer. Kissing her until she quivered, each quick inhalation rocking her chest so her breasts rubbed his palms.

He hauled her higher, taking hold of one nipple and sucking hard enough that she gasped. When he would've let go, she made it clear that wasn't what she wanted, clutching his head to keep him in place.

"More," she demanded.

"Where's the condoms?" he spit out in the scarce second he took his lips off her skin.

She gestured to the side.

He patted his hand along the couch blindly, continuing to enjoy and lick and nip.

Somehow, they got the box open. Somehow, he got his zipper down and his cock out and covered. Ginny had lost her pants and underwear in that time and, gloriously naked, crawled back on top of him to rock her heat-slick pussy over his length.

Sex between them was always good. No, it was always *spectacular*, but today, even more, Tucker savoured the moment when they connected. His tip slipped between her folds, and then her strong thighs flexed as she slowly dropped onto his length.

So hot, so fucking right. Tucker groaned in amazement.

Ginny leaned their foreheads together, grinning at him. Then her eyes widened. She jerked upright, which pushed him even deeper, and both of them reacted with a soft moan.

But her expression—somewhere between panic and *oh my God this was not going to end well* mischief.

"Oh. You're *staying*. At Silver Stone."

Tucker held on tight, because no way was he letting her get away from him, not now. But at the same time, amusement bubbled up until laughter burst free.

"Hold that thought," he commanded, even though the words echoed with his delight. Then he picked her up, shuffling until he'd kicked his jeans off his feet. He brought her into the bedroom and settled on the mattress, stretching out with her over him.

This was not the time for conversation.

Using her hips as an anchor, he rocked up into her. Relishing the slide, the mind-blowing pressure. The way that they fit together.

Ginny moved with him, helping where she could, but

when she cupped her breasts, a shudder shook him from top to bottom. "Give them to me," he ordered.

It was more a growl than clear words, but somehow, she understood. She leaned over and pressed one nipple to his mouth, and he sucked it in, multitasking in one of the best possible ways. He was about to lose his mind, lose himself, definitely lose control, which considering that it had only been a couple of minutes, was pretty damn pathetic.

He slid his fingers between her legs to where they joined, catching moisture and drawing it up to her clit. Stroking in solid circles until she moaned, "*Yes.*"

Bingo. Slowing everything down half a notch, Tucker teased until she was ready to break. The heat rising between them was everything he wanted and needed. He urged her forward again to press a kiss to her breast. A kiss to her heart.

"Going to work you until you come," he promised, switching up his hand motion the slightest bit. A little quicker now with a hint of a pinch between forefinger and thumb on every stroke.

"Oh my God. That, *that*," Ginny moaned, fingernails biting into his shoulders as she rocked her hips hard against him. Riding him, rising over him like the goddess she was.

He couldn't last. Her sex wrapped tight, and her nails scratched his skin. Her lips dropped to meet his as she all but ground on him as if trying to weld them together.

He swallowed her trembling cry, followed her over the edge, and came hard.

Holding her body against his as pleasure rolled on for a while longer—thank God he was lying down, because otherwise he might have fallen over and passed out, it had been so good.

Ginny slowed her restless motions, stroking a hand over his chest in a soothing caress. "Wow."

And his amusement was back. "I've rendered Ginny Stone speechless. I feel quite proud."

She bounced the edge of her fist off his chest but then cupped his face with her hand. "Thank you for taking care of me," she whispered sweetly before offering him a gentle kiss.

Always. Forever.

But those weren't the appropriate words to say right now, and he knew it.

Still, he enjoyed the kiss and offered one more of his own before breaking them apart and rolling her to one side. "Let me clean up, and then we can talk."

"Deal."

He grabbed his clothes and took them with him. By the time he was back from the bathroom, Ginny had gotten dressed and was poking around in the refrigerator.

"You hungry?" she asked.

"Always," he said truthfully. "Luke said he left food for us. For me."

Ginny snorted. "Tamara also loaded the fridge. She must've shown up first, or she would have wondered why there were supplies here already."

"Which kind of leads well into answering that question you had."

She closed the fridge and eyed him full on. "I don't remember asking a question. I remember realizing how completely clueless I had been to how much you sticking around changes things."

Tucker braced himself. "I want things to change. What we're doing, I mean."

"Oh." She got herself busy, digging back in the refrigerator and giving him her back. "Okay, I guess. If that's what you want."

Oh hell. Tucker put a hand on her shoulder and turned her

to face him. "Don't jump to conclusions," he warned. "I don't want to just fuck around with you, Ginny. Only we've never been in the same place at the same time when more was appropriate."

He'd never trusted himself enough to take the chance, but now? He wanted her enough to fight her personal demons.

She was thinking again, that intensely focused expression she got where the magical, mystical program she carried in her brain ran through options at the speed of light. "You want more than just the occasional fling?"

"Yes. *Hell*, yes."

"Oh." She tilted her head slightly. "Spell it out for me. What exactly does that mean?"

He caught her by the hands, his touch gentle and very innocent, considering they had just fucked each other silly not even five minutes ago. "I want to date you. I want to get to know you better and figure out if between us, we can find something that can last."

"Holy shit," she whispered.

Tucker stroked his thumbs over her fingers. "Holy shit, good? Or holy shit, *I never in a million years imagined this would happen and how do I get this asshole out of my trailer?*"

She rolled her eyes. "Please, I'm supposed to be the drama llama in this relationship."

"Go right ahead and drama away, but I still need an answer to the question.

Ginny tilted her head to the table. "Sit. Want a beer?"

"Why not."

She grabbed two then sat kitty corner to him instead of across the table. Then she caught hold of the hand closest to her while she raised her bottle in the air with her other. "To Operation *Prove It*."

They clinked then drank.

Ginny placed her bottle carefully on the table before meeting his gaze. "I think you are one of the sexiest men on the entire planet."

That was a good start. Maybe? "Thank you."

"I've also had a crush on you since I was a teenager, but you know that because I shared those details when I was twenty-one and talked my way into your bed. Even if it was only once or twice a year."

"You did tell me." Tucker ignored his beer and wrapped both his hands around hers. "I think we should do this like a Band-Aid. Rip it off, really quick. Are you about to tell me to take a hike?"

She licked her lips, suddenly—*shy?* Confident as hell and outgoing *Ginny* avoiding his gaze?

"I'm not telling you to take a hike," she said softly. "I think we've got some good history, and some amazing chemistry..."

Fuck it. "I just heard a *but.*"

She looked him straight in the eye. "Timing is everything. You're about to start in a position that's pretty important, and while us dating isn't impossible, it could cause problems. There's Ashton, there are my brothers, and there's the entire Silver Stone crew. You'll have to earn their respect—which you totally deserve because you've got the skills. But most of them will suspect you're got an in because of your relationship with Ashton. Add on a relationship with me, and..."

"I can deal with that."

But she continued. "I'm *not* willing to mess this up for you. What we need is some sort of compromise, because I also don't want to go without you. I want time together to do Operation *Prove It,* and I want sex." She wrinkled her nose. "It probably makes me pretty shallow that I included that last part."

"No, I totally want that part as well," Tucker admitted.

She lifted his hand and brushed his knuckles against her cheek. "I'm not saying no, I'm saying slow."

"We wait a couple months before we officially start dating?"

She hesitated. "No set time. We see how things go."

"But I want you in my bed," Tucker admitted. "And I mean that literally, as well as sex."

"I like sleeping with you, too." Ginny made a face. "Yes, as well as the sex, but we can figure that out."

"You're moving into the Hayes cottage, right?" Which was right out in the open hillside. Everyone and their dog would see if he stopped to visit. "We'll get creative. But I mean it, Ginny. As soon as things are going smoothly, I'm officially asking you out. And prepare to be spoiled."

"I look forward to it." The delight on her face was very real and very ego stroking. "I really want you to be my boyfriend, Tucker Stewart, but we've been patient this long. What's a little longer?"

It was a wise sentiment, but Tucker was pretty sure agreeing to this would come back and kick his butt in more ways than one.

"Then I hope you don't mind us burning up a little energy a couple more times tonight. Maybe again in the morning." He pressed a kiss to her knuckles. "I talked to my boss. I have to head back to Winnipeg for a week."

She offered him a cheeky wink, trailing her fingers over his shoulder as she rose and headed back to the refrigerator. "Well, I'm disappointed we won't get that solid two weeks trapped together in this love cave, but the sooner you go, the sooner you get back. Let's make some supper so we'll have enough energy to ravish each other as much as possible tonight."

As plans went, it sounded rock-solid to Tucker.

~

Early the next morning, Ginny let the covers fall back into place as Tucker closed the door behind himself.

It was better to let him do all the things he needed before setting off on his long drive, and there was nothing she could do to help him right now anyway.

She stretched lazily, appreciating the little aches and pains in her body from what had ended up being a spectacular sexual marathon. She was glad she'd nabbed the condoms.

Tucker Stewart wanted to date her.

Ginny stretched her arms over her head and let out a squeal of delight. Okay that thought was every bit as thrilling as fourteen-year-old her could have wanted.

But she was serious about not interfering with him getting established at Silver Stone. Maybe if things had been different, like if Tucker had been around every year, or if her parents and the Hayeses had still been there. Being mentored by a solid group of older men would've given Tucker so much of a head start.

She was pretty sure her brothers would approve in theory. Caleb obviously did, and Luke thought the world of Tucker.

But if she was in the picture, would her brothers get tangled up with thoughts of her as their little sister to protect, instead of focusing on Tucker as a cohort to encourage and bring up to speed?

She sighed. Being an adult sucked, but here they were.

Which meant her plans to juggle the next thing while making frequent booty calls got adjusted. In a way, it might be good to focus all of her attention on catching up with old friends and future plans for staying on the ranch.

The package on top of the dresser caught her attention. She was revved up enough from the excitement bubbling inside and the sneaky suspicion that she would be an emotional wreck that night anyway once it sank in that she didn't get to cuddle with Tucker.

She grabbed the package off the dresser and sat back on the bed.

Unraveling the ancient twine gave her time to reconsider, but now her curiosity was in high gear.

She carefully undid the brittle tape holding the parchment paper in place and discovered a plain but sturdy cardboard box. The lid lifted off easily revealing two matching hardcover journals.

A rush of memory slipped in...

"Mom?" Ginny kicked off her boots at the back door and made her way farther into the house. Something bubbled on the stove, so her mom had to be somewhere nearby.

"In here," her mom called. "Just a minute."

Ginny rounded the corner into her mom's office in time to see her pick up her shiny red journal and tuck it into the top desk drawer. "Oh. Writing in your diary," Ginny teased.

Her mom folded her hands. "Yes, I was. Someday you'll appreciate it."

"Not if you're writing stuff in there about you and Dad. There are some things I don't need to know," Ginny insisted.

"Wait until you fall in love. Then you might be curious to hear other people's stories."

Ginny shrugged. "Maybe. Don't hold your breath. Anyway, Dusty is hiding in the barn. He refuses to come in the house because he failed a test, and now he thinks he'll get kicked out of Grade Two, but even worse, that Dad might take away his riding privileges."

Deb Stone made a face. "The kid is probably not wrong

about that last one. What kind of test?" She eyed Ginny hard. "How come you know this, and why are you telling me?"

"Because I, as his beloved big sister, who is nearly eight years older, know all and see all."

"Ginny. Spit it out without dramatizing it any further, if that's possible," her mother demanded.

"You're no fun. Fine, Dusty was cranky on the bus ride home from school, so I asked him what was wrong, and he told me. The reason he failed was he was actually sitting in the hallway being disciplined when the teacher handed out the test."

Their mother folded her arms over her chest. "You're not making things better for your brother right now."

Ginny held up a finger. "Ah, but here's the part that neither the teacher nor Dusty will tell you. I happen to know Dusty got sent to sit in the hall because he told Jeremy Dane to stuff it and stop teasing Fern Fields about having a prosthetic arm. And when Jeremy made a rude gesture, Dusty sat on him. Which was probably really uncomfortable because Jeremy is lumpy like a bag full of rocks. Personally, I hope Dusty didn't bruise himself."

Deb pinched the bridge of her nose. "Thank you for that little bit of colour commentating."

"Anyway. Rose and Tansy told me about that part, because Fern told them, so I told Dusty that I was sure you would understand he did the right thing, but if it came down to it, I would help him study for a makeup test. And I'm making peanut butter cookies so when he comes in, he has something to make him happy, okay?"

Her mom rose from behind the desk and came to offer her a hug. "That sounds fine. I guess I'll put my boots on and go on a Dusty hunt."

"Look for the nearest set of kittens. The last batch we

found are in the south corner of the loft," Ginny suggested as they headed back to the kitchen and her mom began layering on outdoor gear. "Mom? What *do* you write in your journal?"

Deb adjusted her toque and pulled on warm winter gloves. "Memories. Joys and sorrows. Dreams. Sometimes I write the most outlandish thing that I possibly can, just to make myself smile."

"Something absolutely wild and outrageous like Dad taking over the accounting books?"

Her mother laughed. "So disrespectful. No, but I do sometimes try to imagine the future."

"The immediate future includes the heavenly scent of peanut butter cookies wrapping around you and your beloved son when you return from your quest," Ginny said, offering a dramatic bow.

"I love you, kiddo. Now let me go find your brother."

IT WAS ONLY ONE MEMORY. Ginny had seen the journal many times over the years, at least the red one on the right that was bumped and banged and a little worn. The second one was identical, only the shine on the cover was still pristine, and instead of red, the cover was sky blue.

Ginny's favourite colour.

She traced her fingers over them both, and a knot grew in her throat as she thought back to all the times and places she'd seen her mom holding it. Curled up in a chair by the fire. Sitting on the porch swing. Hanging out in the hayloft, the journal spread in her lap as she either wrote or read back over well-worn pages.

Oh, dear God, Ginny was going to cry again. At least this

time there was no one around to witness as she lifted the little piece of the past and cradled it carefully.

A sticky note that had lost all its stick fluttered to the bedspread beside Ginny's hip.

All it said was 2 *of* 3.

Ginny opened the red journal in the hopes there would be some further explanation. Another folded note addressed to her in her mother's clear beautiful handwriting waited between the pages.

You're always asking what I'm writing in my journal, so as your second present on this milestone birthday, I'm going to show you.

This is a loan, mind you. Some of what's written in these pages is very personal, to me and to others, but I trust you to keep the things private that should remain that way. But I'm also trusting you to share what should be shared when and if appropriate.

I suppose it's a bit old-fashioned and slightly misogynistic to automatically think you should someday become the family record keeper. That chore seems to typically fall to the women, but I never complained because it's something I enjoy. I hope it's something you do as well.

There are always questions, there are always the do you remember *moments, and that's part of why I journal. No one's memory lasts forever, so putting things down on paper is a good way to look back.*
Sometimes we do it to celebrate the good choices we've made. Sometimes we do it to see where we got on the wrong path, to make a course correction.

Either way, you don't have to do this alone. I've done some of it before you, and I've done some of it for you (peek in your new journal and you'll see what I mean.) And as the summer passes, I look forward to sitting on the deck with you, writing in our journals. Sharing our hopes and dreams and, as is inevitable with you involved, I'm sure there'll be laughter.

I love you. Here's to making memories.
Mom

Somewhere in the middle of the letter, tears slipped free. As much as Ginny hurt inside, the moment was still beautiful. Yes, it was painful that she hadn't been able to enjoy the summer her mom had envisioned.

But looking back over the years, Ginny could honestly say there had been other joys. There had been experiences with her brothers—good experiences—that would never have happened if their world hadn't turned inside out so terribly.

She turned a page, examining non-sequential the dates. Noticing little pockets that had been added to some of the pages with additional papers stuffed inside. Her mother had turned the journal into a mass of notes and doodles.

It was a treasure Ginny had not expected.

She carefully put it down and picked up the new journal. Flipping open the pages she stopped in surprise to discover it wasn't empty and pristine. At the top of the page here and there were notes from her mom. Questions, or commands from beyond the grave.

Something I like about myself.
Who is my best friend, and what do I do to show them that's true?
If I had an entire day all to myself, what would I do?

There were more. Ginny pressed the journal against her chest and held it tight as she let the sadness inside escape one last time.

Then she wiped her eyes, washed her face, and made breakfast. The journals were carefully put back on the top of the dresser like the treasures they were.

Today was about a different kind of treasure hunt. She got out her phone and made a few calls.

10

———

Crawling out of a warm bed and away from an even warmer and softer Ginny had been hell. Tucker consoled himself by focusing on the fact that the sooner he got out of there, the sooner he could return.

He tracked down Ashton in the barn, surprised to find Luke and Jack there as well. The three men leaned comfortably on the wall and side rail outside a stall that held one of the prettiest mares Tucker had seen in a long time. She was pregnant, and Luke affectionately patted her nose as he spoke.

Tucker moved into sight slowly to avoid spooking the mare.

"You're up early," he said before focusing on Jack. "I thought you were on holiday."

Jack grinned. "Diane kicked me out of bed. Said I needed to go entertain myself elsewhere for a while."

"Getting a little too handsy, were you?" Luke chuckled evilly as he moved away from the mare and still managed to avoid the jab to his shoulder from his friend. "Hey, either you've got a woman who likes sex in the morning, or you don't."

It was terrible that the first thought that rushed to Tucker's mind was that Ginny liked sex no matter what time of day it was. In fact, she usually woke him, and the memory of that morning hit with a rush of heat.

His only saving grace was that Ashton had folded his arms over his chest and offered a disapproving look. "Stop bragging about your sex life."

"Nothing says you can't join—" Luke shut up instantly then looked upward, as if admiring the rafters.

"Hooligan," Ashton muttered.

"Interrupting this scintillating conversation," Tucker offered dryly. "Ashton, does Luke know?"

"Do I know what?"

Obviously not. Tucker would've loved to have dragged this out longer and made Luke suffer, but he wasn't willing to waste that much time. "Ashton offered to take me on as his apprentice. Caleb approved yesterday."

"Congratulations." Jack bumped his fist into Tucker's arm with a solid hit. "Good for you."

"Holy shit. That's fantastic." Luke not only pounded him on the back but pulled Tucker into a tight embrace as well. "About time we got to see more of your ugly mug around here."

Hopefully that was the way Luke continued to see things once Tucker's plan to start up more seriously with Ginny came to fruition.

"Thanks," he said sincerely. He lifted his gaze to Ashton. "I got in touch with Raymond back at the stables in Winnipeg. He needs me to clear things out right away, plus I need to pick up Braggart. I thought I'd head out now. Work for you?"

Ashton dipped his head. "Last I checked, the weather looked friendly for a few days."

"If you need me to sign anything while I'm gone, just email."

A muttered conversation between Jack and Luke broke off

as Luke stepped forward. "We're coming with you," he announced.

"Get out," Tucker protested. "It's a full day's drive, twice, and it's going to take me at least a couple of days to help my old boss with some final tasks."

Jack answered this time, smile flashing as he grinned. "I'm on vacation, remember? Part of what I'd love to do is see more of Canada."

A snicker escaped Luke. "Nice try, but no one will believe that's the selling feature for us to get away. We'll be driving east through some of the flattest land God created."

"Good point," Jack returned. Then he looked Tucker in the eye. "I've been foreman for my family stables for over fifteen years, and I love to talk. Consider me your own private question and answer service."

Which was a gold mine of an opportunity. Still...

"You think your wife—your *wives*—won't mind you leaving for a chunk of days in the middle of your visit?" He included Luke in the question.

"They were already plotting some girls-only thing that we can't be around for." Luke shrugged. "They'll be fine. Give us twenty minutes and we'll be ready to go."

Tucker would be a fool to turn down time with his friend and time with a willing resource who could make his future life easier. "If you're sure, I'd love the company," he admitted.

Jack hooted. Luke slapped him on the back, and the two of them took off running like they were teenagers with a free hall pass.

Even Uncle Ashton was amused. "They're good people," he told Tucker. "I'm glad you didn't ignore their offer and insist you could do it on your own."

He usually would have, Tucker realized, except that option

hadn't felt right. "There's something about Silver Stone that makes me want to make it a group effort."

Ashton's expression turned serious. "You know, that's nearly word for word something Walter Stone used to say a lot. The group effort part. How it was everyone doing their part that made the job easier. That got the important things dealt with."

His uncle sent him off with a promise to look into a different living situation for when he got back. "I suppose if you have to, you can stay in the trailer, but that's only temporary."

As far as Tucker was concerned, as long as Ginny came with the accommodations, he had zero problems with it.

He drove his truck up to Luke's house where it overlooked Little Sky Lake to grab his drive buddies. While he waited, he got out and stood in the cold, admiring the snow-covered landscape.

Luke had built on a small rise, and while the main ranch buildings and Caleb's house were close enough to the left, the actual house faced slightly more to the northwest, offering a pristine wilderness view over the smaller of the two lakes.

This wintery picture wasn't one that Tucker had gotten to enjoy often. He'd spent so many summers here, but the first time he'd come out to the ranch in the winter had been the February of the accident. He'd visited every year after that for some non-official memorial sharing. It had felt right to make sure he was around.

It had been one of those non-official winter visits when Ginny had talked her way into his bed.

Smiling now at that memory, he let his gaze wander, tracing trails into the bush, following them into the distance where Heart Falls would be ice-locked and beautiful. He looked to the south and spotted men already at work in the arena. There were trucks leaving the ranch hand parking area outside the bunkhouse as workers headed out to whatever tasks Ashton had assigned them.

Something akin to terror filled his veins. He wanted this so bad. To be a part of Silver Stone. To have the right to be here, and not just the job. To be the man Ginny needed.

Her Operation *Prove It*—he felt the urge to succeed all the way down to his soul.

Luke poured out the door with Jack on his heels. "Whoohoo, let's get this party bus on the road."

Kelli and Diane poked their heads out and waved farewell.

Luke handed Tucker a travel mug. "I was ready to pour you a manly drink, but Kelli interfered."

"I love you, Kelli," Tucker called toward the door. "Anytime you want to leave this loser, give me a shout."

"But I've got him half trained," Kelli complained. "Have fun storming the castle, boys."

Feminine laughter followed as the ladies disappeared back inside the warm house.

Tucker was still grinning as he turned onto the main highway and headed them on the shortest route cross country. "Thanks for the coffee."

"You need to stop flirting with my wife. Get yourself a woman of your own," Luke said dryly.

Tucker wasn't going to touch that. Not yet.

Didn't help that Jack stuck to the same tune. "Anyone you have to say goodbye to while we're packing your stuff?" he asked from the backseat.

"No one," Tucker assured him. "Packing won't take long, but my boss needs some help moving horses. Before we leave, I'll grab my trailer so I can bring my ride with us on the return journey."

"Braggart is a sweet thing," Luke informed Jack. "Ashton

trained her, and I swear she can read Tucker's mind sometimes."

"The best kind of woman," Jack said with a grin. "Human or equine."

Tucker chuckled. "I'm pretty sure that's the sort of talk that gets you kicked out of bed in the evening as well as the morning. You know, comparing her to a horse."

"Are you kidding?" Jack said. "Diane knows it's a compliment of the highest order when I start talking horsey."

"That's just wrong," Luke complained. "You're giving me so many openings for crude jokes, when I'm working to be polite and not shock Tucker."

"I think you were one step away from shocking my uncle," Tucker said. He wasn't about to share what Ashton had confessed, but he was curious how well his uncle had been keeping secrets.

"With my little 'why don't you simply confess what you've been up to' oops? Yeah, not my business, but damn is it tempting to poke the man at times." Luke took a sip of coffee and eased back in his seat. "He didn't take me apart too badly when I got involved with Kelli, so I like to give him a little slack when it comes to his love life."

"I hope my relationship situation is a whole lot less complicated when I'm in my sixties," Jack said. "Good to get it established while we're young."

"So your ladies can train you up right?" Tucker teased.

"Definitely." Jack laughed. "Let me know if you need help finding someone. I've got a couple skilled trainers I could send your way who are single."

Tucker glanced at Luke. "Is he pimping me out?"

"Not my fault," Luke insisted. "Maybe you should take him up on it. Get some new blood happening. There's no one around town. Of course, I shouldn't say that. You know the Fields sisters. And there's a few others who—"

"I'm not looking to get set up," Tucker said quickly.

Thirteen hours on the road. This would be one hell of a trip if he had to spend the entire time convincing his friends he wasn't in need of female companionship.

Tucker glanced beside him to discover Luke grinning from ear to ear.

"We'll stop now. You're probably focused on the whole mentoring thing, and I get it. I'm pretty pumped myself," Luke admitted. "And what a way to start. Road trip for the win. Although I should not be shotgun, but behind the wheel."

"Hell, no," Tucker returned. "When your dad taught us to drive, he said I was a far better student than you. Safety-conscious and astute."

"Boring brownnoser. You're lucky he didn't see you doing doughnuts in the community hall parking lot a month later," Luke snapped back.

"You were too chicken." Tucker said it dryly, then braced for the inevitable.

Sure enough...

His entire body rocked when Luke smacked his fist into Tucker's biceps. "Jerk."

"Ass."

Laughter rolled from the backseat. "It's like a Canadian comedy show, with less *eh*'s than expected."

Tucker raised a hand and flashed his middle finger, snickering hard when he realized Luke had done the exact same thing beside him.

"You guys crack me up." Jack groaned then sighed heavily. "Wake me when we're five minutes from our next pit stop, will you? I'm still not adjusted from the time zone difference."

"Will do," Luke assured him. He dropped his voice a notch

and spoke quietly to Tucker. "In the meantime, let's get caught up. What have you been doing for the last while?"

Tucker shared the everyday, ordinary events of his life since the last time they'd been together, and it was a bit of perfection.

The only thing that would have made it better was to have had Ginny beside him as well.

~

GINNY WAS HALFWAY across the yard when Dustin came running up. "Hey, Gin. Wait up a sec."

He was so annoying.

She glared at her little brother. "I'm pretty sure you have enough strength to get out the two syllables that make up my name. This is your final warning, or I will convince everyone to go back to calling you Dusty."

His cocky grin grew bigger than it should have. "Fine. I was only teasing. Real news of the day, Tamara and Caleb gave me a heads up about you moving into the cottage. I wanted to let you know, there's no problem."

"Thanks." Ginny was actually a little surprised he was that willing to give it up so easily. Maybe Tamara's premonition about Dustin not hanging around for too much longer was true, which in that case, Ginny wanted to know now so she could make sure her little brother planned some smart moves. "You have plans?"

He snickered. "I swear you sounded just like mom right then."

A wave of sadness rolled in and over her, gone in a flash. "I'll take that as a compliment."

"There's a lot I don't remember, but I do have these scenes in my head. Sometimes I wonder if I've half made them up, based on pictures I found in photo albums or stories people told me." Dustin gave her a wry smile. "I think she used to get people to admit stuff without ever actually coming out and asking directly."

"That was her." Ginny laughed softly. "Mom would ask a direct question that was a hundred and eighty degrees from what you would actually end up confessing to. It was like magic," she shared.

Dustin nodded, thoughtful now, and Ginny was reminded all over again how young he'd been when their Mom and Dad had died. How few memories he really had of time with them.

"Anyway, to answer the question you asked *and* the one that you didn't," Dustin teased, "I'm not a hundred percent sure I want to try my hand at rodeo. Not with all the possibilities around here. But in the meantime, Shim is sticking around for at least a couple of months. He is dying to live in crew quarters, so Ashton found us space in the bunkhouse."

"He's..." Ginny wasn't quite sure how to say this without it coming out sounding offensive. "He's not from around here, is he?"

Her kid brother wiped at his mouth, covering a laugh. "No. Very urban upbringing, very straightlaced, intellectual and non-outdoorsy parents. But he's a good guy, so I figured, why the hell not? I've lived in crew quarters before."

"Plus, you don't mind eating at the mess hall, do you?" Ginny said dryly.

"We've got one of the best cooks in the county." Dusty checked his watch. "I need to get going or Ashton will have my ass. Everything's cleared out of the cottage, so you can move in any time you want."

That was unexpected. "Already?"

Dustin shrugged, walking backwards. "Didn't have much stuff in the first place."

He strode away, suddenly looking so grown up that Ginny

could've mistaken him for one of her older brothers. She called after him, "Hey, Dustin. I'll have you guys over for supper sometime, okay?"

He offered a thumbs-up but kept walking.

She knew the feeling. Being late for a meeting with Ashton was not something that a person did on a regular basis...

The sudden realization hit her. Holy cow. That's who *Tucker* would be. The man who, when he said jump, men would stop in the middle of their conversation and hurry back to work.

Yeah, being careful starting a public relationship between her and Tucker was pretty damn important. That said, she really didn't want to give him up. Not even temporarily.

Time to give herself something else to think about rather than brooding. Ginny made her way past the main ranch house to the long, low greenhouse that had been her domain before she'd left.

It was well below freezing outdoors, so stepping inside was like instantly changing seasons. The heaters were still on winter settings, barely enough to keep pipes and materials from freezing. Warm enough that when Ginny took a deep breath in through her nostrils, the rich scent of soil and growing things temporarily at rest filled her senses.

The roof overhead and the walls were all made of a semi-clear polycarbonate material. It let in the light but was nowhere near as see-through as a regular glass, helping stop plants from burning in direct sun. It also retained heat better than clear glass, turning the inside of the building into a secret hideout that glowed with warmth and light.

At this end of the greenhouse there were a number of raised beds covered with boards for now. The grow lights above them were turned off, but everything was prepared for the next go-round of planting seeds and getting a head start on spring.

She walked slowly between the rows, past where the raised beds stopped and into the area with well-fertilized and screened soil where she could plant directly into the ground.

Outside, to the west and south, lay the rest of the expanse of gardens. They were covered now with a blanket of white, but as she peered through the one clear glass window at the far end of the greenhouse, it looked as if everything waited.

Waited for her to make a decision about what to do next.

Too bad she didn't know what the answer was yet.

Was it right to change course and veer away from the path she'd walked for years? She might not have spent the past three growing seasons at Silver Stone, but she'd spent them at operations that were very similar. Farms, and vineyards, and in one case, a community that had banded together to make a garden for everyone. Work at all of them had followed the seasons, and Ginny would have to here as well. Which meant deciding soon—this wasn't something she could sit on for weeks or months.

Which was why she needed inspiration.

For the next hour, she wandered from one end of the greenhouse to the other. She dug her fingers into pots of dirt, sniffed buckets, poked under the sinks, and basically got herself dirty. This, even more than the house where Caleb and Tamara lived, had become her home after her mom and dad died.

The greenhouse had been Ginny's domain. She'd liked having something to be in charge of.

Oh.

She stopped dead in her tracks, sitting in the middle of the path and tracing her fingers over the rough pressed concrete under her butt.

"I feel as if I'm not in charge of my life anymore." She said it out loud, quietly, but in the stillness, it was a profound statement. It also wasn't true, because she absolutely got to decide.

But what?

Do the next thing, sweetie.

Ginny sighed even as she answered back to the voice in her head. *Great advice, Mom, but there's no current to-do list anymore.*

And until she made one, there was no use in starting anything.

She scrambled to her feet, brushed off her hands, and headed back to her truck. Right now she needed something more to listen to than dirt. She needed her friends.

Half an hour and one text message later, Ginny pushed through the door at Buns and Roses.

"Incoming."

It was the only warning Ginny got before being wrapped up in a huge hug and squeezed tight. Tansy Fields gave her one more fierce squeeze before pulling back far enough to grasp Ginny by the head and give her an exaggerated set of kisses on her cheeks, one side, then the other, then the other.

"Stop manhandling her," Tansy's sister Rose demanded before taking over and hugging Ginny just as tightly. "About time you got here."

Ginny went warm to the base of her toes. "Didn't know for sure if I should stop at your place of work. I don't want to interrupt."

Tansy tugged her to the side of the room where they obviously had a table. "Sunday is our day off. Well, after I finish the morning baking."

"Not Monday anymore?" Ginny should've figured that out during her visits over the last six months, but most of those brief excursions had been straight to the ranch to take advantage of every minute she could spend with her nieces and nephew.

"Sunday *and* Monday," Rose said happily before gesturing toward the counter. Their youngest sister Fern waved back, her shiny prosthetic made up today like an android arm. "Fern is helping during the holidays, but we've got a couple of other people hired on so that we can take more time off."

"Good for you," Ginny said, impressed and happy for them.

Tansy sat, keeping an arm wrapped around Ginny's shoulders. "Did you get all the travelling out of your system?"

"And then some," Ginny admitted quietly. She leaned her head against Tansy and glanced at Rose. Took in these two friends who had been in her life for as long as she could remember. "I want to get caught up. I want to know about all the changes, especially the good things, like that you're doing well enough you can hire extra staff. But I also just want to spend time with you."

"Same," Tansy agreed. She slipped away far enough to lean her elbows on the table and meet Ginny's gaze straight on. "Everyone feels like that, so gird your loins. We're having a girls' night out this week, and you are the main event."

Ginny didn't need to be the center of attention. "I just want to see everybody."

Fern brought over a tray with drinks and brownies and pieces of pie that were big enough to make even Tucker blink. "Hi, Ginny. Nice to have you back. Your brothers were so excited. Dustin must've told me ten times that you'd be home in a few days."

Interesting. Ginny kept her expression neutral. Was her little brother making a move on Fern? "Did he now?"

"He and his friend helped me make the props for the Christmas fundraiser." Fern put the last cup of coffee in front of Rose. "Shim seems nice."

Oh, now there was a plot twist. "He's very nice. He'll be staying at Silver Stone for a while longer."

Fern tucked the tray under her arm and blinked a few times before jerking herself upright. "Oh, that's good."

She turned and walked away even as Ginny stared after her, grinning from ear to ear.

One glance at her friends only made her amusement rise. "Come on. Tell me this isn't the first you've heard about Fern having a crush on Shim?"

Rose still looked absolutely confused. "Who is this Shim fellow?"

"I thought she was making cow eyes at Dustin," Tansy whispered before catching hold of Ginny's hand. "Quick. Spill the tea about the guy so I know whether I need to poison him or not."

"Please. You can't poison him. That would ruin Buns and Roses reputation."

Rose got an evil glint in her eyes. "I'll use hemlock."

"And that won't ruin our reputation?" Tansy demanded.

"Of course not," Rose sniffed. "It's got a horticultural lean to it. Right on brand for me."

Laughter welled up, and between the delicious scents in front of her and the familiar banter of her friends, Ginny finally, *finally*, felt as if things were truly going to be okay.

She wasn't on the path she'd intended to follow, but that was okay. Maybe the best new adventures meant starting right here in her own backyard.

11

———

*M*onday was icy cold, with a wind that made the idea of being outside the last thing Ginny wanted to do. Luckily, she had plenty of other things to occupy her time.

"You don't have to help me do this," she said again to Tamara as they stood in the small living room—slash—kitchen area of what was originally the Hayes cottage.

Tamara raised a brow. "No, I really do." She paused, listening to the childish giggles escaping from the second bedroom. "And they really do as well. Cleaning up the cottage is a good task for everybody to take a turn with. Considering just about everybody has stayed out here at one time or another."

Ginny tried one more time. "Dustin said he cleaned."

"Ha." Tamara coughed then excused herself. "I'm sure he *thinks* he cleaned. I hate to say this, but I can tell your youngest brother was trained by someone who cleans barns."

"Our barns are clean," Ginny said defensively.

Tamara tilted her head. "They're very clean for barns. I, however, used to work in a hospital."

Enough said. Ginny lifted the bucket in her hand. "I'd better get at it, then. Sounds as if the inspections will be fierce."

They worked hard, but as much laughter as elbow grease was involved, especially as the girls dug in and helped. It was a good opportunity to get to know Tamara a little better and ask some pointed questions.

"Since you weren't here the last time I was in charge of the gardens, you don't know what's changed. Let me ask you this instead." Ginny leaned across her kitchen table toward her sister-in-law during a break from scrubbing the cottage clean. "Is there something you wished you only had to walk outside your door to find? Is there something you had back in Rocky Mountain House that you haven't found a replacement for here in Heart Falls?"

Tamara looked thoughtful. "The first one is actually harder to answer, because I grew up on a ranch. I was trained by my aunts that you used what you had and made do. When I go to make meals, I don't sit there wishing for asparagus when it's not asparagus season." She took a sip of her tea and continued. "I have the house garden. Also, you gave the lease to the gardens to the Singh family. They let me have access to produce early when they could."

Ginny had wondered if the family would do that. It wasn't required, but most Community Supported Agriculture projects tried to operate on the barter system as much as possible.

She'd set up a meeting for the start of next week, which meant a deadline. She had to know what to tell them by Monday. No problem.

"I'm glad things worked out well for them." Ginny said. "Sounds as if they've had a couple of good growing years."

"No flooding, no dry spells. Plus the greenhouse, which is

such a big help," Tamara pointed out. "To answer your second question, herbal teas, which sounds like something right up your alley. One of the local ladies in Rocky was obsessed with drying herbs and putting together her own concoctions. I ordered them in for the first year I was here, but last year she decided to retire the online portion of her business. Now I get packages when my dad visits." She made a face. "When he remembers."

Every time Ginny bumped into someone over the next two days, she asked similar questions. She wasn't going to live her life by committee, but if part of what she wanted to do was make life better for her family, providing something they wanted to begin with was a good place to start.

By suppertime on Tuesday her brain was full of ideas. She was also completely settled into the cottage, which seemed very unreal.

Her phone rang, and she grabbed it, sticking it under her ear as she hurriedly pulled on boots and her coat. "Hey."

"Hey, yourself," Tucker said, his deep voice stroking her skin in a caress. "I've only got a minute, but wanted to let you know I've been thinking about you."

"Is this a sex call?" Ginny teased. "Because that's totally on my bucket list, but I'm heading out the door right now."

"Girls' night out at Luke and Kelli's. I heard."

The man had connections. "How's your man-bonding going?"

The sheer happiness in his voice said it all. "Luke is solid as always. Hysterically funny, and I still occasionally feel the urge to kill him. Then while I'm in the middle of debating exactly how to commit said murder, Jack spouts these gems of wisdom and I drop whatever I'm doing to take notes."

"I bet he'd repeat everything as often as you'd like."

"You'd be right. They're good people," Tucker told her.

"And we're sharing tight quarters, so I'm calling you quickly while they're out of the room. Hope to be back late tomorrow."

She didn't bother to tell him about the change of living arrangements. He didn't need to worry about it right now. "And then a whole new game starts."

He swore softly.

Ginny laughed. "You'll do great. I've got to run. Drive safe, and I'll see you soon."

She hurried across the distance to Kelli's house, meeting another familiar friend on the doorstep.

"Brooke." Ginny gave her a hug then leaned away to examine her closely. "So, this is what *married* looks like on you."

The tall mechanic grinned. "It's been a blast. But let's get inside before I freeze my butt off."

"I'm supposed to be the one complaining about how cold it is after not having experienced winter in Canada for three years," Ginny said.

An instant later there was no need to worry about the cold. In fact, Ginny stripped off not just her jacket but the sweater she'd put on underneath. Luke and Kelli's house was far warmer than the little cottage. Ginny would have to figure out a way to deal with the heating issue.

The sound of voices and laughter beckoned, and as soon as they got their boots off, Brooke grabbed Ginny by the hand and led her into the house proper.

"The star of the show has arrived," Brooke announced.

"Ginny." The shout went up from everyone at the same time, the hands thrust in the air already holding filled glasses.

Ginny took a deep breath and looked around, putting names to faces. And then for the heck of it, she said them out loud, pointing at each in turn. "Kelli, Rose, Brooke, Tansy. Although two of you have changed your last names since the last girls' night out I attended." Those were her friends from way back. Now to the newcomers. "Diane and I met on Christmas Day. And you're Yvette Wright, veterinarian."

Yvette waved.

Then Ginny examined the final woman in the room who was at least a few years younger than the rest of them but confidently coming forward with her hand outstretched in greeting. Beautiful dark skin, a mass of curls that bobbed freely around her head.

"Charity Gruzing, yes?"

Charity looked shocked but pleased. She glanced toward the other women. "You're right, she's got that spooky voodoo woman vibe." She shook Ginny's hand. "Do I have a nametag on somewhere?"

"I have two nieces in your ballet class," Ginny reminded her. "They spent the afternoon singing your praises and doing pirouettes into my walls."

"Ah, yes, Sasha and Emma are very...enthusiastic."

"You have more patience than me," Yvette said. "But you honestly seem to enjoy working with the kids, so good for you."

"You're pretty patient yourself," Charity returned. "I saw you convince that abandoned dog to get in your truck."

A story which it seemed most of the women in the room had not yet heard. Which meant to Yvette's embarrassment, Charity proceeded to recite the entire story while Brooke took Ginny to grab a drink.

By the time they were all curled up in the comfortable living room, the faint trace of butterflies Ginny had felt earlier in the day had vanished.

Part of it was having new women in the room—it made her feel as if she weren't the only one who wanted to know *more*. She wasn't the only one who had missed things that had happened recently.

In fact, by the time the buzzer on the oven went off, Ginny's nerves were a thing of the past.

"Pizza," Kelli shouted. "Come on. Serve yourself at the island. There's green stuff on the table for anyone who wants to pretend to balance their meal."

Ginny ended up seated next to Yvette.

"I've heard good things about you," Ginny told her. "My big brother is good friends with Josiah Ryder, and Josiah said you're doing a fantastic job. That even the old grumpy guys like you."

Yvette nodded slowly. "That's good to hear. The bit about Josiah being happy. The part about the old grumpy guys is a little less *hurrah*, because they're still grumpy, and I still have to deal with them."

"I hear you. When I used to drop off the CSA boxes, some of the customers would be cranky and grumbling even as they said thanks, and I was pretty sure they were annoyed because I was making them eat their vegetables."

"Kind of like Kelli?" Yvette asked.

"I heard that," Kelli said then went back to her conversation with Charity.

They both laughed. "You plan to start up the garden boxes again?" Yvette asked.

"Still deciding," Ginny said honestly. "Tell me more about you. Have you got any veterinarians in your background? Grow up on a ranch? Win all the 4-H awards growing up?"

The other woman shook her head. "About as far from that as you can possibly get, to be honest. Most of my family is in the home-building supply business. Plus, my mother and sister are allergic to absolutely everything, so I didn't even have a pet."

Not at all what Ginny had expected. "Wow. What made you decide to take a new course?"

Yvette shrugged. "I like animals. I like caring for them and making them feel better. It might not be something my family ever considered, but when I really sat down and thought about what would make me happy to do for a whole lot of years, being a veterinarian hit all the high points."

"Good for you." Ginny meant it sincerely. Then she leaned forward and asked a variation on the same question she'd been asking nonstop for the past two days. "What's the one thing you wish you could get here in Heart Falls?"

"A local surprise box," Yvette said instantly.

Ginny had no idea what that meant. "Explain."

"They're all the thing on social media. Cause boxes or book boxes or art boxes. Subscriptions, so once a month or once a quarter, you get a selection of things sent to you." Yvette's cheeks flushed slightly. "I like to collect knickknacks, but with how busy my job is, the opportunity to wander through collectible shops isn't there. Plus, I like the idea of supporting local, so when I can order stuff online, I don't want to have stuff shipped long distances. Small footprint impact, but still a lot of fun."

Ginny scooped her jaw off the ground. "You're brilliant. Plus, you just articulated a big part of what I've been looking for, and I didn't even ask you the right question. Thank you."

Impulsively she put her arms up to give Yvette a hug.

Somehow, she jerked herself to a stop right before making contact. "Oops. Are you a hugger?"

Yvette grinned. "Not always, but I'll make an exception for you."

She scooped Ginny in for a tight squeeze.

The party went on for a while. Ginny ate far too many pieces of pizza, followed by one of Tansy's enormous cinnamon buns. And they talked and showed each other pictures on their phones, and in some cases exchanged phone numbers for the first time.

At the end of the night, Ginny felt as if she'd been wrapped up in the biggest, most enormous fuzzy blanket in the entire world. Her belly was full of good food, her female friendships shored up or begun.

That seed of an idea that had tickled in her brain before was now firmly planted and ready to be watered.

Now to get the rest of the garden ready, figuratively speaking.

~

THEY WERE on the road bright and early Wednesday morning for the trek back to Heart Falls.

Tucker's boss Raymond had nearly fallen over when he got not just Tucker, but Luke and Jack's help as well for two days. The man had bought them dinner at the end of each shift plus given Tucker a bonus along with his final check.

A whole lot of things came to mind he could spend the money on. The first place his thoughts went was to a celebratory dinner and a getaway with Ginny, which was kind of how they had operated in the years before she'd left the country. He'd book a couple of nights somewhere modestly comfortable—the limit of his abilities. He'd never had enough money or time to spoil her the way he wanted, but considering they usually spent most of their time in the room, clean and comfy had been their highest priority.

They'd had a whole lot of sexual energy to burn. Still did.

"Lots on your mind?" The question came from Luke, who was once again riding shotgun.

Since Tucker couldn't really explain that he was bemoaning his inability to set up a sex-fest with Luke's little sister, he scrambled for an equally valid excuse. "Mentally making lists of things I need to do. Lots of lists. Lots and lots of to-do lists."

A slightly evil chuckle drifted from the passenger seat. "You know, Ashton's been around for so long, this is going to be rather amusing."

Tucker didn't even think about it. His hand automatically lifted and swung, fist smacking into Luke's raised forearm. "Jerk."

"Yeah, this will be highly entertaining." Luke rubbed his arm, little more thoughtful now. "You done any fighting recently?"

"Only when I have to." Tucker glanced at his friend. "You?"

Luke shrugged. "The occasional time. Usually when someone is getting out of line, but Ashton runs a tight ship. Ranch hands who can't follow the rules don't last long."

Which was pretty much what Tucker had figured. And it just pointed out again exactly how big the boots were that he hoped to eventually fill.

Ashton had been at the ranch since nearly day one. He'd worked beside Walter Stone and Joseph Hayes, and out of everyone there, even more than Caleb, Tucker's uncle knew what the direction and hopes had been when they'd established the ranch.

Yet it wasn't trepidation in Tucker's gut about taking over, not when he really thought about it.

"You all set a solid course for Silver Stone," Tucker said slowly. "You, Caleb, Walker. You're making it your own. Not just now, with the change in finances. But every step over the past years—you've truly made a difference."

Luke looked pleased. "You think so?"

A snort rose from the back seat. "Please," Jack drawled. "You need your ego caressed a little more, sweetheart?"

"Ass," Luke said affectionately. "And yes. I want to hear all the good things we've accomplished praised."

"Of course, you do," Jack said. He laid a hand on Tucker's shoulder and squeezed, speaking in a mock-whisper. "That's part of what a good foreman does. Good for you for figuring that out."

Tucker knew exactly what was going on, but he met Jack's gaze in the rearview mirror and offered a wink. "It's my job to remind my bosses what they've achieved?"

"Pet them on the back and give them cookies," Jack returned. "Children work much better when they're rewarded on a regular basis."

"Hey." Luke twisted in the seat and glared sternly at his friend. "Whose side are you on?"

"Yours, of course," Jack said, deadpan serious. "You want a blankie? Stuffed animal? Glass of warm milk?"

Luke threw his empty coffee cup at the back seat.

Amusement rumbled up from low in Tucker's gut. "Hellions. No fighting in my truck."

That initial feeling of being on the outside looking in had vanished completely over the past couple of days. The sensation had been replaced by something new and wonderful. Luke was still his best friend. Having Jack in the picture hadn't taken away from that years-solid base, but instead added to it.

Another one of those changes from the past that was good to see and understand at a core level.

Tucker met Jack's gaze again. "Let's talk about my first to-do list, if you don't mind."

"Not at all." Jack's patient enthusiasm was a gift. "I'm all yours."

The drive home passed quickly, but it was still late enough

when they arrived that Luke and Jack were eager to get together with their wives.

Tucker unloaded his horse into the stall that had been arranged for her, then hurried back to the trailer.

Ginny and all of her things were missing.

A note lay on the table.

Tamara and Caleb moved me into the cottage already. Hope you had a good trip home. Watching movies with the girls tonight. I'll try and catch you in the barn sometime tomorrow.

Operation Prove It now begins!
X, Ginny

Disappointment and exhaustion battled for top billing. Tucker decided to take advantage of the unexpected dose of quiet, made a simple meal and hit the sack early.

The next morning, he found himself swept into a meeting with Ashton and Caleb. Paperwork was signed, and they took a tour around the main ranch buildings. Not even a week ago when Tucker had first arrived, Ashton had showed him around, but the information hit a whole lot harder now.

Caleb rested a booted foot on the bottom railing as they stood by the arena, hands draped casually on the top bar as he, Ashton, and Tucker paused to watch Kelli and Luke work one of the new horses.

"She's got a gift," Caleb said.

"She does, and she's not the only one," Tucker agreed, casting an experienced eye at some of the other ranch hands. His brain was full to the brim, and in spite of Jack's help narrowing down where to start, the moment still felt overwhelming.

Ashton folded his arms over his chest and sighed contentedly. "Things are good overall."

"Even better than I expected," Tucker confessed. He went for straight-up honest, because working with the man, it would be better to not tiptoe around issues. He met Caleb's gaze straight on. "The only thing I don't understand is your lack of focus."

Caleb blinked. "Explain."

Tucker shrugged. "You've branched out into a lot of areas. That's not a bad way to put money on the table, but it's not how Silver Stone becomes established as the best at what she does. You've got the breeding program, you train horses for everything from personal rides to rodeo stock. You raise cattle, you had a semi-commercial agricultural arm."

"Only made sense," Ashton said, a little more gruffly than usual. "Diversifying brought in money."

"I'm not saying it's wrong," Tucker insisted. "But I am saying that it's something you need to think about going forward. If you like what you're doing, then we'll carry on and find ways to make each part of the operation stronger and more lucrative. Or, if you don't want to keep that many pots on the fire, you could pick the ones you like best and specialize. Since you're no longer fighting to keep finances balanced."

Caleb's expression seemed stern, but he blinked more than usual, which Tucker recognized as a tell the man was considering brand-new thoughts. "You're saying I need to take my own advice. The way I told everybody on Christmas Eve to dream about what they'd like to do."

Tucker dipped his chin. "If you want to bounce ideas around, Ashton and I are more than willing to listen."

"Huh." Caleb stared at Luke and Kelli, but his gaze seemed far more distant. "I might take you up on that."

Conversation shifted to other topics. Eventually Ashton

hauled Tucker into the mess hall for lunch, the cook serving up an eclectic mix of classic ranch food and tasty, spicy Indian dishes that created a mouth-watering aroma that set Tucker damn near drooling.

He settled opposite his uncle and dug into his food, the empty hole in his stomach messing with his manners.

When he finally paused, he looked up and discovered Ashton sitting across from him, arms once again folded over his chest and a highly disapproving expression back in place. "Sorry. Didn't realize I was that hungry."

"Your lack of table manners isn't the part I'm pissed about," Ashton growled.

Yeah, Tucker had figured this was coming. And yet, same as he had with Caleb, he figured it was better to start as he meant to go on. Which had in fact, been one of the bits of advice that Jack had offered that made a hell of a lot of sense.

"You mean me asking Caleb to consider the overall direction of Silver Stone going forward?"

Ashton's frown deepened. "I thought you planned to apprentice under me, not take over the first chance you got."

Tucker put down his fork and wiped his mouth clean with his napkin, considering his words. "I absolutely want to apprentice, but what I said to Caleb goes for you as well. With the changes available to Silver Stone, plus me joining the mix, you need to think hard about what you want. There's not much use in training me to do something that will be obsolete a year down the road."

Ashton made a harrumphing noise.

The fact his uncle wasn't tearing a strip off him at that moment was a positive thing. Tucker went on, allowing amusement to slide into his tone. "Plus, I figure you have no intention of retiring completely."

"Damn right."

"So tell me I was wrong to nudge the two men with the most influence to consider all their options." Tucker leaned forward and winked at his uncle. "Nope. Thought not."

"Ungrateful brat," Ashton murmured, but he picked up his fork and went back to his plate instead of continuing to harass Tucker.

And so it began.

12

———————

ew Year's came and went in a flash, and as they rolled into January, Ginny found herself retreating to the cottage at the end of each day far more exhausted than expected.

Finding a new path forward meant a lot to do, and all of it seemed to involve other people. There were her friends who felt they had years to catch up on, and rightly so. Her nieces and nephew wanted to spend time with her. Plus, sharing time with each of her new sisters-in-law—who were, thank God, nothing like Caleb's first wife—was also high on Ginny's daily activity list.

Thoughts of the cold-blooded creature still gave Ginny nightmares if she were being honest.

She quietly said something to that effect to Tamara while they were cleaning up after lunch on Monday. Emma's happy laughter echoed in the room, simultaneously driving guilt and happiness into Ginny's heart

Ginny eyed her niece. "I had no idea how much damage

Wendy caused. I'm so glad you're in their lives," she admitted as she and Tamara worked quietly beside each other.

Tamara paused in the middle of washing and laid her hand on Ginny's. "You couldn't have known."

"I lived right here," Ginny said gruffly. "I should have seen that Wendy's attitude was more than simply someone uncomfortable with her surroundings. When I heard she'd had been abusive, I kept thinking back for some sign that I missed. I wish with everything in me I had stopped it."

Dishes forgotten, Tamara grabbed Ginny by the hand and tugged her until they were face to face. "It was not your fault," she said clearly, still softly though, as the girls entertained their brother in the living room only feet away. "Caleb does this at times, as well. He beats himself up for not being perfect. And it's useless, because it's in the past. If you had seen, you would've changed things, but now things are different anyway. We move forward, we don't look back."

Which was usually Ginny's way, but the thought still haunted her. "I was too tangled up in my own head," she confessed.

Tamara stole the dishtowel from her hands, stepped back as she twirled it a couple of times, then applied a well delivered *snap* to Ginny's thigh.

"Ouch," Ginny exclaimed loud enough to draw the attention of small children playing nearby.

Tamara was winding up again. "If you don't stop, I'll give you something else to worry about."

Ginny raised her hands, backing away. "Okay, okay. I'll behave."

Emma came rushing to her defense, which emphasized Tamara's point even more. "Auntie Ginny, you need to be good," she teased. "Mama only hits Papa with the dishtowel when he's been naughty."

"Very naughty," Tamara said, totally amused. "Which means I don't have to do it very often."

Sasha wandered up, Tyler on her hip. His little toddler arms were wrapped in a stranglehold around his big sister's neck. "Tyler says he wants to go look for kittens."

Tamara rested her fists on her hips and offered her oldest daughter a *look*.

Sasha opened and closed her mouth a few times before speaking again. "Oops. Sorry, Mom. Tyler, tell Mommy what you want to do now."

Tyler bared his little teeth and made a meowing sound.

"Then I guess that's what we're doing next." Tamara slid over and gave Ginny a squeeze. "You're a wonderful auntie, and wonderful sister. Never forget that," she chided softly in Ginny's ear.

Emma caught Ginny's fingers. "Are you coming to the barn with us?" she asked

It would've been nice to try and catch a glimpse of Tucker, whom Ginny hadn't seen since he got back, but unfortunately, that wasn't an option. "I have to meet someone at the greenhouse," she informed her niece.

Emma patted her hand sadly. "Don't work too hard."

Ginny was still snickering about the serious tone in the little girl's voice as she made her way across the yard and into the warmth of the greenhouse.

Devjeet and Janae Singh were waiting for her, their concern clear even as they welcomed her back.

Ginny hurried to put them out of their misery as quickly as possible. "I have heard nothing but good things about how well you ran the CSA boxes the past years," Ginny assured them. "I want to know if you're interested in continuing to run it going forward."

The couple exchanged glances before turning back with

both excitement and confusion. "Don't you need to run it now for your family?" Janae asked.

Ginny wiggled a hand from side to side. "I have an opportunity to make some changes. I thought maybe we can work together and come up with some new plans that will work for all of us. But I don't want you to carry on unless it's something you want."

"We're interested," Devjeet said instantly.

"Very interested," Janae echoed. "But what kind of changes are you talking about?"

"This conversation requires a pot of tea." Ginny gestured them toward the small kitchen at the side of the building.

The one good thing about Tucker being buried in work was that Ginny had spent her past evenings coming up with ideas. Between her friends' suggestions and everything that had percolated during her time away, she was ready to lay what she hoped were interesting options on the table.

Ginny dove in. "I still want CSA boxes available to Heart Falls and all the communities you've reached. I plan to focus more on growing herbs, both for the teas I used to make and possibly branching into skincare and bath products."

Devjeet nodded slowly. "We've done limited herbs to include in the boxes. The perennials you established are still there, but not that well-tended, I'm afraid."

"That's okay, I'd like to do a bit of a revamp, but it means I will need some space in the exterior gardens until we have time to expand. Plus, I'll need room for seedlings here in the greenhouse."

"We've already ordered vegetable seeds for this year," Janae told her. "The same way we have every year, based on how you set us up that first time. So you'll need to order anything new. I have all the records for you."

Ginny thought quickly. "We can go over them, but the idea

isn't for me to take over. You two still make the decisions, and I get to start brand new mischief."

"But we can overlap a little, yes?" Devjeet suggested. "If you have enough herbs to include in the boxes?"

"We'll discuss that." Ginny promised. "Also, you know my sister-in-law, Ivy, assistant principal at the school?"

Janae nodded. "She teaches our daughter in Grade Two. Our son is in Grade Five."

"I'd forgotten how big they are." Ginny shook her head. "Anyway, she asked about starting a garden at the school this spring. I'll line up some help from a few local organizations to build raised beds, but the school kids would get the garden started. We'll open it up to the community to continue running over the summer."

Devjeet look surprised but nodded. "That sounds like a good community builder."

Ginny nodded. "It shouldn't affect the sales of your boxes. In fact, you might possibly get more subscribers when the kids start asking for local carrots."

"Local carrots taste better," Janae recited in a childish voice, obviously imitating their daughter.

The three of them talked for over an hour, and the longer they brainstormed, the more ideas kept coming up. More adjustments were made to the plans as Devjeet and Janae caught some of her fire and got more and more excited about Ginny's ideas.

In the end, Devjeet shook her hand and Janae outright hugged her before they left.

Ginny wandered back to her cottage, hands shoved into her pockets, whistling into the cold, her breath rising in puffs of white on the chilly air.

It was a plan barely started, but something deep inside said it was the right place. She might not get everything right, but this one might end up making a difference.

Down near the barns, two familiar outlines appeared on horseback. Tucker and Ashton returning from wherever they'd been working that afternoon. Ginny was getting anxious for a chance to see Tucker. To catch him up on where she was at with Operation *Prove It*...

Oh, who was she kidding. She just missed the guy. She wanted to talk to him and hold him *and* jump his bones.

She slipped into the cottage and topped up the wood in the stove, trying to beat back the winter chill that seeped through the little wooden walls far too easily.

She typed off a quick message.

Ginny: *your evil overlords need to give you some time off.*

The paperwork Janae had given her took up the rest of Ginny's afternoon. She made up a new order for the additional herbs and the supplies for the community gardens.

She was washing up her dinner dishes when her phone buzzed, and she opened up Facetime to discover Tucker smouldering back at her.

"I'm sorry, I don't accept video calls from total strangers," she teased.

"Good to know. I'll be sure to warn off all the total strangers who keep asking for your number." He leaned back on the couch in the trailer and rolled his neck gently from side to side. "The evil overlords on this ranch have somehow added extra hours to the regular daily rotation."

"Poor, baby." Her fingers damn near twitched with the urge to head over there and give him a neck rub. "How's it going, though?"

He drank half a bottle of water before responding.

"Good, I think." Tucker leaned forward on his elbows, considering hard. "Let's see. You said for Operation *Prove It* we got to bitch about one thing and celebrate one thing, right?"

"Top points, Mr. Stewart," Ginny said. "You bitching or cheering first?"

"Both at the same time. Silver Stone operations are set to run like clockwork. Which means there's a lot of people who really know how to do their job well."

Ginny made a face. "This sounds ominous."

"Yeah. Part two, there's a few people who don't know how to do their job, but they're pretty damn sure they do, so I'm anticipating a few fights in the future."

Which was one of the things they'd talked about. "You'll manage them."

He shrugged. "I will. I would prefer they got their shit together instead of having to fire them." He looked her over. "How about you? How are you conquering your project?"

She caught him up with her ideas for the greenhouse. "My thing to celebrate? I made a plan. I'm not going to be a garden goddess anymore."

He blinked. "Really?"

"Really." It had taken putting everything down on paper to see it clearly. "Not a kitchen garden goddess, at least. I'm diving into specialization. Herbs—for teas and cooking to begin with, then branching into bath and beauty products."

"Good for you," he said with approval. "That's a very clear business plan you've nailed down in a very short time. Well done."

His compliment made her glow. She leaned in and grinned. "You'd have been so proud if you'd seen me, Tucker. I used at least ten pages and a big thick Sharpie to write out everything I needed to consider. And *then* I used up most of a roll of tape sticking them to the walls so I could order and reorder my goals until I figured it out."

"Hmmm." He waggled his brows. "Dirty girl, seducing me all over again with your talk about spreadsheets and checklists."

"I know. Filthy, isn't it? I even threw in a bunch of 'I am…' statements. Oh, and the Sharpies were all colour-coded."

He groaned at that, deep and husky.

They grinned at each other.

It was good chatting with him like this, but also slightly annoying. "I miss you," she said abruptly. "It kind of sucks that we're less than a ten-minute walk away from each other, and we're Facetiming."

He crooked a finger. "Come on over."

It was tempting. Oh so very tempting, and yet it hadn't even been a week, dammit. Add in he'd just admitted the balancing act of making changes and earning the ranch hands' respect had begun?

She had to be strong and stick to the plan for his sake.

Which meant a little distraction right now would be a good idea. "I was just complaining a little. But that doesn't mean I'm not interested in a good time."

Tucker chuckled. "I'm fairly well endowed, but this kind of distance is beyond me."

Ginny hooted. "Nothing wrong with your ego."

He flashed a brief smile and her heart flipped. Then she focused on blowing his mind. "Good thing we have the wonders of technology to bring us together."

She slowly undid the buttons on her shirt then peeled the front apart to reveal a whole lot of cleavage.

On one level, watching Ginny Stone get naked did not suck.

The fact that he was *here* and she was *there* though? Sucked was beyond an understatement.

As she peeled back the sides of her blue flannel shirt, he could all but feel the soft texture under his fingertips.

"What are you doing?" he demanded.

The shirt slid from her shoulders and she backed her chair away from the table. Whatever she'd propped her phone against, the new position meant he got a front row view of her spectacular tits in a very sheer blue bra.

He dropped a hand over his hardening cock and gripped it firmly.

She nibbled innocently on her bottom lip. "Want to fool around?"

Always. Forever. Neither of which were the correct answer.

He went for casual and light, since that seemed more appropriate. "You're going to break me, woman."

"Again with the ego." She dropped her gaze over him. "Adjust your screen. I want to see."

He slid the heel of his hand over his length, emphasizing the arm movement, because while his groin was out of the picture, no way would she misunderstand what he was doing. "Maybe I'm comfy like this."

Her eyes flashed. "Fine. Then you won't mind if I do this."

She leaned back in her chair, lifting a hand to her mouth. She slipped two fingers past those pouting lips, tongue extending as she licked. Swirling around until moisture shone in the light. The minx kept her gaze firmly on his as she slid her hand down her body. Past her breasts and over her belly—

Out of sight.

"*Ginny.*" A growl of protest escaped as her eyelids fluttered shut and her head drifted back. Her fingers must've hit their target.

She played mean, which meant he needed to fight fire with fire.

He stood, watching his phone to see exactly what the camera was aimed at. When he got a shot of crotch, he ignored his image and went back to watching her. "Want this?"

She licked her lips again, gaze fixed on his hands as he stroked. "Hallelujah. You're finally sending me a dick pic."

"Nothing as crass as that," he returned. "Move your damn camera so I can see what you're doing."

Both of them fumbled with their phones, stripping away clothes, and then he was staring at her clad in a pair of see-through panties that matched the sinfully sexy bra.

Ginny sighed contentedly. "You have filled out in all the right ways," she said.

He slowed his motions, easing the pressure against his dick. Because the sight of her lush curves relaxing back in her chair, fingers diving under the pale fabric with her knuckles moving in an easy rhythm as she stroked herself—

The visuals alone were going to set him off without any effort.

"Put your fingers in your pretty cunt," Tucker ordered.

A shiver rolled over her. "Such language," she scolded even as a sigh escaped her lips. She followed his command, and the sound turned into a breathless moan. "Show me your cock."

"Soon," he promised. "If I'm doing this, I'm going to do it right."

Her lips curled in a smile. "I like your cock, Tucker. Show me."

"No way. There's nothing pretty about male equipment. Not like how your pussy gets all swollen and wet for me. Opening up so I want to lick every soft fold with my tongue. I love tasting you bloom as I tease the little pebble of your clit out from the pretty little cave where it hides."

Her fingers moved faster under the fabric that was now noticeably wet. "Getting pretty poetic there, sweetheart."

"Sweet words for a sweet pussy. Pet her a little harder. That's it. I want to see your legs quivering." Tucker jammed a hand under his sweats, relief at pumping into his fist enough to make his muscles clench.

Her eyelids dropped to half-mast as she fixated on the hand under his sweats. Then the hand drifting across his chest as he stroked a thumb over his nipple.

"Never sent you something so ordinary as a dick pic. But I hear a dick drop is all the thing." He shimmied the edge of his sweats over a hipbone, pressing the front fabric away with his pumping hand until the tip of his cock was exposed every time he stroked.

"*Tucker.*" Ginny shoved aside the gusset of her underwear, propping her right foot up on the chair beside her and opening wide to his view.

Christ, he was going to die right then and there. "*Fuck.*"

Zero finesse left, he shoved aside his sweats and jacked hard. Watching her fingers tunneling into the wet perfection of her sex. Her other hand cupping her breasts, one and then the other.

He rubbed his thumb over the perfect spot, wishing they weren't in separate rooms, separate spaces, wishing he was there to drop to his knees and put his tongue—

"If I was there, I'd lick you right now. Push your hands away and suck your clit into my mouth. I'd fuck you with my tongue until—"

Ginny choked out a sob, fingers faltering as she gasped in release.

Her pleasure was the trigger he needed. His hips pulsed forward helplessly, the pressure of his hand a pale exchange for the pleasure of her body.

Mindless of everything except watching her come and feeling the release from his own body, Tucker collapsed onto the couch before he realized she had laughed softly. "What evil thing are you thinking now?"

"That was pretty good, wasn't it?" She flicked a finger in the air. "Although I think you failed at target practice."

Shit. He focused forward and realized he'd been so caught up in the moment, he'd simply shot his load everywhere. He cursed softly. "Crap, what a mess."

Her giggle increased in volume. "Sorry?"

He frowned. "You should be. You should come and clean up this mess."

"Me?" she asked, utter innocence on her face. "I had nothing to do with you getting into a...*sticky* situation."

Damn, this woman. He grabbed his T-shirt and tossed it at the floor. Cleanup he would deal with in a while. First, he wanted to make something clear. "That was fun, but this isn't a long-term solution," he warned her.

"I know." She pulled herself upright, adjusting back to a normal face-to-face position. "Only it's right for right now."

That was something to be debated, but he'd respect her wishes for now.

Truth was, after having given Luke, Caleb, and Ashton a heads-up reminder to figure out what it was they truly wanted, the wisdom of keeping his and Ginny's relationship on ice grew less and less logical.

"I want to see you sometime in person this week," Tucker told her.

Ginny nodded slowly. "We'll figure something out. I don't know my schedule yet, because I need to get in touch with a few more people, but yes. I want to see you too."

His phone went off. Alex Thorne, one of the lead hands for the ranch. "I've got to take this," he told Ginny.

She blew a quick kiss and disconnected.

He opened the connection to Alex, thankful it was a phone line, not video. "Tucker here."

"You have time to come to the mess hall?" Alex jumped in, but Tucker was already moving to pull his clothes back in place. The shouts and banging in the background didn't sound very orderly.

"I'll be there in under five," Tucker promised.

By the time he hit the mess hall, whatever tempers had temporarily flared had cooled enough that Alex had it under control.

He was, however, standing in the middle of the hall between two full tables of ranch hands who were lingering after dinner for far too long.

Tucker joined him, marching across the room with his stride firm and his expression as disapproving as possible. "Alex."

The other man grinned. "Sorry to pull you back to work, but Ashton said that you got all the bullshit calls from here on out."

Tucker snorted. "Of course he did."

"Can't blame the man. Seems as if it's the perfect decision while training your replacement." Alex tilted his head the slightest bit to the right. "Jeffrey and Jim. I reminded them they can talk politics all they want elsewhere."

Jeez. Some things never changed. "Religion, politics, money —there's always something to fight about."

"Women. You forgot that one," Alex offered softly. "Table to the left are a little less conservative in their views and a whole lot more willing to ignore the *no bullshit in the mess hall* rule."

"Anyone I need to talk to?" Tucker asked, trusting Alex's opinion.

Not only was Alex one of the lead ranch hands, he was an active coordinator with the Heart Falls firefighting team, which made the man a little more balanced when it came to relationships in the community. He hung out with people other than just his fellow ranch hands, and he seemed solid to the core.

Alex shook his head. "Seems the threat of you or Ashton showing up was enough to calm them down this time."

Or was it only Ashton's displeasure?

One step at a time. Tucker looped an arm around Alex's shoulder and guided him toward the drink station. "Can I buy you a coffee?"

"Big spender," Alex joked. "Sure."

By the time they got themselves drinks and settled at a table near the exit door, most of the men contemplating trouble had slunk out of sight as quickly as they could. Only Jim met Tucker's gaze head on, disapproval written all over him.

Tucker didn't bother to change his expression. He didn't need the man to suck up. He needed him to do his job.

Alex stirred his coffee and chuckled. "Damn. That glare you and Ashton have. Is it genetic, or is it something I can learn?"

"What are you talking about?" Tucker asked with amusement.

"That thing you do. That Ashton does, where you look as if you could zap lasers out of your eyeballs, and woe to the man who triggers the beast."

A snort escaped him. "Are you sure you're a ranch hand? You've got a bit of—"

"—literary genius?" Alex offered.

"—bullshit in you," Tucker finished.

An outright burst of laughter escaped Alex. "You're going

to do just fine," he assured Tucker. "While I'm here, if you ever need an extra hand, let me know."

"Going somewhere?"

Alex dipped his head. "Ashton must've forgotten to tell you. Yeah, he's letting me go on short warning. My parents are back in Manitoba, and they're both on waiting lists for major surgery. Hip and knee replacements. My sister fosters high-needs kids, so she can't drop everything."

That made sense. "You're going home to help them until they recover? I hope you're coming back," Tucker said honestly.

Something a little more unreadable crossed Alex's face. "Hell, yeah, I'm coming back. All sorts of things waiting here for me. Just postponing some of it until the right time, you know?"

The right time. Tucker was beginning to hate that phrase. It represented too much of his life that had been put on hold, waiting for the *right moment*.

He had to find a way to make the right moment arrive sooner than later...

13

———

While it was pretty clear both she and Tucker had hoped for more interaction on a regular basis, the next days flowed into a week, which flowed into time passing all too rapidly without getting the chance to talk with the man.

She'd tracked him down a few times, but every time she closed her approach, a ranch hand, or Ashton, or one of her brothers would show up, so she'd casually keep walking and pretend that everything was business as usual.

Diane and Jack were at the end of their visit, so Kelli and Luke set up a final evening together where laughter and outrageous stories were standard fare. Tucker was there for about half the time before he had to respond to a summons from his uncle. Which meant while Ginny saw him briefly, they weren't together.

She distracted herself by sharing a couple of the funnier moments from her time away, saving her favourite for last.

"Going to the spa was an absolute splurge after being in the French countryside with nothing but lukewarm water in the workers' quarters for a month. So I'm in Paris, all comfy in this robe that's like a heavenly cotton ball. I've had a pedicure and manicure, and I'm so relaxed I'm fuzzy-brained when they send me into a teeny sauna room that's like five feet by five feet. The woman helping me takes my robe and closes the door. I figure it's a small enough space, it must be a private sauna."

"Oh, oh," Diane's eyes were wide. "No?"

"No," Ginny said dryly. "About two minutes later, just when I'm starting to sweat, the door opens and in comes person number two. A guy, who also loses his robe. Followed seconds later by guy number two."

Kelli glanced at Luke, then slapped a hand over her mouth as if trapping some truly dirty comment.

Ginny snickered. "I know what you're thinking, and no. They were not remotely within my 'suitable to date' age range. This was not a fun opportunity waiting to happen."

"You're lucky they didn't have heart attacks seeing you there. Good looking woman, that's all I'm saying." Jack ducked from Diane's mock-fist swing.

"So if you're looking for a sauna in Paris, I have one on the *no* list," Ginny said firmly.

"Unless you're into that sort of thing," Kelli said, waggling her brows. "I'm shocked naked surprises aren't right up your alley."

"Naked with the right people, fine. Naked with those people, not so much."

"Do we really need to listen to you talk about being naked?" Luke asked, looking away from her and shaking his head.

"You're such a prude," Ginny teased. "Get over it."

"You're my sister," he repeated, like there was no other answer ever needed.

Ginny found herself being pulled into a hug when it was

time to say goodnight, since Jack and Diane were leaving early the next morning.

"You take care of my girl, now," Diane said as she squeezed Ginny tight. She leaned in close. "You're a shiny star waiting to light up the world. I'm glad you're here. I hope Kelli gets to enjoy as much of that brightness as you can share."

Ginny warmed inside at the compliment. "Kelli is awesome, and it's been good getting to know you."

"You too, girlfriend." Diane winked. "We'll be back."

Ashton's birthday came and went, but even that ended up not being an opportunity to see Tucker as the guys vanished for a men's only celebration at Josiah's house.

It sucked. Big-time. Hugely, enormously, and only the fact that Ginny was busier than she'd ever thought possible made the days roll by.

But the guys' only party brought to mind the idea Ginny had shelved a few weeks ago. An idea that was also poked back to life as she spent time reading through her mom's journal and tentatively starting to write in the new one she'd been given.

Ginny asked the other day if we could go out for breakfast to Connie's. When I asked what we were celebrating, she told me Caleb and Walter went out to Connie's for breakfast every couple of weeks, and there's no way some other woman could make breakfast as good as I could, so there had to be something special about the place.

Humbled by my child yet again. We now have a girls only date on the agenda, because she's right. I can cook far better than the line cooks at Connie's, but going there together makes it special.

Then there'd been the single-line prompt in Ginny's new journal that asked, *What am I doing to pay it forward?*

Which could mean any manner of things, but in light of her niece's recent comment, this one made sense.

Ginny stopped in to run the idea by Tamara before she said anything to the girls.

"What do you think of having a girls' night out type thing for the kiddos?" Ginny asked.

Tamara blinked. "Go on."

"Sasha said something about our girls' night out being just for grown-ups, and rightly so. It's good they know there are some things they need to work up to." Ginny winked.

"Oh. So you're thinking more than a playdate gathering with their friends?" Tamara considered. "They're usually pretty happy with that."

Ginny wanted to tread carefully, because the last thing she wanted to do was imply that Tamara wasn't doing a fantastic job. Because she totally was, and the girls were thriving.

Still, the words itched to escape. "I thought more like a mother-daughter thing, but since you've got two, I could stand in this time with one of them. Something a little more focused than just general play-time for them to enjoy."

Understanding slid in, and Tamara smiled. "That's a good idea, especially right now. I know Hanna would love to do it with Crissy, and Talia's got a new mother figure in her life. Let's make it happen."

Which was how a few days later they ended up with four little girls nearly vibrating out of their skin as they gathered in the kitchen at the Silver Stone ranch house.

Petite Hanna Ford was there with her daughter Crissy. Tamara had both Sasha and Emma leaning against her sides as they welcome Madison Joy and Talia Zhao into the house.

Madison wore a very bemused but happy expression. As if she couldn't believe she was actually there.

Talia wrapped her arms around Madison's neck and laid

her cheek against hers. "Auntie Ginny, this is my new Mommy."

"Hello, new Mommy," Ginny said as Madison blinked hard, obviously fighting back emotion. "I hear you recently made my kid brother wear pixie wings. You're already one of my favourite people."

Madison laughed, and the afternoon flowed easily from there. Cookies were made, stories shared. When Sasha insisted, Tamara taught them all how to do a wrestling move that could pull a bigger, larger person off balance. While it was fun, it was also important. Planting seeds, making a difference.

The fact that Emma planned to take Dustin down the first chance she got was funny as hell to boot.

Part of the joy of the afternoon was telling Dare about it later. Ginny's sister was mostly amused by the entire idea, but also slightly horrified.

Dare: *I'm so glad I have all boys. How did you even know what to arrange?*
Ginny: *Are you kidding? Have you forgotten Sasha and her opinions that quickly?*
Dare: *What was I thinking? So, pedicures? Manicures?*
Ginny: *Pedicures were labelled "icky" by three out of four of the younger participants, so Madison came up with the brilliant idea of tracing our feet on a piece of paper and giving ourselves virtual pedicures.*
Dare: *Get out. That sounds fun.*
Ginny: *I'll send you a picture of everything later.*
Dare: *I'd love to see them. Also, speaking of pictures... Have you made any headway on the strange message from your parents?*

Ginny sighed. She'd been ignoring that part of the problem. *I sent you a picture of it, didn't I?*

Dare: *Nope. Shoot me a copy, and I'll give it some thought.*
Ginny: *Don't show it around yet, though, okay?*

She wasn't sure why, but it felt wrong to be flashing the page around when it was a present to her, and she couldn't even explain what it meant.

Dare sent an eye roll emoji. *Of course, I'll keep it private. Silly rabbit.*
Ginny: *You can show that cowboy who knocked you up. This isn't a keep-secrets-from-him situation.*
Dare: *You are nothing but trouble, but I love you, Truth.*
Ginny: *I love you, Dare.*

Ginny slipped into the greenhouse early the next morning, breathing deep and once again soaking the sensation in to her very soul.

There were few signs of Devjeet and Janae preparing for the season, but it was still too early to start any seedlings. And they'd obviously left the place in tip-top condition the previous fall.

Even with a lot of work to do it felt good to be in that familiar place. Ginny wandered slowly, remembering previous years, planning what she would grow once the seeds arrived.

She did some research for her idea of branching out into natural cleansers and cosmetics.

She was at the far end of the greenhouse, peering at the snow-covered ground outside the plexiglass wall when a small sound echoed. She spun in time for Tucker to catch her around the hips and lift her, pressing his lips to hers and taking her mouth in a hungry kiss.

It had been far too long. She jammed her fingers into his hair, his cowboy hat flying as she gave back as good as she got.

Tongues tangling, breath growing erratic. She tucked her legs around the back of his body, and the heat between them continued to rise.

He twisted and aimed for the nearest bench, dropping to his knees with her butt landing on the low surface. His breathing heavy, one hand slipped under her shirt as he hungrily retook her lips and palmed her breast at the same time.

Not what she'd expected. Not at all, but also very welcome as she caught fistfuls of his shirt and jerked it free from his jeans until she could put her hands on his bare skin. She pressed her fingers over the rigid planes of his muscles, dragged her fingernails back and drew a gasp from his lips.

He shoved her bra aside, lifted the front of her shirt, and leaned back just far enough to stare at her semi-naked in the low lights. "Dammit, Ginny. This wasn't what I planned."

"It's perfect. Don't stop," she ordered.

His serious expression turned smoky hot as he reached for the button on her jeans, popped it open, dropped her zipper, and pressed her back on the bench far enough to haul the fabric to her ankles.

Then he rose over her like some earthborn God, looking down on her partly naked form. "Hard and fast, yes?"

"Hell, yes," she agreed.

But if she'd bet he would simply free his cock and drive her into the bench, she'd have lost. What he did was dip his head between her knees then rise up so that her ankles were tangled in her jeans on his back and his head was right there over her sex.

He grinned. "My favourite breakfast."

Ginny laughed and then moaned, because he dove in as if he were starving, his mouth on her sex doing terribly wonderful things. She was trapped. The fabric around her ankles kept her locked in position so there was nothing she could do, no way to retreat from the rapid strokes of his tongue and his fingers sliding between her folds, dragging forward a release far quicker than she thought possible.

"Oh. My. God." Ginny involuntarily tightened her fingers in his hair, and for all she knew she tore out chunks of it, but she was coming so hard, her legs squeezed around his head, back arched, and stars floated in front of her eyes.

Then he was up, leaning back so the jeans peeled off one of her legs. A moment later he was covered, and covering her, the thick width of his cock pressing her open as her body continued to tighten.

Tucker placed his hands on the bench on either side of her head. Her feet were draped over his shoulders, and she was obscenely, wonderfully open. He met her gaze and pushed all the way in. Withdrew and did it again. Faster this time, harder.

It felt so damn good. Ginny closed her eyes for a moment. "*Yes.*"

"Look at me." The order came out harsh and deep. "Look at us."

Ginny met his gaze again, fingers digging into his torso as he increased his pace, thrusting in until they were on fire, and she was once again exploding. A rocket about to be consumed by the dazzling show of lights and whirligigs and whatever the hell else happened when a firecracker went off, because her brain was trickling out of her ears and she could barely breathe with the pleasure of it all.

Tucker made a tortured noise, hips frozen against her, the heat and rhythm of his response pulsing in time with her heartbeat.

It took a while to come down.

They ended up with Tucker sitting on the bench and

Ginny in his lap, and neither of them completely dressed or in their right minds. Which was just fine, truth be told.

She laid her head against his shoulder, stroking lazy fingers over his chin. "Good morning."

He made a small sound of amusement. "Morning."

Too damn funny. "Come on. That deserves a *good*, doesn't it?"

His lips twitched. "The men are going to think I'm out of my gourd if I go around saying that it's a *fucking fantastic morning*, which would be even more accurate."

Ginny laughed. But she had to agree he was probably right.

TUCKER HADN'T MEANT to fuck her brains out. It seemed that, when it came to Ginny, his plans had a way of getting adjusted last minute by very impulsive ideas.

His lack of control was disconcerting. Still, he could hardly object to how they'd spent the past moments.

Only he'd been spending a lot of time thinking about his own decisions. Prompting Caleb and his uncle to plan wisely had been the kick in the backside he needed as well.

While Ginny had a valid point about the two of them and their timing, it was also bullshit. He could deal with fallout and questions regarding ranch hands assuming he got the job because of his relationships.

The only thing stopping him from throwing the *keep-it-quiet* plan to the wind was that he didn't want anything to blow back on her. That was his biggest concern. People could be assholes, and he couldn't be around to protect her from all random snide comments.

The one thing he had decided was the announcement that they were a couple was not going to come out of the clear blue sky. Which made it all the easier to begin his own step-by-step plans. If Operation *Prove It* was the connection he and Ginny had to find their footing in this new reality, he had his own *prove it* situation when it came to her.

How did he protect a strong woman? How did he support and listen and still take away any burdens she didn't need to bear?

Most importantly, how did he keep him and Ginny from becoming his parents, with neither of them ever truly happy because of agreeing to half-baked compromises?

All of that rattled in his brain as he sat there, sexual endorphins still rushing his system. The weight of her in his lap was perfect, and heat wrapped around them in a mix of tenderness and lingering sexual satisfaction.

She dragged her fingers along his jaw. "We should get dressed. Or I should turn up the heat in the greenhouse so we don't catch cold."

"Sounds intriguing," he teased. "Do you really turn the heat up enough in here that you garden naked?"

Ginny laughed as she slid off of his lap and put her bits and pieces back in order. "What do you mean, do I *turn up the heat*? You're dangerous, Mister Hottie. Good thing we don't have any seedlings up yet, or we would've steamed the bunch of them."

"Mr. Hottie is not an approved nickname," he said dryly. He glanced around as he did up his zipper and tucked his shirt in. "Steamy hot sex notwithstanding, it still feels wintery in here."

"We don't need to turn the temperature up until closer to when we need to put stuff in the ground, and that's not for a while still." Ginny linked her fingers with his as they strolled back toward the main door. "Did you need something? Other than a booty call?"

Shit. That's exactly what he didn't want her to think. He stopped and pulled her against him, lifting her chin so their gazes met straight on. "Don't think the fact that we get on like a house on fire sexually means that's all there is to this."

Her head tilted slightly, and she cupped her palm against his face. "Sorry. I was being flippant. I know we've stepped beyond just sex."

It had never been just sex for him, but now wasn't the time to say that.

Instead, he finally got his shit together and did what he came to do in the first place. "There's talk about heading out to Rough Cut dancing in a couple of days. I want you to show up. No staying home and watching Disney with your nieces."

"Tucker, we can't—"

"I'm not taking you as my date, but I want you there." It was a compromise he could work with, and it fit nicely into his plan for slowly making it clear Ginny was his. That he was hers.

That they were together.

Thankfully, Ginny seemed to catch onto part of the idea. She nodded. "I think my girls were talking about going out. I'll make sure it's the same night, so there will be plenty of reasons for us to be in the same place at the same time. Oh, and we need an official Operation *Prove It* meeting soon."

A rumble of a truck stopping outside the greenhouse snapped Tucker into full attention. "I should go, but I'll send you a message later. I have an idea of where we can meet."

Her eyes lit up, and she pressed a quick kiss to his lips, going up on tiptoes. "Send it secret messenger if you need to, but I look forward to hearing from you."

Tucker dragged himself away from her warmth and headed out the side door just as voices drifted from the main entrance. Ginny greeted someone who had come for a visit.

He dragged his feet, though, as he headed back to the barns. He hated not having their relationship out in the open.

It wasn't as if he didn't have enough distractions to keep him busy. Between Ashton and Caleb, Tucker began the work in earnest of slowly getting to know all the tasks his uncle kept rolling as foreman for Silver Stone.

After nearly fourteen years of being in charge, Caleb was definitely the manager. He and his brothers set the direction for the ranch operations, but it was Ashton who made sure everything got done.

Like a juggler keeping a dozen balls in the air while spinning plates, and the entire time keeping his cool—

As the days passed, Tucker admired the man more and more.

"You keep staring at me. Do I have mud on my face?" his uncle asked gruffly as they stopped in the mess hall for a quick bite after a day of looking over every piece of machinery on the property.

Tucker shrugged. "Sorry. Didn't mean to. Just thinking how grateful I am that you're willing to stick around for the next while."

Ashton glared back. "What did you do?"

"Nothing," Tucker protested. "How the hell did you get from me saying I'm happy you'll be around to I've done something wrong?"

"Pretty much what you used to do. *Uncle Ashton, you are so good with horses. By the way, I think I broke my saddle.*" Ashton attempted to imitate a childish Tucker, which just made Tucker snort all the harder.

"Please. Do not take up acting."

Ashton lifted his chin. "I'll have you know the *Heart Falls Star* reported my rendition of a goat was one of the best in the Not-So-Nutcracker performance this past December."

Video of which Luke had shown Tucker on the sly, the two of them howling with laughter. Definitely not the thing to share with his uncle.

"I'm sure you were a fine goat."

Ashton glowered. "Are you poking at me, boy?"

"Would I ever do such a thing?" Absolutely deadpanned.

His uncle *harrumphed* again, but a hint of a smile twitched at the corner of his lips.

Tucker was getting ready for bed, well pleased with the work that he had done on the sly up in the hayloft that evening. A secret that he couldn't wait to let Ginny know about.

His phone rang, a text message arriving simultaneously.

He put his clothes back on and hurried to the barn where Alex and Luke were in the stall with the pregnant strawberry roan.

She was agitated, stepping uncomfortably with her head wavering from side to side. Luke did his best to calm her while Alex came forward to get Tucker up to speed. "This is early, and she's definitely not right."

"You call the veterinarian?"

"On his way."

Luke spoke quietly, soothing the mare. "Quiet, darlin'. You'll be okay."

Tucker moved carefully, sliding a hand along the mare's extended sides as he checked her. Her skin rippled under his hand, twitching as he passed.

This wasn't Tucker's area of expertise, but he knew enough to agree it wasn't something simple gone wrong.

The three of them worked together best they could to ease the mare's discomfort. Tucker was very relieved when the barn door swung open in the distance, announcing the arrival of the expert.

Only it wasn't Josiah Ryder's familiar face that appeared.

Instead of the sturdy veterinarian who had become a Heart Falls mainstay, it was the far smaller woman he'd hired as an assistant.

Yvette Wright strode forward with an easy confidence though. Laying a hand on Luke's back, she spoke quietly to the horse. "Hey, beautiful. Sounds as if you need a little help."

"Where's Josiah?" Alex asked.

"Busy." Her gaze danced over the horse as she shrugged her way out of her coat then pressed it into Alex's arms. "Here. Make yourself useful."

Tucker blinked at the change in her tone of voice from sweetness with the horse to dry disdain for Alex.

He examined the other man's face. Alex stared after Yvette with something akin to puppy love.

Oh boy. Tangled webs always showed up at the most awkward times.

It only took a few minutes before Yvette was ready. "Tucker, come help me," she ordered quietly. She gave him directions that he followed explicitly as she slipped a hand into the mare, confusion slowly shifting into comprehension.

"Well, sweetheart, no wonder you don't feel so good. Your babies are a tangled mess. I'll get you straightened out as soon as I can," Yvette promised.

It took an hour and a half, and by the end of it Tucker felt as if his arms had been put through a wringer. He had no idea how Yvette stayed on her feet, working inside the horse to untangle the limbs of a rare set of viable twins.

By the time the tiny beasts arrived, the crowd around the pen had expanded by a few. Ashton had shown up. Luke had contacted Kelli, who had obviously sent a message to Ginny in case she wanted to get in on the action.

Ginny brought a thermos of chai, and once Yvette had washed up, she wrapped her hands around the mug Ginny handed her and took grateful sips. "Thank you. That hits the spot."

"Glad to help," Ginny said quietly.

Inside the pen, Strawberry Delight was now resting comfortably, one of the tiny foals fast asleep as the other nursed.

"That's a sight we don't see too often," Ashton said with approval.

Tucker couldn't take his gaze off of Ginny's face. The wonder in her eyes, her happiness as she glanced between the newborn fillies and Yvette. The young woman finished her drink, and Ginny moved ahead of her, grabbing her coat and helping the veterinarian into it.

Constantly helping. Constantly aware of others—

"It's turned out to be a good evening," Luke said, coming forward to shake Yvette's hand. "Thank you."

Yvette dipped her chin. "Glad I could help."

Alex moved forward as well, hand outstretched. "That was wonderful to see."

She eyed his hand as if expecting a joy buzzer, then shook it firmly as well. "Thanks."

It looked as if Alex would say something else, but Tucker stepped in. Exhaustion was written all over Yvette. "Come on. I'll get you home," he offered. "Alex will drive your truck for you."

Yvette blinked. "Oh, no. That's fine."

But when an enormous yawn escaped her, Tucker held out a hand and tugged her forward. "Don't fight it. I'd offer Josiah the same deal. Honest."

Which meant instead of finding Ginny, Tucker finished the evening by acting grateful chauffeur to one very tired but thrilled veterinarian.

She laid her head back on the headrest and closed her eyes,

sighing softly, the sound happy and content. "That makes it all worth it, you know? The moments when you're not sure things will work out, the mental questions if you're doing the right thing, and even the fear." She glanced at him quickly. "Don't tell Josiah I said that. About being afraid."

Tucker snorted. "He'd understand completely. No way any of us on the ranch get through a day without being afraid of something. Not when we're really trying to live to the fullest."

She nodded and yawned again. "Pretty little fillies. I'm glad they're going to make it."

On the trip home, Tucker and Alex sat in silence until they were nearly in sight of Silver Stone.

"I'm an idiot," Alex offered.

Tucker wasn't even sure what the big picture problem was between Yvette and Alex, but he didn't need to know, not to share one bit of advice.

"Maybe," Tucker replied. "But knowing you're the problem is more than half the battle."

Alex snickered, then nodded. "Yeah, pretty much."

A peaceful quiet resumed, and Tucker breathed deep.

It was a solid ending to a good day.

14

Saturday was warm enough that when Ginny crawled out of bed and looked outside, she decided it was time to take a page out of her sister Dare's book.

She made herself a cup of tea, bundled up, and went to sit on the porch as sunrise slowly stretched golden fingers over Silver Stone.

Last night had been amazing, and she'd only been on the periphery of the magic. Watching Yvette at work reminded Ginny what the woman had said about finding what she wanted to do for the rest of her life that made her happy.

It was clear Yvette had not only chosen well, but she was also making others happy because of her choice.

Two beautiful animals that might not have survived, three possibly, considering their mama had been in danger as well, were all safe and sound in the warmth of the barn.

Ginny held onto her mug a little tighter. She had no skills like that. Nothing that could truly make a difference, and that lack tugged places inside.

But as her nieces poured out of the homestead and headed

for the nearby hill, toboggans in hand, Ginny pushed aside her momentary blahs. Enough moping. She was blessed beyond belief and able to enjoy some pretty sweet choices.

Somewhere along the line she'd find a way to make a difference.

Meanwhile, she needed to spend a little time dealing with the puzzle. If she didn't, Dare would be poking at her with another reminder like the one she'd gotten the previous night.

Dare: *I love you, Truth. Solve any puzzles lately?*
Ginny: *I love you, Dare. Go away, you're annoying.*
Dare: *This is your subconscious speaking. Send me a copy, girl. Don't make me come over there.*
Ginny: *Like that's a threat. The door is always open.*

Ginny reached into her pocket and pulled out the folded paper covered with cryptic drawings.

She thought at first it was something like a rebus puzzle. But while she was usually smart enough to solve those, this one still made no sense.

Twelve different images, including the one with some sort of equine animal—it was unbelievable to think it was a horse because surely her father could draw better than that.

She tried writing down what each symbol made her think of at first glance. Then she tried her own hand at drawing them in stick figures to see if any of that turned into letters or words.

A half-dozen attempts later, her tea was cold and she was no farther ahead than she'd been at the start when a small voice interrupted her.

"What are you doing, Auntie Ginny?"

Ginny glanced up in surprise to discover Emma standing at the base of the porch. "Hey, kiddo. You snuck up on me."

Emma shrugged, the pom-pom on her pink toque bouncing as she wiggled on the spot. "You were reading your book."

"I suppose I was," Ginny admitted. She glanced around. "Where's Sasha?"

Her niece looked at the ground but didn't answer.

"Emma?" Ginny repeated, more sternly this time. "Is Sasha somewhere she's not supposed to be?"

Emma nodded, still staring at the ground.

Drat. But also hurrah that the kid was willing to squeal on her sister.

Ginny put her things down and held out a hand to her niece. "Come on. Show me where she is, so we can maybe stop her before it's too late."

The little girl spoke softly, the teeny bit of the flashback to the hesitancy she'd had so many years ago. "I don't *want* to get Sasha into trouble."

"I know, sweetie, but sometimes we get people we love into a little bit of trouble to keep them out of even more." Ginny squeezed little fingers as Emma tugged her toward the barn. "It's in the sister rule book. Honest."

"Did you ever get *your* sister into trouble?"

The first time Dare had decided to hold a wake for her family flashed to mind. Ginny had made a choice and called Luke to squeal before her sister could get too drunk to walk. The same night, coincidentally, that Ginny had gathered her courage and seduced Tucker, which meant the memory was all the sweeter.

She jerked back to attention and nodded seriously at her niece.

"All the time. Even now, when we're all grown up," Ginny said. She grinned at the shocked expression on her niece's face. "Because I love her very, very much, you know."

Which pulled a giggle from Emma before she added

seriously, "Sasha wanted to see the baby horses. Papa said he would take us after lunch, but she said she wanted a quick peek now."

They should've realized the draw of two foals would be too much for Sasha to resist.

Thankfully, while Sasha had chosen to disobey the standing order to stay out of the horse barn unless she was accompanied by an adult, she'd done it in the smartest way possible. Ginny spotted her ponytail poking up over the edge of the loft as she stared into the horse pens from a safe distance. Well away from the traffic of the ranch hands, and nowhere near enough to spook Strawberry Delight.

Ginny took Emma up the old side ladder to the loft. They paused, looming over Sasha until she rolled and gasped in surprise.

Then she blinked guiltily and offered Emma a dirty look. "Tattletale."

Oh, no. Nipping that one in the bud. Ginny lifted a finger and spoke quietly. "Tell me what you did wrong."

Her oldest niece curled up to a sitting position. "I came into the horse barn without permission."

"That was your second mistake," Ginny informed her. "The first and more serious crime was expecting your sister to lie for you."

Sasha's eyes widened. Emma pressed her lips together.

Ginny glanced between them, still speaking softly enough that no one else would know they were there. "You two are best friends as well as sisters, which means you need to look out for each other. That's what Emma did. If you can't trust each other to do the right thing and always take care of each other, even when it's hard, you'll miss out on something magical and special."

Sasha's lower lip trembled. She scurried back from where

she sat and rushed to hug Emma tight. "I'm sorry. I didn't mean to make you sad."

"I'm sorry, too," Emma sniffled.

Ginny did her best to not grin, because the whole conversation was a flashback to moments between her and Dare, and damn if she didn't want that same wonderful *friends forever* for these two kiddos.

Sasha gave Ginny a hug as well and apologized. Then Emma had to give her a hug, and Ginny had to kiss them both and wipe away their tears.

After all that was done, they once again shuffled to the edge of the loft and looked down at the two perfect little foals snuggled in with their mama.

"Can we go pet them?" Sasha asked.

Ginny shook her head. "Let's leave that for your dad to get to do when he thinks it's right."

Sasha looked disappointed, but she nodded obediently.

"We could, however, go find some kittens," Ginny offered.

Emma's smile flashed from ear to ear, and suddenly Ginny was being tugged over the bales and into corners in search of the slightly larger-than-last-time kittens.

They were in the middle of furry cuddle time when Emma caught the paper as it fell from her pocket.

"You dropped something, Auntie Ginny."

Ginny took it from her and opened it up. "Maybe you can help me solve the riddle," she said in a mysterious tone of voice.

Sasha leaned in, nose wrinkling as she stared at the paper. "Is this a puzzle game?"

"I have no idea what it means," Ginny admitted. "But can you guess what any of these are?"

"That's a goat." Emma stabbed a finger at one picture and nodded decisively. "I drew a picture of Meany that looked just like that."

Ginny grinned. "Well, Meany is very handsome then."

And it appeared artistic talent did not run in the Stone family.

There were a few other guesses, but nothing absolutely shocking. Sasha thought one of the things looked like a fancy candelabra. One they guessed was a ball with legs.

It was Emma, other than the goat suggestion, who made the most amazing discovery. She pointed a finger at one picture. "There's numbers in there," she said.

Ginny peered closer. "Where?"

Emma put a finger against the paper and traced the numbers as she recited. "Five. Twelve. Thirty. See, there's little lines between them, so I think that means it's not just one big number."

Ginny pressed a kiss to Emma's temple. "Smart little girl. That is a wonderful discovery."

Absolute approval rushed from Sasha. "Emma is very smart. She's the best at math, and someday she's going to work for Silver Stone and do all of the accounting."

A fact which would make Caleb ecstatic, Ginny decided. "If that's what you want to do, that's wonderful."

Not to be outdone, Emma had to share as well. "Sasha wants to train the horses."

Her sister made a face. "But I'm still too little," Sasha complained.

"Too little to train the rodeo horses, definitely," Ginny said firmly. "But that doesn't mean you can't practice training right now."

Sasha and Emma looked at each other with wide mouths and surprised eyes before turning back to Ginny.

"How?" demanded Sasha.

Ginny shrugged. "I thought you were training the goats."

Sasha made a rude noise. "Goats aren't horses."

"I should think not, but if Emma wants to do the accounting for the ranch down the road, do you think she knows everything she'll need for later? Even though she knows her numbers really well, and things like adding and subtracting and multiplying."

Emma wrinkled her nose. "I don't have all of them memorized yet," she confessed.

Sasha nodded slowly. "If I get really good at training Eeny, Meany, and Miney, that'll help me train horses?"

"Plus, we have lots of ranch dogs," Ginny pointed out. "It's always a good idea to train them to be better behaved." She tapped her niece on the nose. "It will all add up, a little bit at a time."

Emma turned to Sasha. "Like Mr. Tucker. He knows lots of things, but Papa says he's going to 'prentice with Mr. Ashton until he gets really good as a foreman."

"I want to apprentice with someone," Sasha said seriously.

"You should tell Papa," Emma said. She caught Sasha's hand in hers. "I'll come with you. And if you have to practice lots, I'll come and help you practice. Because you're my big sister, and I love you."

"I love you too," Sasha said.

Then the whole thing dissolved into another round of little girl hugs. Then Ginny was being tugged into the fray, and the paper with the doodles was put back in her pocket because being in the middle of so much current happiness and joy was more important than solving a mystery from the past.

AFTER SETTING things up so he could take Ginny dancing, or at least innocently ask her to dance while they were all there in a crowd, Ashton messed with Tucker's plans. They headed out on Thursday night to the Pincher Creek area where the Stones' Uncle Frank had land.

Tucker still didn't like the other man very much. He was pretty sure Frank didn't like him either, simply because Tucker had witnessed the first time Caleb took charge and refused to cave to his uncle's requests.

Thankfully, it was a short visit, and Tucker only had to work on being cordial for a few nights.

When they got back, another weekend had passed, and the end of January approached. It had been more than a week since he and Ginny had touched base for their last Operation *Prove It* meeting, and Tucker had every intention of another happening sooner than later.

The next thing he knew, it was the afternoon and he was seriously wondering if he'd see her before the spring.

"There you are." Luke poked his head into the office where Tucker was pouring over employment records. A room which, thank God, had a window facing toward Big Sky Lake. Luke patted one of the piles of the papers on the desk in the ranch office. "Looks ominous."

"Ashton gave me the dubious privilege of taking over the portion of payroll he's been responsible for up until now. I might like spreadsheets, but I already know this will be one of my least favourite tasks," Tucker shared. "Thank God, I'm nearly done."

Luke slapped his hands together and rubbed them. "Good. Because we're going fishing."

Tucker eyed the to-do list open beside him. "Maybe."

"Come on," Luke said. "I know you're busy, but someone really smart recently made a comment about making sure we took the time to do the things that are important. Which means if Ashton's been doing the job of two men, you need to think about hiring somebody else as an assistant."

"Damn if I want to look as if I can't keep up this close to the beginning," Tucker complained.

"Bro, you put in full days. You're allowed to take some time off." Luke dropped the joking and spoke far more seriously, which cut through Tucker's wavering.

"You're right."

Luke winked. "Finish up. I'll pack what we need."

"I'm game, but I don't want to go anywhere too far into the bush or be gone overnight," Tucker insisted. He was determined to see Ginny today, even if he had to burn the midnight oil to make it happen.

"Fishing right in our backyard." Luke gestured out the window where the sunlight reflected on the frozen surface of the lake. "We'll drill a few holes and drop in a line."

Perfect. "You're on. I need half an hour to finish here, then I'll bring the whiskey."

Luke slapped him on the shoulder. "Good man."

Ice fishing less than ten minutes from home seemed a decadent experience but one that Tucker could fully get on board with. The ice was thick enough Luke hauled out a fishing tent and a heater, and two comfortable camping chairs were lined up at the edge of the hole.

Luke held his coffee mug forward and waited until Tucker poured a healthy measure of whiskey into it. "There we go. By the way, Ginny calls ice fishing *Canadian Pong*. You know, that drinking game when you try to get ping-pong balls into red solo cups?"

Tucker snickered. "How on earth does she connect the two?"

Luke thrust his coffee cup in the air. "The less luck you have bouncing balls, the more you drink. The less luck you have catching fish, the more you drink. Canadian Pong."

A laugh escaped. "She's a hoot."

"She is. I'm glad she's back," Luke said seriously. "Something didn't feel right when she was gone. Even though she's never done a lot with the livestock, she's always somehow been in the middle of every major event."

Because she's always taking care of everyone. The thought came instantly.

It was time to change the topic off Ginny before Tucker said something he shouldn't. "You plan to finish the basement of your house anytime soon?"

Luke eased back in his chair, gaze fixed on the bobber floating in the hole in front of them. "Definitely. I hired Dustin and Shim to pound some nails over the next while. Figured if they got the framing done, I can hire someone to do the drywall and mudding—hate those parts of the task."

"What's the story with Shim?" Tucker asked. It was a question that had constantly slipped his mind as he dealt with everything else.

"Dustin had him as a pen pal during high school, if you can believe it. His parents are both college professors. Sounds as if they're rather horrified that their son is spending time daily dealing with manure."

Tucker raised his cup in the air. Professors and researchers had a lot in common, it seemed. "To parents who have no clue."

Luke blinked. "That's right. And it's not that I forgot, but it's just that you never talk about them. Are your parents still as out of touch as they were when you were growing up?"

"More," Tucker admitted. "Only now it's fine. I think they've decided the experiment of having a child has been completed. They raised a fairly productive member of society, so now it's on to the next thing."

His friend frowned. "That sucks."

"No, really, it's fine. If they'd been more attentive while I was growing up, I wouldn't have gotten to spend as much time with you. Getting to hang out with Uncle Ashton, and your parents, made a huge difference in my life, and I appreciate it so much. Heck, for years your parents phoned me while I was at home to check in with me. I probably talked to Walter as much as I talked to my father some months."

"I remember you telling me that," Luke said. He offered a wry smile. "I remember Dad sometimes knowing what you were up to before I talked to you. Just made him more God-like and know it all."

Tucker smiled at that. "He was a good, good man. I think about him and Deb often, and the things they taught me. Makes me even more appreciative that my parents don't try and interfere in my life now."

"Your folks still kind of suck," Luke insisted.

Tucker chuckled. "Fine. They kind of suck."

Luke narrowed his eyes. "Are you managing me?"

"Heaven forbid."

"Because I don't need to be managed," Luke said, amusement rising. "You're such a jackass."

"Okay. If that's what you think." Tucker hid his smile behind his cup.

"Damn, I've missed this." Luke eyed Tucker. "Not the part where you're being a jackass."

"Definitely not that part."

"Stop it," Luke said before allowing his grin to fade to serious. "It's funny. I've always had my brothers around. But Walker was out on the circuit for a while, and Dustin's a good kid, but he's still young. Caleb had his head full of all the things he needed to worry about." Luke made eye contact. "You're like a brother and a best friend all rolled into one. Something was off when you weren't here."

Tucker took the comment at face value. "I'm sorry."

Luke shook his head. "Not your fault. You had to get on

with the things you needed to do. I probably didn't help, getting tangled up with Penny for a while."

Yeah, that hadn't helped at all. Luke's ex-fiancée hadn't felt right to Tucker. "I never liked her," he confessed.

"So you told me," Luke said dryly.

Well, shit. "I did? I don't remember that."

"I think I raved about her at some point in the beginning, and you pretty much told me to take a second look." Luke looked away. "You're a smart man, Tucker Stewart. In retrospect, I now know that any time you poke me about something, I should listen."

It was quite a compliment. "I'm sorry things didn't work out, but I am damn glad you're with Kelli. She's awesome."

"She's the best." He eyed Tucker speculatively. "Now we need to find someone for you."

Hell, no. Or, more like *hell, yes*, but Luke wasn't ready for that revelation yet, and Tucker couldn't say anything until Ginny agreed.

Luke probably would've pushed it and said something else but at that moment, his bobber jumped into action and the two of them had to grab for their lines.

For a while the fish arrived. Every time they dropped a hook into the water, they had a strike, so the relaxing was over and the fishing had begun.

After they'd caught their limit, Tucker got out a fillet knife and cleaned while Luke packed up their gear and loaded it onto the back of the snowmobile.

"I've missed having time like this with you," Luke said. "I really am glad you're back. No matter how busy things get, we're going to take time for this kind of shit, yes?"

Tucker didn't have the heart to draw it out and tease. He agreed whole-heartedly. "Yes, we will do the shit. As much as our— Your wife and our jobs will allow."

Luke grew quiet for a while. They packaged up a bag of fish to drop off for Tamara, and a bag for Ashton, as well as one for each of them to take home.

Then Luke shocked Tucker by pulling him in for a hug. He pounded him on the back briefly before tilting his head toward the skidoo. "Come on. I'll give you a ride."

"Sounds good."

Tucker slipped into his trailer and grabbed what he needed. Then he sent a message to Ginny to meet him in the old hayloft in half an hour.

He waited for her return message, which thankfully came only minutes later.

Ginny: *What are you up to?*
Tucker: *Come to the barn, and you'll find out.*

15

*S*he'd seen the fishing tent out on the water earlier but had deliberately stayed away. Not only was it good for Tucker to have time away from work with his guys, fishing was not one of her favourite activities.

Figuring out what Tucker was up to now? That hit all of her interest buttons.

She grabbed a couple of important contributions to their meeting and headed out the door, striding through the crisp snow toward her destination.

She passed her brother Caleb headed the opposite way and waved a greeting. "Say hi to Tamara for me."

"Why don't you come and join us for dinner?" Caleb asked, pausing in the path.

She thought quickly. "Nope. Thank you for the invite, but I don't want to stop in too often."

He chuckled softly. "Ginny, you're family. You live five minutes away, so stopping in on a regular basis is kind of expected."

"Good thing I like to do the unexpected then," she teased.

"Seriously, thanks for the invite, and I will have you and everyone over to my place sometime. But not tonight."

He dipped his chin, began to turn away then paused. "Where are you going?"

"To the barn."

He frowned. "*Ginny*."

"What?" she asked innocently.

"What are you doing in the barn that you don't want me to know?" He said it in the same tone of voice he had used back when he took over for the family. Back then it intimidated the hell out of her, but now she was less cowed. "I am doing something that a grownup Ginny is allowed to do without further explaining herself to her brother."

A snort escaped him. "Fine. Tell me to mind my own business."

"Mind your own business," she said obediently.

He downright snickered.

"I have to say, your sense of ha-ha has really improved since Tamara came on the scene."

He mock-glared. "Go do whatever it is you don't want to tell me you're doing. I have dinner to get ready for."

"I love you, big brother." Impulsively, she threw her arms around him and planted a big kiss on his cheek.

He patted her back. "I love you too, brat. Get."

"Getting."

Inside the barn were familiar scents and warm contentment. She took her time walking the long line of stalls toward the old central building. Kelli was ahead of her, sweet talking one of the horses and petting its nose.

Ginny paused beside her. "You're usually done by this time of day."

Kelli glanced up. "Hey. Yeah, my grandpa called earlier, and I ended up talking with him for over an hour. Figured I should make up the time now, especially since Luke was out fishing with Tucker."

"Still blows my mind that you've got a grandpa in the picture." Ginny dipped her chin. "He's a good one, too. I approve."

Kelli snickered. "Good for Grandpa Timothy, because if you didn't approve, I'm pretty sure he'd have boot prints on his butt right now."

"Darn tootin'," Ginny said, raising a hand and waiting for Kelli to give her a high-five. "You and Luke heading out dancing this Friday?"

Kelli nodded. "Tansy will be there as well. Rose might have to do something with their little sister. Driving her to Calgary for a prosthetic fitting or something."

"We should suggest Dustin give her a ride," Ginny said innocently. "You know, so Rose can come out dancing."

Her sister-in-law looked confused for a moment. "Why would Dustin want to give Fern a ride? I mean I know they're friends, but he's busy hanging— Oh. I see what you're doing." Her eyes flashed. "If Dustin is driving, it's pretty sure Shim will come along, is that what you're thinking?"

Ginny blinked innocently. "Heaven forbid I interfere in someone's driving schedule, but maybe it's an option."

They looked at each other for a moment then burst out laughing. "You know, I'll mention it," Kelli offered. "We'll let Tansy and Rose decide if they want to meddle in their little sister's love life."

Ginny sashayed past and left Kelli to her tasks, slowing as she moved into the oldest sections of the barn.

She had memories tied up in every inch of this place. The worn wood, the hooks on the walls. The scents and the sounds and the dust motes dancing in the overhead lights. All of it as familiar as breathing.

Lost in a daydream, Ginny rounded the corner too quickly and bumped full on into one of the ranch hands.

"Jeez, sorry. I wasn't looking where I was going," she admitted, grateful he'd reacted fast enough and caught hold of her before they both bounced to the ground.

The man was tall and solid, with dark scruff neatly trimmed into a beard, but when he held onto her a little longer than necessary, Ginny stepped back, forcefully swinging an arm to knock his hand away.

"No need to get feisty." He looked her up and down, lingering on her chest too long for politeness.

Ginny had had guys staring at her boobs ever since she started to blossom at age thirteen. He wasn't the first man to try and hold a conversation with her chest, and he probably wouldn't be the last.

But she didn't have to like it.

"Hey." She clapped her hands then pointed upward. "My face is up here."

"Not admiring your face, darlin'," he drawled far too confidently.

And when he took the longest time to actually lift his gaze, Ginny was pretty sure she had daggers shooting out of her eyes. "What's your name?"

"Jim Allen." He took a small step closer, towering over her as he once again slid his gaze over her body. "And I hear you're one smooth, cool drink of gin."

"Lovely. Did you also hear that I'm one of your bosses?" She stepped back, because as much as she wanted to make a point, she wasn't stupid enough to think about physically challenging the bastard. "Mind your manners. I'm sorry for running into you. Now, get back to work."

He lifted a hand and saucily tipped his hat. "Yes, ma'am."

She kept an eye on him as he turned and wandered off, heading out the door and toward the bunk houses.

Well, fuck.

It didn't happen often. Not at Silver Stone, where one of the first talks with new hires regarded the women working the ranch. Kelli had been a lead hand for years, and before Ginny left, while she hadn't worked in the barns, she'd been around often enough that Ashton and her brothers had made sure nothing ever got dangerous.

Ginny knew the rules. It was a ranch, and with animals around acting like—well, animals—sexual jokes were a given. But she and Dare had been told from the very start they were to report any hand who went beyond the comfortable level of teasing.

Shit, shit, *shit*. Because the person she should report this to now was probably Tucker.

She quickly thought back. Jim hadn't really said anything terrible, had he? Was she overreacting? There were plenty of times she'd been out in public and admired a good-looking man. Was it wrong for Jim to check her out when she knew she was put together in a way that made guys take a second look? Maybe she'd done something to encourage him...

...and the fact that she was even having this mental debate with herself meant the answer was she needed to talk to Tucker. But damn, it wasn't a conversation she wanted to have.

The door opened behind her, and she snapped her head up, worried that the man had returned.

It was Tucker with an oversized gym bag in one hand and wearing a pleased expression. "Hey. Sorry it took me a little longer than expected."

"That's fine," she offered cheerfully. "What's the big secret?"

He tilted his head toward the hayloft. "Head-on up. I've got something to show you."

She snickered but kept any dirty comment to herself. She also decided she would tell him about Jim, but first things first.

They were in the oldest section of the barn now, solid as a rock, with only a couple of window openings on the west wall. She followed Tucker, admiring his broad shoulders as he led her to where someone had obviously put in some time and created a perfect seating arrangement out of the bales.

She stepped into the neat little hideaway, with a wide comfortable bench seat facing the window, backrests behind it and a footrest in the front. When Tucker reached into his duffel bag and pulled out pillows for them to sit on and put at their backs, Ginny smiled.

"This is comfy."

"This is Operation *Prove it* headquarters," he told her seriously.

"Get out." She ignored the pillows and jumped up to catch Tucker around the neck, squeezing hard and enjoying the feeling as he wrapped her up tight.

They stood there for a few moments, just holding each other. Ginny took a deep breath and felt herself synchronizing with him. Chests moving easily as they found a rhythm and a pace.

He tucked his knuckles under her chin and lifted her face to his. "Missed you."

Then he kissed her. Gentle and soft. Sweet even, which after the hug made her feel one hundred kinds of wonderful.

"Missed you, too," she confessed.

Then instead of heating things up, he motioned toward the pillows. "We've got some reporting to do."

~

His afternoon spent with Luke had only confirmed Tucker's decision. It didn't matter how busy he was, at the end of the day, he wanted to go home to Ginny, and he didn't give a damn who knew it.

No, correction. He sure the hell wanted *everyone* to know he was the one coming home to the woman.

But this was more than that. He'd seen her, truly seen the way she stepped in and did things, often without anyone noticing. Ginny was always there for her family. Always doing what she thought was right for them.

Doing what was right for herself? Those moments seem few and far between. She knew how to go after what she wanted—seducing him, for example. Heading off on the apprenticeship program.

But her insistence they keep their relationship quiet had been to make *his* life easier. Well, screw that.

He didn't want easy. He wanted her.

He wanted her to know she was potentially the most important thing in his life. Kind of hard to do that when they were living in two different places and barely able to speak to each other except over the phone. Fuck it.

"You're glowering," Ginny teased.

Shit. He settled back on his pillow and put up his feet, deliberately set up so he could look her in the face. "I hope you know I don't plan to stay this busy."

"Some times of the years take more energy than others," she returned. "And you want to do a good job, so diving in at five hundred percent is a given, knowing you."

"Doesn't change the fact that Luke gave me hell today. Rightly so," he added quickly as her expression turned indignant. "It was good to spend some time with him. And I need this time with you."

She put her feet up beside her and curled her arms around

her knees, smiling sweetly. "I miss talking with you in person. The phone and texts are fine for so long, and then I want a real body in the room with me."

He spread his hands. "Real body, right here."

Ginny made a terrible face. "Okay, before we start, I need to tell you something. It's just a heads up, but I don't want this to get away and be forgotten."

She gave him a quick summary on her run-in with Jim.

He stifled his first impulse which was to immediately track down the bastard and teach him some manners. "I'll talk to Ashton. We'll make sure it doesn't happen again."

She nodded quickly. "Thank you, and thanks for not making a big fuss over it. I want to focus on us. So tell me, what's on your report?"

Tucker stared at her for a moment. "Not dropping that topic yet, darling. I won't make a fuss, but we will do what needs to be done, understand?"

Ginny wrinkled her nose. "I know. I just—I don't think I did anything wrong, but I don't want to get Jim in more trouble than he deserves." She narrowed her gaze. "Don't you dare go beat him up in some he-man ritual, got it?"

"He-man ritual?"

"Fists. Cursing. Blood and bruises." Her expression got harder. "You and Luke used to do that all the time, and I hate it."

"It's sometimes inevitable."

"I don't have to like it. And inevitable means stuck in the past, where nothing changes until something changes." Ginny inhaled sharply. "Don't expect me to approve."

"Want to make an herbal weapon for me?" he asked, trying to lighten the situation.

Ginny tilted her head and gave him a very well-executed dirty look. "You're not funny."

"I'm hilarious," he insisted even as he took a deep breath and rebooted, although the incident with Jim was pushed aside, not forgotten. "I want to start with a success," he said, aiming them back into safer territory. "I'll have you know Ashton now thinks I am a minor god when it comes to mechanical repair."

She leaned forward eagerly. "What? Did you fix something he couldn't?"

"Of course, although it was a close call," Tucker said dryly. "I googled the problem when he went to the head, so when he came back, I instantly fixed the wires that had gotten crossed."

She hooted, the sound echoing through the loft as she pressed a hand over her mouth. "Oops. Sorry, our headquarters has very open acoustics."

Amusement rumbled up. "How about you? Something you've been successful with?"

She looked thoughtful for a moment. "It's still too early to plant anything, although I did put in the order for all the herbs and jars that I'll need. Beyond that, I've been pretty laid-back. Poking a little bit into that strange mystery present my mom and dad left me. No success on that quarter, sad to report."

"Bring it to one of our meetings, and we can check it out together," he promised.

"That would be nice." Ginny shrugged. "I've been hanging out with my nieces and visiting with my girls. Spending time getting to know Tamara better. Nothing important, really."

She simply didn't see it, and he was getting damn tired of listening to her downplay her own worth. Tucker folded his arms over his chest. "You know my parents?"

Ginny stalled. "Not really. Never met them, although I've heard a little about them over the years. Never from you, though. It wasn't really something we discussed when we got together the past few years. Ahem."

He focused on the point he wanted to make.

"You wouldn't like them," he said confidently. "Within half an hour of meeting them, you'd call my dad a stick in the mud and ask my mother if she ever smiled. You'd be right on the first one, and the answer to the second would be no."

"Well, that's terrible." Ginny offered him a sympathetic pout. "I'm sorry. I knew you came to spend summers with us, but I thought it was because Ashton wanted you around—rightly so. Because you are awesome."

"My parents are not kid people, and I was an inconvenience."

She swore softly. "Jackasses."

He snorted. "Just not good parental material." He leaned forward, resting his elbows on his knees. "I told you this because you need to understand something. All the time you spend with your nieces? The moments you share with Tamara? Those are important things, so you need to stop putting yourself down and realize your value."

Ginny stared at him.

Anger and frustration rose hard, and he dragged a hand through his hair. "Well, fuck. That's not the conversation I wanted to have, but since we're here, I may as well muddle forward. Yes. What you do isn't always big and shiny, but it's appreciated. Obviously, more than you know. You've got a very giving heart, and I think you're wonderful, Ginny. It's about time you started thinking that you are wonderful as well."

Her lips twitched, and for a moment he thought she might cry.

Then the most beautiful smile spread across her face. She crawled across the hay bales, closing the distance between them so she could straddle his legs and curl her arms around his neck, squeezing him tight.

"I like you, Tucker Stewart," she whispered.

To hell with it. "I know."

She laughed out loud, leaning back and pressing both hands to his face. "You're right. I did a lot of important things this week, mainly spending time with my family. The thing that I disliked the most was not getting to spend time with *you*."

"We're about to change that," he said, "because that's the thing I disliked the most, as well."

Suspicion slipped in. "Tucker."

He held her hips tight. "*Ginny*."

"You're still in the beginning stage of the biggest career change of your life."

"And it's not something I want to do unless I get to do it with you." The confession was wildly ahead of time, but it was true. "If there're complications, I'll face them. But so far, there's been nothing other than the typical small bits of grumbling from a few of the men about having another supervisor in their lives. Ashton is still here, Caleb's rock solid. I don't think the worry is as big as we considered it."

"What are you saying?" She ran her fingers distractedly around his ear, tucking his hair back.

"I'm saying we're dating, Ginny Stone. Officially." He caught her fingers, because they were driving him crazy, and lifted them to his mouth so he could press a kiss to her knuckles. "What I'd like to do is jump about five steps forward and move into the cottage with you, but I think that might cause a few shovels to swing in my direction."

She snickered. "If we're dating, you will visit my house."

"Yes."

"And stay the night, sometimes."

"Yes."

She lowered her lashes and blinked them provocatively. "Take me dancing on Friday?"

He brushed his nose alongside of hers. "Absolutely. You okay if we make that our first official date?"

"Of course. When do you plan to tell Luke that while we're starting to date, this isn't the beginning?" She made a bit of a face. "Because it's not something I will lie about. And while it's still not really any of their business, it's part of our relationship."

"You're right. I will most definitely talk to Luke. Soon."

She eased in closer. "Good. I'll let you take care of that. And trust me. It's not that I plan to stand up and announce to all and sundry that we've been fooling around for the past nine years."

"Jesus, has it been that long?"

She smirked. "But knowing this town, at some point, the information will come out."

"I'm okay with that," he said, still reeling a little at how long it had been. "Does it still count as nine years if you were gone for three of them?"

"It's a little easier to say nine years than to say, 'nine years less the three that Ginny was out of the country,' don't you agree?" She smirked at him.

"We don't always have to take the easy route," he reminded her.

She turned serious for a moment. "I hope this works. I want this to work," she admitted, "but if you need us to take a break. If you need us to do something different, let me know."

He caught her chin, and his fingers shook her gently. "Stop trying to fix things for everyone. It'll be okay. You and I will figure things out going forward. Together."

She took a deep breath and nodded decisively. "Together."

16

The warm glow inside wasn't getting any fainter. Ginny felt like a teenager getting ready for a date. It was pathetic, really.

Before she could stop herself, she sent a text to her sister.

Ginny: *Please laugh at me and tell me to calm down.*
Dare: *LOL. What are you all kerfuffled about? Wait— It's tonight, isn't it?*
Ginny: *I have changed clothes four times. Which you will know is truly ridiculous considering my wardrobe consists of jeans, jeans, and more jeans.*
Dare: *Oh, sweetie. We both know there are umpteen different kinds of jeans. I hope you picked the sexy pair that makes your ass look great.*
Ginny: *My ass looks great in all my jeans.*
Dare: *There's my Ginny! Of course it does. You'll have fun tonight, and you don't have anything to worry about. This is Tucker we're talking about. He's an amazing guy. I'm so glad you're coming out of the shadows, so to speak.*

Ginny: *Great. Now I have this image of him as a giant spider.*
Dare: *LOL. I just meant the whole secret sexy rendezvous thing was pretty spectacular, but this has more long-term potential. That makes me happy.*

That was the bit that scared Ginny to death. The long-term part. She wanted it—she was sure she did. But was she good enough for him?

Ginny: *He is a great guy, and I'm really happy to try the next thing. I hope it works.*
Dare: *It will. If you need me for anything, give me a shout. I will rain down sisterly indignation on anyone who needs it. Now go. Enjoy your evening.*
Ginny: <3

She put her phone away and turned back to the mirror one more time. Her jeans were newer, the dark blue contrasting with the pale powder blue shirt she'd layered over a creamy tank top. She'd left her hair down, which she would probably regret somewhere after the third or fourth dance.

Ginny grabbed an elastic and shoved it in her pocket for the inevitable moment she'd return to a ponytail.

A final check. The faint layer of cosmetics, including a lip balm she'd made, were enough to make her look bright and happy yet not overdone. She looked good, so it wasn't concern over her appearance making her heart pulse rapidly as a knock sounded on the door.

She swung it open to discover Tucker standing in front of her. Sheepskin-lined jean jacket, his dark hair slightly messy as always. Clean-shaven with not a trace of five o'clock shadow.

His face was sheer perfection because of the look of appreciation in his eyes. "Damn, you're beautiful."

She snickered, grabbing her coat and pulling it on quickly. "Thanks. I'm glad your taste runs to low-key and casual."

He stepped inside and closed the door behind him, keeping the warm air inside as she pulled on her boots.

"My tastes run to beautiful women who wear clothes that make their eyes shine." He caught her by the hand and tugged her forward. "Go dancing with me?"

"That's the plan," she teased.

He leaned in close. "Need to steal a kiss before we leave."

She slid her hands up his chest and over his shoulders, easing closer until their torsos made contact. "Is it stealing if it's freely given?"

He answered the best way possible. Hands sliding down to cup her ass. Mouth coming in contact with hers in a way that set her blood pumping and lit up every bit of anticipation possible.

He squeezed her butt gently before letting go and stepping back, reaching for her hand again and tugging her out the door. "Come on. I hear Ryan's got something new happening tonight at Rough Cut."

It was all kinds of incredible to have him help her into the passenger seat of his truck. To have him glance disapprovingly when she went to buckle up.

"Move," he ordered. Then he helped slide her into the middle seat.

Yes, teenager Ginny would have totally approved of getting to sit next to him, their thighs touching, his arm around her shoulders as they drove into town to go dancing.

"Thank you for making one of my adolescent dreams come true," she said impulsively.

Tucker chuckled. "I'm glad I had no idea you had a crush on me all those years ago. It would've freaked me out."

"You should've heard my mother," Ginny said. "She never

came right out and told me I was too young for you at the time. Not in those specific words, but she definitely told me I had to wait."

They were on the highway, a few other vehicles also headed into town. The red taillights ahead of them appeared and disappeared in intervals as the road rose and fell.

"Your mom was great," Tucker said softly. "I hope she would've approved of us."

"I'm pretty sure she did. Just not when I was still a kid." She twisted so she could examine his face as he focused forward on the road. "One of the cool things about my mom was that she didn't give you more than you needed at one time. But she was pretty clear on what she thought was important."

"Have you been reading through her journal?"

"A bit," she confessed. "Sometimes it feels unreal. As if any minute she'll walk back through the door and give me hell for snooping."

That got an actual laugh out of him. "I can see that."

Ginny considered then figured Tucker was the one person she could absolutely trust with this. "I've been opening up the journal at random and reading bits here and there. I was trying to figure out why, and it suddenly hit me that if I start at the beginning and go all the way to the end, at some point I'll be finished."

He caught her fingers, linking them with his and squeezing gently. "You don't want it to end."

She rested her head on his shoulder. "I guess not."

They sat in silence for the rest of the trip, and once again Ginny was thankful that this was Tucker and not some other guy she was attempting a first date with. It wasn't an uncomfortable silence, but a moment of sharing something precious and intimate.

When he pulled into the parking lot behind the bar, Tucker

paused and turned to her to press a kiss on her forehead. "Your mom will always be part of your world. I promise."

Which was exactly what she needed to hear.

"Thank you," she said sincerely.

He dipped his chin.

Ginny took a deep breath. "Ready for this?"

"I was born ready," Tucker drawled.

Which meant Ginny was laughing as he pulled her out the driver's side door with him then tucked her fingers into the crook of his arm to guide her across the parking lot, up the steps, and into the bar.

She'd been there a week ago with her friends, yet as they headed into their corner, music welling around them, Ginny found herself tangling with a strange mix of apprehension and curiosity.

How would her friends deal with the change in relationship about to arrive?

Rose was the only one in their usual spot. She smiled as Ginny and Tucker reached her side.

"You made it," Ginny said. "Thought you had a date with your sister."

"Fern's appointment got changed to yesterday, so we're all good to go." Rose's gaze dropped, eyes widening for a split second as Tucker slid his arm around Ginny's waist. Her gaze snapped up to Ginny's, and a slow smile curled her lips, but she made a typical Rose report without commenting. "Tansy is on the dance floor, regretting her life decisions because she found somebody with three left feet. Kelli and Luke are dancing, and Fern is over there with the rest of her posse, making eyes at your youngest brother and his buddy."

Ginny peered over to where Rose had pointed. "Fern knows Charity?

Rose all but rolled her eyes. "Fern knows *everyone*, and

everything. At least according to Grandma Sonora. Grandma also thinks Fern needs to be careful with her dangerous source of knowledge, because at some point, it's going to get her in trouble."

"Fern doesn't seem the type to go snooping where she shouldn't," Tucker said cautiously.

Rose waved a hand. "It's not that. I think she's openly sneaky. Walks right into the middle of a conversation and stands there, and for some reason, people keep talking. Add in that the girl doesn't forget a thing, and she could pretty much have blackmail material on anyone in this town."

Tucker turned to Ginny. "Want a drink?"

"A little later. First, let's dance," Ginny ordered. And it was an order, because she caught him by the hand, winked at Rose, then hauled him onto the dance floor.

Tucker's confident arms wrapped around her. He whirled her in a rapid two-step full into the thick of things, his lips curled in the smallest of smirks. "I take it we're going for full on *blow their minds* rather than easing into it."

Ginny grinned, trusting he'd keep them from barreling into anyone on the crowded dance floor. "My mom always said when you're going to do a thing, do it up right."

"Seems I've heard that sentiment a time or two from my uncle," Tucker offered.

They danced. For the first couple of moments, Ginny was curious what kind of reaction they might be causing. But the truth was, the longer they danced and the longer she was in his arms, moving to the upbeat music; the longer Tucker looked down at her in that intensely focused manner that sent all her nerves tingling; the longer it all went on, the less Ginny cared to see anyone else's reaction.

This was where she wanted to be. Period.

"Your brother just spotted us," Tucker informed her quietly.

Ginny didn't care. Or maybe she did, because she stroked her fingers along the back of his neck a little more intently. "If the next song's a ballad, I dare you to kiss me."

Another near smile. "You're an evil woman, Ginny."

"Yeah, but you like me anyway."

An outright laugh escaped him, and he gave her an extra hard twirl, dipping her back over his arm and smiling down with his eyes set to *Smolder, Level-Ten*. "Challenge accepted."

Definitely not the move she'd expected. She teased, he responded, but in this case, he flipped all her expectations out the window.

Tucker pulled her upright, firmly against his body. With the hand pressed to her lower back, he sealed their torsos together. The other hand he brought to the back of her neck, fingers tangled in her hair to tilt her face up so he could lean in and kiss her. A slow, hot, demanding kiss that made it clear this was the type of evening that ended in the bedroom.

Somewhere between their lips making contact and his tongue dipping between her lips...

Somewhere between him accepting her teasing challenge and taking absolute control...

Somewhere between the start and the finish of all that, Ginny's brain simply fizzled out. When he finally pulled her upright, and the two of them stood in the middle of the dance floor while amused patrons danced around them, it happened.

Ginny Stone fell in love.

17

———

Once again, Tucker had gotten a prime example of how being involved with Ginny never went to plan.

The next song was thankfully slower. Tucker kept Ginny in his arms, swaying together. It gave everyone plenty of time to gawk and talk, ripples spreading visibly around the room.

He wasn't terribly surprised when Luke and Kelli were suddenly dancing beside them, his friend's expression absolutely hysterical.

Unexpected was Luke stealing Ginny out of his arms while Kelli stepped in to replace her.

Tucker watched Ginny dance away with reluctance. "Well, drat. That's a conversation I was supposed to have," he complained, turning his attention on Kelli. "Hi. Having a good evening?"

"I don't know if I should give you an award or hogtie you right now," Kelli said sweetly.

"Let's go with the award."

She laughed. "I thought Luke was about to lay an egg."

"So that's what his expression meant."

Kelli snickered again. "You're terrible. Also, I think you and Ginny will make a great team, so please put up with whatever nonsense happens over the next few days until this all settles, yes?"

Interesting observation. "Ginny and I will do just fine," he assured her. "I'm in it for the long haul. Or at least, that's what we're aiming for, a fact Ginny knows."

Kelli nodded. "Luke's not upset that you guys obviously..."

Her lips twitched as she seemed to struggle for the right word.

"Like each other?" Tucker suggested.

"Have carnal knowledge of each other seems more appropriate," Kelli suggested.

Well. "It was a better kiss than I expected."

Kelli fanned her fingers in front of her face. "Hell-*o*. Every one of Ginny's cohorts plans to interrogate her as soon as possible. Just in case your ears are burning later tonight."

It was impossible to keep in his smile. "I really do like her," he said more seriously. "I'm glad she's got all of you in her life again. She needs you, Kelli. She needs you and all her girlfriends more than she'll probably ever admit."

Kelli nodded slowly. "Yeah, she does. But you can't help somebody who doesn't ask. Know what I mean?"

Boy, did he ever. "We'll have to figure out how to be the best secret *Team Ginny* supporters."

Kelli patted him on the shoulder and tilted her head toward the side of the room where their things were. "Come on. Time to face the firing squad."

Tucker braced, uncertain exactly what would happen next. But Luke simply gave him a brief chin nod then took Kelli back out onto the dance floor.

Then, because Ginny insisted, Tucker danced with Tansy

who was downright gleeful about the kiss. Then he took Rose for a spin before handing her over to Alex.

It was a normal, ordinary evening out dancing with good friends. The only change was that he had a pretty woman he wanted to call his by his side most of the time.

A number of the ranch hands were there. Ginny accepted their invitations to dance, coming back each time to Tucker with amused updates.

"Some of them are buttering me up in order to get on your good side," she said with a grin, stealing a long drink from his beer. "You okay with this?" she asked, leaning in close so she didn't have to yell over the music.

"Being here with you, or you dancing with other guys?"

"Both."

He shrugged. "You like to dance. As long as they're respectful, I'll put up with it tonight." She blinked in surprise. "They've got questions. Some of them are probably double-checking you're okay with what's going on. They'll be happier hearing it come from you."

She curled her arms around his biceps and squeezed for a moment. "You're smart. And you're right."

"I'm smart, yet I also fucked up royally." Tucker saw Alex making his way over and gestured to the man. "Dance with him. I need to talk to your brother."

Ginny frowned. "I told Luke—"

"This isn't about us," Tucker assured her. He pressed a kiss to her forehead and turned her toward Alex. "Go. Dance."

Alex raised a brow. "That's incredible timing."

"Don't be a jackass," Tucker told him.

Ginny snickered. "Come on, Alex. I have questions for you."

Now Alex was the one who looked worried. "Tucker, what are you getting me into?"

"Not me. This is all her," Tucker drawled. He watched them dance away and slid farther to the right to where Luke and Kelli had taken possession of a low table. He hauled a chair next to his friend and sat down close.

He leaned back, watching Ginny as she laughed with Alex.

His position put him close enough that his head was only inches away from Luke's. "Thank you for being a whole hell of a lot smarter than I was a few minutes ago."

Luke stretched his arm along the back of Tucker's chair and leaned in even closer. "You're my best friend, and if we go outside right now, I will rip your spleen out through your throat."

"You would *try* to rip my spleen out," Tucker corrected him. "I'm still a better fighter than you. But I should've given you a heads up, and I'm sorry."

"What the hell," Luke complained. "You're lucky Kelli clued in faster than me what kind of trouble it would make if I threw a fit in public."

"That's what I'm apologizing for," Tucker explained. "Dammit, this was supposed to be a gentle transition into people seeing Ginny and I as a couple."

"Good job. There is no doubt whatsoever that you have a thing for each other," Luke said dryly. "How long?"

Damn, Tucker really didn't want to say nine years. "Long enough that we know we like each other."

His friend laughed. "You're such a fucking bullshitter. Answer the damn question. When did you start up with my sister?"

Reluctantly Tucker told the truth. "Remember the year Ginny called from the bar because Dare decided to hold a wake for her family and things were getting out of hand?"

Luke leaned back, exasperation in his body as he shook his head. "Holy crap, man. Seriously? That long ago?"

Tucker shrugged. "She told me it was something she really wanted, and since we were both grown-ups—"

"Don't give me the details," Luke complained. "Because I don't want to know."

Tucker stayed silent. Not much else he could say in that moment.

Luke took a long drink of his beer, then shook his head, leaning in to continue to curse Tucker out. "Christ. Not once in the past nearly ten years you felt like you should tell me?"

"What was I supposed to say?" Tucker asked seriously.

Luke made a face. "How about 'I like your sister'?"

They'd been friends for too long. Instinctively, Tucker responded the way he would've to any other prompt. "Luke, I like your sister."

His friend grimaced. Then his lips quivered, and his eyes rolled back in his head. Then he full on laughed, smacking a hand on Tucker's shoulder a touch harder than a friendly good-old-boy pat. "You're such a jackass. Fine. I'm glad you like my sister. Good luck dealing with her because while she's one of the most wonderful people I know, she is a fucking handful."

"Thank you for not blowing a gasket and making things tougher for me and the whole apprenticeship deal."

Luke shrugged and took another pull on his beer. "What you should be thanking me for is the fact that I'm not going to beat you up later."

"You mean you're not going to *try* to beat me up."

His friend shook his head disbelievingly. "You didn't tell me you slept with my sister."

Ginny was back. Settling, of course, into Tucker's lap. She glared at her brother. "For fuck's sake. We already talked about this. Leave Tucker alone. Besides, I talked him into it. It took three hours before he caved."

Luke blinked then glared at Tucker. "Why did it take that long? Didn't think she was good enough for you?"

Delight rolled in hard. "Now you want to beat me up for *not* sleeping with her fast enough?"

"Sounds about right," Luke agreed.

Ginny sighed, a huge, exasperated thing. "*Luke.*"

Tucker was so stinking amused. "Is there any scenario in your brain where I *don't* get beat up?"

Luke considered for a moment. "Not that I can see."

Kelli outright laughed. She shoved at Luke's shoulder then gestured to the dance floor. "Come on. Instead of threatening to beat people up, we'll burn off energy on the dance floor, deal?"

"Brilliant." Ginny was on her feet, hauling Tucker after her. She spoke to Kelli on the side. "Dinner at my place tomorrow for the four of us, yes?"

"We'll be there with bells on," Kelli promised.

Then Ginny was back in Tucker's arms and everything was right with his world.

The music turned slow and soft. As Ginny swayed in his arms, she looked thoughtful. "I hope that went better than expected."

"I screwed up," Tucker admitted. "I know Luke doesn't have an issue with us being together, and he's not really talking about sex. But I did blindside him. We're best friends, and until now, we've shared about the important things in our lives. That's on me, and I'm grateful he reacted in a way that keeps things rolling forward with this new job. I'm grateful he's my friend."

She wrinkled her nose. "I'm sorry. I shouldn't have teased you into moving too fast."

No way. "Goddess, you do things to my brain that I don't expect, but you're not responsible for my actions. I'm an adult, and if I can't think things through a little harder before I act, that's on me. Never you."

She dipped her chin. "Okay. I still feel a little guilty."

"Well, feelings are feelings, but I'm saying you need to remember it's not your fault. And in the end, things turned out fine." He twirled her a little closer, savouring the feel of her body's heat. "Let's focus on that part, okay?"

She twisted her head to rest it on his shoulder, swaying comfortably against him. "Okay."

A great evening on the dance floor turned into an even better evening in Ginny's bed. Tucker caught himself whistling as he crossed the distance between her cottage and the barns the next morning.

Of course, if he'd wanted an example of how fast the rumour mill operated, he had it in spades. As he grabbed a cup of coffee in the mess hall, more grins were aimed his way than usual. A few hours later, he turned the corner in the barn and came face to face with Dustin, who was definitely not wearing a grin.

"We need to talk," Dustin said gruffly, staring accusingly at Tucker.

Tucker pulled in his patience. He was pretty sure the topic wasn't Dustin's chore list.

The young man was the little brother Tucker had never had, and while there were enough years between them that he'd spent more time quasi-babysitting than having deep heart to hearts, he also knew what it had been like growing up in the Stone family.

Hell, Walter Stone had been the one to explain the birds and bees to Tucker, his own dad having zero interest in answering those types of questions.

No—scratch that. *Deb Stone* had gotten in the first round of information, much to Luke and Tucker's youthful embarrassment. His summertime mom had discussed the logistics of the deed in clear black and white. She'd not only told them most women needed clitoral stimulation to climax, she'd told them to watch women-friendly porn if they needed tips.

God, Tucker could still hear her voice, and his cheeks heated at the memory.

Sex with the right person is fun, but it comes with lots of responsibilities. If you're both enjoying yourself, then you're doing it right. If you can't figure out how to make sure she's happy first, stick to using your hand.

Walter had followed up, clearly amused as all get-out at their flushed faces. He'd given them each a box of condoms and the strict admonishment to never go without.

Dustin would have been too young to have had his parents explain the facts to him, but the next generation? Caleb had a healthy sense of right and wrong when it came to sex. Neither Luke nor Walker had been hound dogs, but they hadn't been dismissive of the women who enjoyed getting together with the men on the circuit. Tamara didn't seem the wilting-flower type when it came to straight truths and facts.

Blunt it was. Tucker figured if he considered himself a substitute Luke at this moment, things would work out fine.

"I can't believe you never said a word about you and Ginny getting together for all those years." Dustin's frown deepened. "I can't believe you thought it was a good idea to sleep with her."

"Why?"

Dustin paused. "Why what?"

"Why wasn't it a good idea? We're adults. We spent time together in a way that made us both happy, but private enough it didn't need to be shared."

If ever a man seemed uncomfortable with a topic of

conversation…poor Dustin all but twitched. "But you shouldn't have slept with her unless it meant something,"

"Now you're digging yourself a hole." Tucker gave the young man his driest possible glare. "You're saying no one should ever have sex until they're in a long-term, committed relationship like marriage?"

Dustin was more indignant than embarrassed. "Don't be ridiculous."

"Are you saying that your *sister* isn't allowed to make responsible adult decisions about whether she has sex with someone who cares enough to make sure she has fun and stays safe? Do you think she shouldn't have sex, period?" Tucker paused but didn't give up, because this was a point about more than the sex. "I really hope you can untangle your brain around this one, because Ginny and her friends need to make choices that are right for them. Fitting their behavior into some antiquated 'men can enjoy sex, but women who do the same thing are whores' idea just makes you look bad."

Dustin looked as if he were debating between crawling into a hole or punching Tucker in the face. Or both at the same time.

Before the kid could decide, Tucker shrugged. "Also, *I* wasn't just having sex. It definitely meant something." He paused. "But if nothing permanent comes of it, we still did nothing wrong. Understood?"

"Stop being all reasonable. You're making me twitch," Dustin complained.

"Sorry to be the voice of reason, but this is important. Both in how you treat Ginny and how you deal with this in the long-term."

"I'm not going to call her names," Dustin insisted.

"No, you're smart enough to know she'd kick your balls through your spleen if you did. But this isn't just about Ginny.

Great that you know better than to insult your sister." Tucker looked the young man over. "You know enough to not insult other women? Or better yet, you ready to tell any of your friends who are being jackasses and making rude comments to stop, even if it's not your sister involved? Because when I see that, I'll know you've learned this lesson."

Dustin sighed, his shoulders all but caved in. "You're right."

"Of course, I am," Tucker said dryly, hiding a smirk when the kid's head snapped up to see if he was kidding around. Then Tucker deliberately raised his arm and examined his watch. "Don't you have somewhere to be?"

Dustin noted the time and swore softly, snapping upright. Before he took off at a sprint, though, he paused and met Tucker's gaze straight on. "You're okay."

"Thanks for the vote of confidence." Tucker meant it.

The kid was already gone, probably now doubly scared that he'd be late for work.

Life was damn funny at times, Tucker thought. Ginny was totally going to get a kick out of knowing Dustin went to bat on her behalf, misguided as it was.

Tucker headed back to his own unending to-do list.

Once again, whistling.

18

Ginny stared at the hard cover journal in her lap. She stroked her fingers over the surface then slowly opened it to a clean page.

Pen in hand, she started writing, fully aware that she'd chosen a spot about a third of the way through the book. Deliberately avoiding page one. The same way she'd still avoided reading the opening pages of her mother's journal.

She shoved all that aside and put pen to page.

I'm dating Tucker Stewart.

Even writing that makes me feel squiggly inside, because I think back to all those notes I used to write to Dare, gushing about how handsome he was. How strong and muscular—and that's when my teenage brain couldn't quite understand exactly what fun all those muscles could add to a relationship.

It's been a week since we officially became a couple in public, and things have gone quite well. No trouble reported yet from Tucker in terms of smartass remarks from the men. My brothers have all been strangely well behaved, the mystery of why solved the other day when I discovered Tamara's younger sister Lisa had, at some point in the recent past, laid bets that Tucker and I would become an item in the future.

That woman is freaky. Based on nothing but stories she'd heard over the years, she somehow put two and two together and made a hundred bucks. She's either very, very smart or very, very lucky.

Anyway, I'm not quite sure what I'm supposed to write in this journal. I've read through some of the stuff mom wrote, and it wasn't a daily here's what's happening/here's what needs to be done kind of thing. More about the aha moments, I suppose.

So what's my aha *reason for writing today?*

I like dating Tucker. He's sinfully sexy, and any time we can get physical, it's hot and yet special. But being with him has become about more than sex.

I catch him looking at me sometimes, and I just want to ask him what I can do to make him happy. I hate that his parents weren't there for him when he was little. I might hate that my parents died when they did, but I got to have them for some very important years. His parents aren't dead, but for how much impact they had on his world, they may as well be.

I am a tangle of emotions.

Maybe that's my aha moment today, because I'm very happy

about many things, and still so confused about what the next step is.

How did you decide, Mom? How did you know when it was time to change direction in how you guided us? To let us fly or to guide us back to the nest a little longer?

How did you know you were making the right choice?

She stared at the page a little longer, suddenly aware that the fire in her stove was dying. That she still had breakfast dishes in the sink, and that in spite of everything that was going well in her world, she was on the edge of tears.

What the hell?

Ginny gave herself a firm scolding. "Damn, you're mopey. You need to get some energy tea brewing and snap out of it."

Only one cup of tea later, when she was still feeling cranky, Ginny wrapped herself up and headed to the barn, climbing into the hayloft and dropping herself into the Operation *Prove It* headquarters.

Sunlight beamed in through the old window, turning the bales golden brown and lighting up the small space like a cathedral.

She laid back on the pokey surface, not even caring that she'd forgotten to bring a protective layer. She just stared at the rafters overhead and slowed her breathing as she listened to the distant sound of voices and animals. The rattle of feed pails, doors opening and closing, the occasional neigh or burst of laughter.

Familiar. Peaceful.

A soft creak on the floorboards brought her to a half-seated position as Tucker slid into the space and settled beside her. He rested his hands on the bales then sat quietly.

Ginny slipped her fingers over his. "Hey."

"Hey. Everything okay?"

She shrugged. "I feel unsettled."

He made a soft noise then picked her up, cradling her in his lap as he braced his feet on the center bale and leaned back. "Makes sense."

"Really?"

"Goddess." He pressed a kiss to the top of her head. "You forget what day it is?"

Ginny considered. "Wednesday?"

Tucker rocked her softly as if they were in some sort of giant easy chair. "It's February tenth."

Oh. "It's the anniversary day."

The anniversary of the accident. The day when everything had changed.

They sat in silence for a little longer, Ginny's throat closing up in a most unwelcome way. "How come it still hurts so much?"

"Because you love them as much as you ever did, and you wish they were here," he said quietly.

She couldn't stop the tears. She wanted to, because this wasn't her. Like she'd told Tamara before, she *wasn't* weepy, she was strong. She could get things done, she could help others. She could make a difference.

But the one thing she couldn't do was bring her parents back.

"I miss them so much," she confessed, the words coming out broken and high-pitched.

Tucker gathered her closer, rubbing her back gently. "I know, baby. I know."

It took a while until she cried herself out, and by then her sinuses were plugged and her throat was sore, which made her even madder at herself.

Then there was the other matter. "I'm keeping you from your work," Ginny complained.

Tucker shook his head, still holding her close. He had provided a clean tissue so she could clean herself up. "This is what I'm doing right now, and it's important," he assured her.

She tucked the soggy tissues in her pocket before wiping a final time at her eyes with the back of her hand. "How did you know I was here?"

"A little bird told me," Tucker drawled.

Ginny rolled her eyes. "Seriously."

"Kelli saw you come in and mentioned it. I thought I'd pop my head in to see if you were looking for some company."

She grimaced. "Such wonderful company. Sobbed all over you—"

"You trusted me with your tears," he corrected her. When she would've protested, he raised a finger and shook it. "Life is not always laughter and sunshine, Ginny. I don't want to be with you only when it's easy, remember?"

He was a good, good man. Ginny dipped her chin. "I remember."

He glanced around the space. "Is it time for an Operation *Prove It* meeting?"

Maybe, but there was something she needed his help with even more. "Would you go with me to Mom and Dad's graves?"

Tucker's expression went solemn. He dipped his chin. "I'd be honoured."

First things first, though. Ginny wrapped her arms around his neck and squeezed tight. Completely innocent. Completely intimate, because this man was quickly becoming an anchor for her very soul.

They had company at the graveside.

Ginny sent a message to Caleb to let him know what they

were doing. Tucker had done the same for Luke. And then it only made sense to shoot a message to Walker and Dustin...

An hour later, a long solemn line on horseback shuffled along the trail up the hillside to where her parents had been buried. All of her immediate family were there except for Dare. Ashton had joined them, along with Kelli, and when the group dismounted and came forward, it was another one of those bittersweet moments.

Someone had been out earlier, because the graves had been cleared of snow, and bright plastic flowers poked up from the holders near the headstones.

After impulsively organizing the gathering, Ginny suddenly felt at a loss. What did she do now? What did she say?

Dustin looked on the verge of tears. Walker stared into the distance, nodding gently as if holding an internal conversation. Kelli had her arms wrapped around Luke's torso, head against his chest. His lips were pressed together in a thin line, and Ginny realized he too was fighting for control.

Even big brother Caleb—strong, reliable, willing to do the impossible because it was the right thing to do, Caleb—even he had turned slightly away from the graves and held Tamara as if she were the post keeping him upright.

Somehow, she could do this. She was a Stone, and they were strong. She was a Stone, and they did the next thing. Her family needed her as much today as they had all those years ago, but inside she felt as if she had nothing to give.

Even as she took a deep breath, strong fingers tangled around hers. Tucker glanced down at her for a moment. Then he looked around the gathering and spoke in that clear, firm tone she'd come to love so much, and was strong *for* her.

"I ever tell you about the time I ran away from home?"

All heads swiveled their direction, curiosity replacing the sorrow and sad memories that had been the main focus.

Tucker casually wrapped an arm around Ginny's shoulders, leaning back and looking up slightly, and damn if there wasn't a smile on his face.

"It was spring. About the time every year when I'd start thinking summer couldn't come soon enough. I was thirteen, which meant I knew plenty about buses and was cocky enough to consider hitching a ride if I had to. Because, truth told, I wasn't running away, but more running to what I considered my real home. Silver Stone." Tucker looked across the circle and met Luke's gaze. "Amongst other things, my best friend was here, and it didn't seem right that I had to wait another three months to see him."

Ashton nodded, laughing softly as if remembering the story faster than Tucker was telling it.

"I was smart, all right. I packed a bag, bought a ticket, and rode all the way to Black Diamond. Pretty damn proud of myself, because I changed buses three times and hadn't lost a thing the entire day and a half it took."

Dustin looked awed. "What happened after you hit Black Diamond?"

"I called your father, of course," Tucker told him seriously. "Figured I had made it that far and no way would anybody send me away. I *deserved* to stay."

Walker chuckled. "Oh, boy. This isn't going to end well."

"Thirteen-year-old me didn't think so," Tucker agreed. He took another look around the circle, meeting everyone's eyes in turn. "Your dad came to the bus stop and picked me up. What's more, your mom was with him. Walter and Deb drove me straight to a restaurant, and we went and had a meal together. The first since I left home, because I hadn't planned *that* well."

Ginny was fascinated. "I don't remember you coming for an extra-long summer visit."

"That's because the next thing they did after that was put my ass back on the bus. But they didn't send me on my own. Walter rode with me, because he said I obviously couldn't be trusted to make grown-up decisions, so I got baby treatment the way I deserved."

"Ouch." Luke grimaced.

Caleb looked as if he remembered it all too well. "The wrath of Dad. He didn't get *mad*, but boy, did you know you were out of line."

Tucker nodded. "I went from feeling as if I was ten feet tall to a toddler being sent to timeout after a tantrum. He escorted me all the way home—still have no idea how he simply took off a couple of days like that on an instant's notice. Only, here's the part I want to tell you. The entire time on the trip home, we talked. He talked about the ranch. He talked about his best friend, Joseph. He talked about his hopes and dreams, and he did it as if I were an adult. As if I hadn't just screwed up big time and acted absolutely childish."

Tucker's arm around her waist tightened a little. Ginny curled her arms around him and gave him a squeeze. Giving him back a bit of strength so he could finish.

He smiled at her. "Your dad talked about each one of you. His kids, who he was so proud of for so many reasons. Some of you were good at one thing, some of you were good at another. He said he knew the day would come when it would be you taking care of Silver Stone, but that was okay. Because you knew about working together. About trusting each other and being there for one another."

Caleb nodded. "He wasn't a lone wolf, our dad. He relied a whole lot on Mom, too." He curled his arm around Tamara, and she smiled.

Tucker slid his hand down until his fingers linked with Ginny's. "Ginny told me today how much she missed them. I know we all do. Not just today, but every day. But—and I don't know if this helps—but when I look around, I still see them here. In the work that you do, and the way you support each other." He squeezed Ginny's hand. "In the way you love each other. It's a pretty amazing legacy your parents gave you, and it's absolutely still true today."

Ashton nodded. "Amen."

On their left, Luke reached out a hand to Tucker. Only when he took hold, Luke pulled him into a tight embrace, patting him on the back. "You're right. It's a damn good legacy they left us. And a damn good story."

"I can't believe you didn't tell us about that trip before now," Walker said the moment before he too hauled Tucker into a hug.

The entire gravesite party turned into a rotating series of embraces.

Ginny found herself being held extra tight by Tamara before her sister-in-law pulled away and shook a finger, gently chiding in a soft voice so no one would overhear. "I recognize the look in your eyes over the past couple of weeks. That's the same look my sister Karen gets when she's struggling with something. Listen to what your guy just said about how the Stones work together as a team, okay? If you've got something you need help with, I'm here for you. We're *all* here."

Enough with the tears. Ginny smiled. "Thanks. I will," she said decisively. "Only I can't guarantee that everything I share will make sense."

Tamara blew a raspberry. "You need to hang around me and my sisters more. Lisa thrives on turning gibberish into words."

"I have noticed this about her," Ginny said dryly.

A whole bunch of hugs later, everyone mounted up and left.

Ginny found Dustin standing beside her.

He still looked on the edge of tears, but he also grinned sheepishly. "Thanks. I came this morning to clean things up a little and..." He swallowed hard. "I'm glad you got everybody together. It was the right thing to do."

Tucker slid into position behind her.

Ginny gave Dustin another quick hug. "It just kind of happened, but I'm glad it did."

Dustin glanced up at Tucker, hesitating then speaking a little on the gruff side. "That was a good story you shared. Thanks."

Tucker curled his arm around Ginny then dipped his chin in response. "The flowers were a nice touch. I'm glad they were here. It means a lot you took care of things like that."

Her youngest brother's eyes widened. "How did you know it was me?"

Tucker shrugged. "Ashton's teaching me how to read minds."

Dustin jerked upright then snickered. "Right."

Tucker patted him on the back then turned him toward the horses and pushed him gently. "Let's go. I think you still have some jobs you need to finish this afternoon."

"Yes, sir."

The response came so quick and natural, Ginny had to hide a smile.

The warmth inside her was back. It lasted all the way until they got the horses to the barn and everyone headed home or returned to work.

Ginny caught Tucker by the hand and pulled him toward her. "I know *you* probably have some jobs you need to finish this afternoon, but come to my place when you're done? I'll make supper."

He nodded. "I'll be there in a couple of hours if that works for you."

They both took off in different directions.

The first thing Ginny did when she got home was hop into the shower, steamy water all around her heating her up until every bit of tension washed right away.

Then she made another tea, mixing a couple of different combinations together before curling up on the couch and once again lifting the journal into her lap. Once again opening to a random page to write.

I don't know how to do this right, but I suppose that's part of the journey.

Every day we have to take the adventure as it comes, and while sometimes the road is not one we want to travel, today I learned a very important lesson.

The companions with us on the journey are vital.
I think that's some of what you tried to teach us, Mom. About picking friends at school who were the rock-solid type and not ones who would only lead us in mischief. I think that's why you and Jacquie Hayes got along so well. You knew how to fight about what was important so that you could learn from each other.

Dare and I don't always agree. We don't always like the same things—although she's totally going to get a kick out of the fact that I'm writing in this thing. Considering she's the one who's been journaling since she was sixteen...

Is that karma, or fate, or just some weird coincidence?

Doesn't matter.

What does matter is that I have people in my corner who love me and care for me and want nothing but the best for me.

I don't have to be strong on my own.

Ginny closed the book slowly, fingers slipping from between the pages in an almost caress. That had felt different. So very different from before.

It'd felt...right.

Then, because she had no idea when Tucker might get there, she headed into the kitchen and got started on dinner.

She may as well admit it. While there were a lot of things she couldn't do, feeding a man—*her* man—was a thing she truly enjoyed.

To borrow Tucker's favourite phrase, screw the rules.

When he got there shortly after five, he paused inside the door and took a deep appreciative sniff. "Ginny, it smells like heaven in here."

She stepped forward, taking the colourful bouquet of flowers from his hand. "These are beautiful." She went up on her tiptoes and pressed a kiss to his cheek. "Thank you."

While he took off his boots, she went and put the flowers in a vase and arranged them on the table, then returned and brought him with her to the loaded kitchen table.

He paused with one hand on the back of the chair. "Wow. You went all out."

Ginny laughed. "I had a few things in the freezer, but yes. I figured you deserved your favourites."

She had warmed up leftover roast, made spiced cauliflower,

and a mountain of mashed potatoes. "There's also green bean casserole with rosemary, and bumbleberry pie for dessert."

He still had hold of her hand and lifted her knuckles to his mouth to kiss them softly. "Just to be clear, I really, truly adore your brain."

After the highly emotional day, it was good to laugh. "Look, I can't help it that you're getting a fantastic package deal. I've got a great body, I love sex, and I love to cook. Face it, you hit the jackpot, Tucker."

He pulled her against him for a brief, but firm hug. "Not going to argue. Like I said, you're the smartest woman I know."

If writing in the journal earlier had felt right, this felt even better.

Ginny wasn't about to confess it out loud, but she admitted it to herself. She liked the idea of being a homemaker. Travelling had never been about being wild and free, but about finding that bit of home in every place she visited.

After dinner, Tucker washed the dishes while she put things away, easy conversation volleying between them about the tasks they looked forward to in the coming week.

Then they curled up on her couch, Ginny nestled under Tucker's arm, her head resting on his chest as he opened Netflix and they settled in to watch a movie.

Homey. Peaceful.

After the show was done, Tucker clicked the screen off and pressed a kiss to her temple. "I want to stay the night."

She looked up and traced a finger along his hairline, pushing away a curl. Sliding her fingertips farther down to rasp lightly on his five o'clock shadow. "I notice you didn't mention sleep," she teased softly.

"We'll get around to that eventually," he promised.

He walked her to the bedroom. Looked into her eyes the

entire time as he undid her buttons, as he stripped her naked and removed his own clothes.

Strong, firm muscles pressed against her softness, Tucker crowded over her until she was blanketed by his body.

Slow, drugging kisses followed, his touch as well, mixing up pleasure between his fingers, his lips, and tongue, and teeth. Ginny closed her eyes and let her hands drift. Teasing back until both of them were vibrating with need.

Tucker rolled them both to their sides then pulled her top leg over his hip so they were in a tangled embrace as he slid them together. Slow thrusts, his hands on her breasts briefly before sliding over her belly to the apex of her sex.

She sucked in a gasp at the sharp shot of desire.

"Right there. That's it," he encouraged. "Let go. I'll catch you," he promised.

Ginny couldn't have stopped if she'd wanted. Like springtime runoff, everything welled up to the point of no return until together they tipped over the edge and cascaded into pleasure.

They lay together for long moments after, stroking each other, staring into each other's eyes.

Tucker left for just long enough to deal with the condom before coming back and folding her in his arms again. Face-to-face, hearts beating in time.

She watched as his lashes slowly closed, a hint of a smile lingering on his lips. Contentment rose from him like fresh, spring growth.

He was sound asleep, and Ginny was still staring. Still stroking her fingers over his body.

"I love you," she whispered, just to try the words.

That too sounded very, very right.

19

―――――――

 lex summoned Tucker over during coffee break a few days later. "I have a request to pass on from a friend."

"Sounds intriguing," Tucker said.

"My friend Ryan—owner of Rough Cut. He and his girlfriend have decided to tie the knot."

Tucker had done his best to get up to speed on all the local happenings, which included all of the main players in the community. Uncle Ashton, surprisingly, had turned out to be a wonderful source of information, and considering Ryan was also part of the volunteer firefighters where Ashton volunteered time every week, the bar owner's recent relationship adventures had been thoroughly discussed.

"Ryan and Madison are getting married? Man, that's quick," Tucker said. "Didn't she show up in December?"

Alex shrugged. "When it's right, it's right. Besides, they've been good friends since they were young." He gave Tucker a pointed look. "You might know someone like that. Someone who's currently involved with a woman he spent a lot of time with when they were young, and who knows where it could lead?"

"Enough," Tucker said, but he was amused. It was nice to have someone like Alex around who was willing to banter back more than just a 'yes, sir.' "What does Ryan need?"

"They're holding the wedding over at Red Boot Ranch, but they hope to have all their friends join the party. Can you make sure everyone on the list has Saturday off?"

Tucker whistled. "Wow, talk about getting the job done double quick."

"Ryan's talking about them trying for a baby right away. Seriously, the man is very action-oriented, shall we say." Alex grinned. "And that's not me gossiping. Ryan has been telling absolutely everyone the same thing. Madison has given up getting him to stop oversharing. She thinks it's funny."

"Hey, whatever works for a couple's relationship," Tucker said. "Give me the list, and I'll see what I can do."

Which meant if he had to work a double shift, he would. Impulsive last-minute activities like this needed to be encouraged as far as he was concerned—

A second later he caught himself. "Damn, I must be feverish."

Alex frowned. "What?"

Tucker pressed a hand to his forehead. "I just caught myself thinking being spontaneous and impulsive was a good thing. The Tucker of a couple years ago just got indigestion and went and checked a few spreadsheets to calm down."

Laughter burst from the other man. "You're all right." Alex looked him over with satisfaction. "It's been good to have you around. Seriously."

"Thanks. Get me the list as soon as you can." Tucker took off, because if he needed to juggle the schedule, he needed to get a couple other things done first.

"I will," Alex called after him.

Tucker had just stepped from the warmth of the training barn and into the darker passage between buildings when something solid barreled into him and shoved him against the wall.

Tucker moved instinctively, rolling away from the force and bringing up his hands protectively as he found his balance.

"Fucking asshole. Course you'd hide behind her skirts. Know who's got the balls in your relationship." A fist snapped toward him.

Tucker ducked to the side, blinking hard to focus. "Jim. What the hell? Back up and talk this out." Tucker ordered.

Instead, another fist flew at his face. Tucker deflected, but not hard enough, and the blow made contact with his shoulder, spinning him slightly.

"She told you to get rid of me, didn't she?" Jim demanded.

"Still don't know what you're talking about," Tucker said, retreating quickly toward the second door. While he could defend himself, fighting with one of the men was not something he wanted to do unless it was absolutely necessary.

Jim jerked his chin upward. "That cold Stone bitch. I didn't even touch her. I guess I should've, considering you've managed to fuck your way to a pretty prime position. Next time I see her, I won't be so polite. Maybe track her down in that greenhouse of hers and have some fun, right?"

Which meant the dammed bastard had watched Tucker and Ginny fool around. He wouldn't have seen much, not with the frosted tint on the windows, but Tucker's fury shot to high.

Yet it was the rest of what Jim had said that crossed a line there was no coming back from. Somehow, instead of killing the man, Tucker shoved open the door behind him, light pouring into the space. "Get your ass out there."

Jim rushed him, catching hold of Tucker's arm at the last

moment to spin him into punching distance. "Fight, you fucking pansy. Cut my hours? Make me redo training? It's all that damn bitch's fault."

Tucker and Luke had spent a lot of years fighting. Fighting because they wanted to learn, fighting sometimes because they were seriously pissed at each other.

Jim might've been in a few bar brawls, but he'd never actually *fought*. That much was clear as Tucker stood back and got into position.

"You don't want to do this," Tucker said. "Walk away, and I'll let Ashton deal with you. But you're done. You're not working another day at Silver Stone."

"Eat shit," Jim shouted, snarling like a rabid dog.

He would've been better off simply swinging instead of working to look fierce. Tucker avoided the next blow and got in a satisfying jab to Jim's ribs.

A crowd moved toward them, which had been Tucker's hope in shifting them into a more public place. He had zero objection to taking the man down, but legally, he needed to stay on the right side of the law for the ranch's sake. Which meant staying in defensive mode.

But defensive with a reckless opponent meant hurting Jim enough to make him stop the bullshit. Tucker dodged another wild roundhouse, jabbing a fist into Jim's gut that sent the other man staggering backward.

"Stand down," Tucker ordered again.

Jim rushed him, screaming in anger. Fists flying, knees rising up. Tucker dodged the best he could, but some of the wild blows landed. By the time a set of ranch hands had pulled Jim back, Tucker had been hit by a sheer fluke in the eye and the nose, blood dripping over his lips.

"What the hell is going on?" Ashton stepped into view.

"He figures since he's fucking the boss's sister, he can do

anything he wants." Jim snapped a finger at Tucker. "She got all pissed at me the other day. Didn't do a thing, but I knew she was gonna tell some lies to get me in shit."

Ashton folded his arms over his chest and stepped directly in front of Jim. He looked him over with disdain. Tucker was happy to see that the other man's face looked worse, in spite of Tucker only defending himself.

"If you're talking about the fact you were put on probation and re-training, that was me," Ashton said.

Jim's head snapped up. "You?"

"Me. Because that's what we usually do around here when a man's not doing his job but has the potential to make things right." Ashton shook his head. "But this nonsense is a clear violation of everything you agreed to when coming on board this ranch. You're fired."

Jim swore, but Ashton ignored him. He glanced at the hands standing nearby. "Mason. Cooper. Walk Jim to his room so he can clear it out. Be in my office in an hour and I'll cut you your final cheque."

"You can't just kick me out." Jim complained.

"I'm not kicking you out," Ashton said calmly. "You broke the terms of your contract, so you terminated yourself. Now get the hell out of here. If you don't go willingly, we'll call the RCMP."

Jim spat at the ground in front of Tucker. "Bastard."

"Take care how you act right now," Tucker said softly, a mirror imitation of his uncle. "Ranching is a tightknit community, and there's not a whole lot of places out there that want to deal with your kind of bullshit. You want a new job anywhere local, you need an attitude adjustment."

Jim left. He didn't go quietly, but he did go, kicking things out of his way until the two men on either side of him moved in and all but straight-armed him into the snowy yard.

The men still gathered looked back and forth from Ashton to Tucker as if waiting to see what happened next.

"The troublemakers always make themselves known." Ashton said it loud enough that everyone around them heard.

Tucker glanced around, meeting the men's eyes. "Any questions?"

One hand rose in the back. "You really dating Ginny Stone?"

Tucker chuckled, slipping a hand across his mouth and examining the blood he wiped off. "I really am. So mind your manners, same as you would with any woman who comes around Silver Stone, understood?"

"Yes, sir," the young man said quickly. Then he grinned. "Would it be improper to say good for you?"

Ashton made a noise that sounded remarkably like a smothered snicker before he growled out another order. "Back to work, all of you."

Tucker waited until the crowd dispersed. "Okay with you if I finish taking care of Jim?"

His uncle stared at him for a moment then nodded slowly. "Don't do anything that'll get you arrested."

"I'll try."

Tempting as it was to head off on his own, it was probably good to have some checks and balances in place. Tucker gave Luke a call and asked to meet at the mess hall.

His friend arrived quickly, eyeing Tucker's bloody face with curiosity and concern until Tucker explained what had gone down, and then anger rose to take its place.

"He's gone?" Luke demanded.

"Packing. I want to make sure he leaves with a full understanding of the situation." A sense of dread slipped in even as Tucker made the decision to go ahead. His anger and sense of justice made the next step logical and inevitable, but it was also potentially trouble he couldn't walk away from unscathed. Ginny was not going to approve. "This is mine to deal with, got it?"

Luke reluctantly nodded. "Don't kill the man."

"No guarantees," Tucker murmured.

The door to Jim's quarters stood open. Mason and Cooper stood outside with their arms over their chests and frowns fully in place.

They both snapped upright when Tucker and Luke appeared.

"We got this," Luke said quietly, gesturing toward the mess hall. "Grab a coffee if you need one, then get back to work."

The men eyed Tucker before offering a nod of approval, taking off quickly as ordered.

Jim must've heard something, because he marched through the door, sneering in their direction as he tossed bags in the back of his truck. "Come to gloat?"

Luke stepped back.

Tucker gestured toward the room. "You empty it out?"

The other man folded his arms over his chest. "What do you want?"

Tucker spread his hands in a *come and get me* attitude. "Since you're no longer an employee, I'm no longer your boss. Which means if you want to take a shot at me, I'll give you the chance."

An evil sneer scurried across Jim's face. "Fucking right, I want to take a shot."

Jim moved like the snap of a slingshot, fist flying to make contact with Tucker's jaw. Tucker turned at the last moment and let most of the impact slide off.

Then he raised his fists and stepped forward. "My turn."

Jim threw another punch, but Tucker pushed it aside easily before slamming his fist into Jim's face. The other man toppled to the ground, arms flung back, legs askew. He lay there motionless for a moment, shocked, before scurrying away crab-like.

He was too slow. Tucker caught him by the front of the shirt, lifting him skyward to deliver another punishing blow.

And another.

The temptation was strong to keep letting the man have it, because while Jim had only been moderately rude to Ginny in person, his threat to stalk and hurt her was fucked up. This was the kind of man who would escalate. Somewhere, sometime, things would go too far.

What if Tucker wasn't around to protect Ginny? What if some other person ended up on the receiving end of Jim's bullshit attitude?

"Tucker, that's enough." Luke spoke softly. The voice of reason, cutting through the haze of Tucker's anger.

His friend was right, dammit anyway.

Tucker hauled Jim to his feet one final time and shoved him toward his truck. The man grabbed the door and clung to it for support.

"That was for threatening my woman," Tucker said quietly. "Here's your final warning. I have enough contacts, so trust me when I say you will be watched. If you *ever* intimidate or scare or lay a hand on anyone in the future—woman, man, I don't care—I will hear about it. You will not like what happens when I hunt you down."

Tucker turned on his heel and left without a backward glance.

Blood pounded in his ears so hard he didn't realize Luke marched beside him, his usually happy face turned thoughtful.

They were nearly at the arena when Luke laid a hand on Tucker's shoulder and squeezed. "I told Kelli I'd meet her in a few. She has some crazy idea I'll let her up on the back of that new bronco we brought in."

"Jeez. The woman is fearless," Tucker said.

"Scares the hell out of me sometimes," Luke agreed. He pulled Tucker to the side of the barn where there was a sink and handed over a handkerchief. "Wipe off the blood before you scare someone."

"A little fear might be a good thing," Tucker growled.

Luke waited until Tucker had removed the surface evidence of the fight, then cleared his throat. "Thanks."

Tucker glanced at his friend. "For what?"

Luke tilted his head toward the crew quarters. "For not killing the bastard, but also, for putting the fear of God into him. Kelli might scare me with how she acts sometimes, but I don't have to wonder if she's safe from being assaulted right here in our own backyard. Ashton's been a big part of why that is, and it's clear you've got the same mindset." He stuck out his hand. "So, thanks."

Tucker ignored the hand and went for a hug, pounding Luke firmly between the shoulder blades. "Aw, I love you too, sweetheart."

Luke shoved him, and the two of them play-wrestled for a moment.

A sharp whistle rang out, followed by a laughing call. "Hey, get to work, slackers, or I'll tell Ashton on you." Kelli strode up, all light and happy, and Tucker felt deep satisfaction roll right down to his toes.

Yeah, Luke was right. There were a few things that his uncle Ashton had been doing over the years that were absolutely worth keeping a priority. For Kelli's sake. For Ginny's. For Caleb's little girls who would eventually be a part of Silver Stone's daily operations.

For a second, a vision of a little girl with Ginny's dark hair and big brown eyes flashed to mind, and Tucker kept his feet through sheer willpower alone.

Only he also knew Ginny's opinion on fighting. What if his actions had just destroyed his chance at happiness with the woman he loved? Fear at a level he'd never known before rocked through him for a split second before he forced it back.

Ginny was not like his parents. Ginny was reasonable—sort of. He had to trust that what they'd built between them was solid enough to deal with a difference in viewpoint.

There would be no compromise on this, though. Nothing less than her safety, and the safety of others, was acceptable.

He just hoped that when the dust settled, he would still be standing.

20

Something was up.

Not only did heads pivot to follow her as Ginny passed by stalls on the way to unsaddle her horse, but low murmurs followed as well.

"Let me get that for you." Alex hurried forward to help lift off the saddle, ready to carry it to the tack room.

"Thanks." She caught him before he could vanish, leaning in close to whisper her question. "Why is everyone suddenly acting as if we're in church?"

Alex blinked for a second, obviously trying to figure out some non-controversial thing to tell her.

"Alex," she warned. "Lie to me, and I will set Yvette up on a date, and it won't be with you."

His jaw dropped. He snapped it shut. "You're mean."

"Motivated," Ginny volleyed back before taking pity on him. "I won't do that. I can tell you like her, and from what I've heard, she doesn't hate your guts. Much."

He sighed. "It's complicated."

She snickered. "Tell me about it." Then she narrowed her

gaze. "Literally. What's up with the peanut gallery? They're all acting as if I'm about to go off like a firecracker."

Alex hoisted the saddle to his shoulder. "One of the hands got fired."

"Really?" She considered, but couldn't imagine why that meant eyes on her. Unless... "Jim?"

"Damn, you're good," Alex said, backing away from her. "That's all I'm telling you. Talk to Tucker."

"Thanks for the help," she called after him.

"Any time."

A moment later, her phone buzzed with a message.

Tucker: *You got time for an Operation Prove It meeting?*
Ginny: *After I groom Prancer, sure.*
Tucker: *Meet you in the secret hideout.*

The exchange made her smile and increased her curiosity. Having big strong Tucker message her to meet him at the hideout was rather hysterical.

Only when she rounded the corner to their out-of-the-way gathering spot, adrenaline rushed in and drowned all lingering amusement. "What happened to your face?"

He raised a sheepish gaze. "Good to see you too."

She dropped to the bale beside him and softly stroked the corner of his eye. "Tucker."

He covered her hand with his and lowered their joined fingers to his thigh. "Operation report—things came to a head today with one lone dissenter. He's been dealt with. My uncle was the one to start the process, but I will admit I finished it. Jim Allen will not be bothering you or anyone else in the future."

Shit. "That sounds scarier and more final than I think you intended. He's still breathing, yes?"

Tucker snorted softly. "Luke made sure of that. I wasn't as concerned."

Ginny sat in silence, gathering her thoughts while she examined the man before her. He was rigid with tension.

Why now, when he'd obviously done what he'd thought was necessary?

"I don't like fighting," she said, the words sharper than intended.

"I know." He didn't defend himself or offer excuses. Just sat there with eyes full of sadness. As if waiting for her to...what? Chastise him? Break up with him?

As if.

She sighed hugely. "How do I tell you that I worry you might get hurt without implying you can't take care of yourself? Or that you can't take care of me, because neither of those are true."

Tucker paused. The furrow between his brows deepened. "You don't like it when I fight because I might get hurt? That's your concern?"

She made a face. "Dude, I've seen you after tussling with Luke. It's not always been pretty, although I expect that's currently more luck on my brother's part than skill. Don't tell him I said that."

His confusion seemed to grow instead of lessening. "My parents said fighting was a clear sign of a low intellect and a morally bankrupt individual."

"Fuck off." The words escaped before she could stop them. "Them, not you. Did they really say that to your face?"

He dipped his chin, refusing to meet her eyes. "The summer I was fourteen I went home with bruises, and got the mother of all lectures. They nearly stopped letting me come back. It took Ashton and your father persistently calling to make my summers continue."

"That is so much bullshit, and cruel, and one hundred percent wrong." Ginny was ready to go to war on his behalf. "It's a good thing I don't know where they live."

She might reconsider her no fighting rule if it meant getting to kick their butts.

"I don't understand," Tucker said softly.

"I'm a really good shot. I wonder if they'd consider a backside full of buckshot a more civilized way to deal with asses." She glared into the distance, sending nasty thoughts on the airwaves to his unbelievably dense parents. Then she shook her head to refocus and looked him straight in the eye. "Back to the topic at hand. With the way you've beefed up? Promise me that you won't actually throw a punch at my brother. Luke's profile can't take his nose being broken. Then again, if you really fought, I bet you'd still hold back for old time's sake, and then *he'd* mess up your pretty face, and I don't want that either." She threw her hands in the air dramatically. "See what dilemmas your fighting causes me?"

The next second, she was airborne, landing in his lap.

He cupped her face in both his hands and took a long, deep breath. "You're amazing."

It was impossible to resist. "I know."

His lips twitched. "You really aren't mad?"

She considered her words. "Your parents were wrong. Not only about the fighting, but about a lot of things. The way they were never there for you when you were growing up, the way they discarded you. It's all wrong. You know that, right?"

Tucker dipped his head slowly.

"Why did telling me this scare you so much?" she whispered. "Why?"

He swallowed hard. Her confident and powerful man, uneasy as if this was life and death to him. "I've said it before. You're one of the smartest people I know. What if..." He stalled. Looked away from her as if he didn't want her to see how much he hurt inside. "What if I don't deserve to be with you?"

In that moment, Ginny well and truly hated his parents. "The only thing you don't deserve are the jerks who were your biological donors," she said bluntly. "Did my mom and dad ever make you feel as if you were lacking?"

Tucker didn't even pause. Just shook his head instantly in denial.

"Of course not. In fact, you're far less annoying than any of my brothers, which means you were probably my parents' favourite."

A soft snort escaped him.

"Promise me that you'll duck faster if this situation ever comes up again." She said the words softly, but with everything in her. "You have to do what you think is right, even if I don't like it. I understand. I still get to worry, okay?"

The instant her final word escaped, his mouth was on hers and she was being kissed senseless. He groaned, though, and not in a good way, when he finally let her breathe and rested his forehead against hers. "My lip hurts."

So stinking amusing. "Sorry, but kind of my point."

He snorted. "Okay. I promise not to permanently damage your brother in the future. *You* have to promise not to shoot or poison my parents at any time in the future, because it would simply be a waste of energy. And finally, I promise to be careful and only use my powers for good."

Ginny snickered. "You *are* a superhero. I knew it."

He hummed as he stroked his hands down her back, settling on her hips and dragging her forward into full contact with some very interesting body parts. "You're a goddess. Make magic with me?"

Sex in the barn when she was pretty damn sure at least half the hands knew where they were, and what they were doing?

There was more than one way for her man to prove he knew how to take care of her, she supposed. Although she did her best to keep her moans and shouts to a minimum.

The next three or four days flew past as Tucker got busy again and Ginny dove full on into research and planning for her new venture. But even checking out recipes and designing product delivery systems for her herbal concoctions only occupied so many hours.

All her extra time was put toward solving the damn puzzle. Only she tried everything in the book, and it still wasn't enough. Time to pull out the big guns.

Ginny took a picture of the well-worn birthday puzzle paper and finally sent the image to her sister.

Then she printed out a half dozen additional copies, folding them up and sticking them in pockets so she could haul them out and shove them under the nose of everyone she met to ask for ideas.

2 of 3

The clear message of the sticky note poked her again and again. If the puzzle page was *one*, and the journals *two*, that meant there was a *three* out there somewhere. She couldn't stand the idea of not having the final gift from her parents fully understood.

At the coffee shop, down in the market, everywhere Ginny went she showed people the page. Everyone tried their best, but none of the suggestions helped, and her frustration continued to rise in spite of the other good things progressing in her world.

Good things like Tucker Stewart smoldering at her across the dinner table as he appreciatively inhaled the roast chicken dinner she'd made for them. Tucker, washing dishes at her side and telling her all about what he'd done that day. Listening with real interest as she shared about her tasks.

Tucker, scooping her into his arms and carrying her to the bedroom, laughing together until they couldn't do anything more than make incoherent noises, pleasure overwhelming them.

Except for the unsolved puzzle, Ginny had to admit her life was pretty damn perfect.

When outdoor temperatures finally rose enough to enjoy the evening outdoors, Tucker curled his arm around her a little tighter as they sat together on the porch to watch the sunset. "Want to go over it again?"

"Please." She leaned her head on his chest. "I must be driving you wild with this unending puzzle."

"I don't mind," he said, stroking a strand of hair behind her ear. "And I can't wait for the moment you solve it. You'll be on fire."

"You like me on fire?" Ginny pressed a palm to his cheek. "Silly question."

He snickered. "Dirty girl." But he tucked his fingers under her chin and lifted her face so he could kiss her, and once again all puzzles and long-lost mysteries vanished. Nothing but his taste, his touch...

She had a Tucker addiction that would not stop.

He hummed lightly when he finally pulled back so she could breathe. "Where were we?"

"Who cares?" Ginny mumbled, twisting to straddle his lap.

A small smirk arrived. "Now, now. No getting distracted."

"Evil man," Ginny complained.

"Tell you what. Let's go over it from the very beginning, and if we find something new, I'll give you a prize."

"Ha," Ginny snorted. "Oh, look, I discovered something new."

Tucker clicked his tongue. "Try again. Christmas Day evening, Tamara gives you your present. You bring it home to the trailer..."

"Wait—" Oh my God. How had she missed this? Ginny lifted her ass far enough off his lap to pull her phone from her back pocket. Tucker looked on with confusion as she connected through to Tamara. "Hey, question for you."

"What's up?" her sister-in-law asked.

"Putting you on speaker," Ginny warned before doing just that and continuing. "Tucker and I are poking at the puzzle thing. When you gave me my present, did you say there were other packages stored away?"

"There were. Ones for Caleb, Luke, and Walker. I passed them on ages ago. Not sure how that helps." Tamara hummed for a minute. "I can tell you what Caleb got because it was strange enough to make us wonder."

"That might help," Tucker said.

"Lego bricks. About a dozen of them."

Ginny's excitement faded slightly. "Ugh. This is getting more complicated instead of less."

"Right? Considering Caleb would have been twenty-four when your mom wrapped everything up, Legos don't seem like a logical gift." Tamara sighed. "They've been added to the main Lego bucket, but I can find them if you'd like to see if there's any other clues on them."

"That's an astonishing yet underappreciated skill," Tucker said.

"They were painted like haybales," Tamara returned with a laugh. "The only ones in the pile."

Interesting.

"Put them aside for me, please?" Ginny asked. "Now to find out what the other guys got."

"Good luck," Tamara said before hanging up.

"I'll contact Luke if you want, and you can call Walker," Tucker offered.

"Deal. Report back in five," Ginny ordered.

"Yes, ma'am." His eyes flashed. "Hmm, that gives me ideas."

She waved him off as she hit her brother's number. "We can get kinky later."

"Promise? Let me break out the ropes?" he said before snorting. "Hi, Luke. No, ignore that." He rolled his eyes. "I said ignore it, or I'll cave and tell you exactly what I plan to do with your sister."

Ginny crowed with laughter, unfortunately right when Walker answered her call.

"Dammit, brat. Phone etiquette is a thing for a reason," Walker grumbled.

"Sorry. Quick question, and I promise to keep it at low decibels."

Five minutes later, Tucker waited for her as she finished her call with Walker.

"It gets even more impossible," Ginny complained. "Walker got a Christmas ornament. Square, like a treasure chest you'd put in a fish tank."

Tucker shook his head. "I don't see a theme. Luke says his present was a cross-stitch of a horse."

"Did it look like a horse?" Ginny grumbled. "Or did my dad butcher it into having five legs and three heads?"

"Frustrating, I know." Tucker pressed a kiss to her forehead. "Now, I said something about a reward for new information, and there's been mention of a rope, and kinky sex. I vote we go inside and see what kind of mischief those three things can combine into."

"You're distracting me again," Ginny said, but she was on

her feet and tugging him after her into the house. "Get naked. I'll get the rope."

"Nice try." He caught her by the hand and pulled her flush to his body for a moment. "You get naked."

She stepped back far enough to take an appreciative glance at him from top to bottom before reaching for her buttons. "How about we both get naked?"

Naked time with Tucker was truly the best way to drown disappointments.

Another good distraction was set up for a few days later as some of her friends gathered in Kelli's house to help Ginny work on some of her herbal body products.

Because her future direction had begun to come clear. It involved a steep learning curve but also a lot of fun.

Kelli stood at the stove and stirred the pot in front of her slowly as directed, sniffing cautiously. "I'm not a very good cook," she warned.

Ginny laughed. "It's for outer body application, not inner, remember? Keep going, you're nearly done."

"Thank you for keeping us at the island, because I was worried that we'd mix up the stuff we can eat with the stuff we can't," Tansy teased. She and Yvette were busily stripping leaves from stems as Ginny had demonstrated. None of the herbs were fresh grown from the Silver Stone garden yet, but Ginny figured making mistakes with store bought supplies would hurt her ego less.

"You have plenty of experience cooking," Yvette said. "Now if it was me having to decide if this was a body product or a pizza seasoning, then we'd be in trouble."

"Wait till I really confuse you and we make a basil body cream," Ginny said with a smile.

"Do I *want* to smell like a pizza?" Yvette asked.

"Are you kidding? How many people love pizza?" Kelli

glanced over her shoulder and gave a knowing wink. "I'm pretty sure it's a good way to get someone to start nibbling on you."

Tansy and Yvette snickered while Ginny looked around the room with satisfaction. She still had a long way to go, and yet every step of the way had become part of the adventure.

Doing the next thing was working.

It wasn't just about the herbal concoctions, either; it was about community. About spending time with these friends and others, and making a small difference, one day at a time.

Ginny carefully poured the batch into tester containers, one for each of them. The girls sniffed appreciatively.

"Smells delicious."

"Peppermint foot cream. I'm looking forward to my next foot rub from Luke. Hey, that reminds me." Kelli grabbed something off the side counter and held it out to Ginny. "He said you wanted to see the cross-stitch he got in that mystery gift package."

"*Ohhh*, more puzzle solving." Tansy rubbed her hands together then wrinkled her nose. "I have herbal hands."

Laughter drifted over the room as Ginny accepted the home-crafted picture, examining it closely.

"It's definitely my mom's work." A single filly, brown with a black mane. Simple, nothing fancy. She flipped it over and discovered a date written on the back in Sharpie, bracketed top and bottom by a seagull shape. "February twenty-eighth. That's right. Luke was lucky he's not a leap year baby."

"He's a Pisces, though. Through and through," Kelli insisted.

"Likes water sports, does he?" Tansy asked as deadpan as possible. Her stoic expression failed an instant later as shrieks of laughter rang through the room.

Kelli shook a finger at her. "You're terrible."

"Yup," Tansy agreed, hand held forward for the cross-stitch. She examined it as she spoke, flipping it over. "Pisces—oh my God, Ginny, where's your gibberish page?"

Hope rushed in as Ginny shoved a copy forward. "You see something?"

Tansy nodded, scanning the page then stabbing one image firmly. "It's half of a Pisces symbol and constellation, the latter drawn with a ton of artistic license."

"What? Wait—the *zodiac*?"

"I think so."

It suddenly made a ton of sense. "That's it—that's the clue we needed." Ginny spun in a circle before squeezing Tansy and pressing a sloppy kiss to her cheek. Ginny shook the tattered page in the air. "If this is all about the zodiac then my father's drawing skills might suck, but there's a book in the house library that I think is what we need. If it's still there."

Kelli waved her arms as if she were herding geese. "What are we waiting for? Time to invade."

Five minutes later, Tamara looked over the four women all but vibrating on her porch then stepped aside. "Of course, you can come in."

Ginny didn't wait to explain further. Just kicked off her boots and raced for the office where the floor-to-ceiling library wall still held a multitude of books from her parents' days. She found the one she wanted far off to the side and in the top row, then darted back to the kitchen with it.

"*The Complete Book of the Zodiac,*" Ginny said, dropping it on the table. "Not so complete now that it's nearly twenty years out of date, but please let this be the clue we needed."

The other women gathered around the island, watching with fascination as Ginny flipped pages and then shook the book by the cover. No papers fell out, though.

"The numbers Emma found." Tamara reminded her. "Can you use those?"

"Right." Ginny snapped a finger. "Emma also said this picture was a goat. Which Zodiac is goat-like?"

"December-ish. Capricorn," Yvette offered. "I think it's actually called a sea-goat, which maybe excuses your dad's drawing."

"Nothing excuses his drawings," Ginny said dryly. A moment later she had the book open to the Capricorn title page. "Numbers?"

"Five—twelve—thirty." Yvette looked up. "Page, paragraph, line?"

"Page first," Kelli suggested. "So you can see if there's a clue there."

Ginny carefully counted pages, and when there were less than twelve paragraphs on that page, she counted lines for the second number instead.

She wrote down the thirtieth letter on that line on a piece of paper Tamara found for her. "That's one. Eleven to go."

When the first four letters actually spelled a word—WORK—Ginny felt a little light-headed. By the time they'd looked up half the symbols, the room had grown even more crowded. Caleb and Luke had shown up, as well as Tucker.

Ginny stopped what she was doing to accept his kiss, barely aware of her brothers exchanging glances in her peripheral vision. "Didn't mean to interrupt you guys."

"Are you kidding?" Tucker settled beside her. "This is important. Success is imminent."

When they wrote down the final six letters, the message was clear, but absolutely useless.

W-O-R-K

T-O-G-E-T-H-E-R

Kelli frowned. "Work together? *What* works together? You

and your brothers? An ornament, a cross stitch, and a kid's toy?"

Tamara wrinkled her nose. "I don't understand."

Ginny couldn't bear to see the people she cared for so disappointed.

"I am so happy right now," she declared, realizing she wasn't lying or trying to make things better. She lifted the paper in the air and met Tucker's gaze. "We solved part of the unsolvable riddle. I'm so proud of us. And maybe someday we'll find another clue that will let us figure out the next part. What could be better?"

Tucker wrapped a hand around the back of her neck and leaned in slowly. "You, Ginny Stone, are one in a million."

"I am," she declared, winking at Kelli, who was tucked under Luke's arm. She looked around the room at her friends and family. "How about everyone comes over to my place for a celebration time around the firepit. I baked this morning, and I have marshmallows. You haven't lived until you've made Brownie S'mores."

A cheer went up and there were nods of agreement. The party moved to outside her small cottage.

Somewhere between the sugary treats and the company, the biggest truth of all became clear.

Maybe the puzzle wasn't solved yet, but as far as Ginny was concerned, she had already found a treasure.

21

————

The final days of February approached, and mischief was afoot. Luke's birthday, and Tucker's, were just around the corner, so ideas were being bandied about behind closed doors and out of ear shot of two curious men.

No. Not *two*.

Honestly, Luke was being a royal pain in the butt, popping out of the woodwork every time Ginny and Kelli attempted to make plans.

Tucker? Seemed to have zero inkling that anyone wanted to celebrate with him—another reason to despise his parents.

Especially after the entry Ginny had found in her mom's journal a couple of days earlier. Just thinking about it pissed her off and made the need to plan a super surprise all the more important.

Like poking a sore bruise, Ginny opened the book just to read it again.

I'm so stinking mad right now, I could spontaneously combust.

Tucker called this afternoon to say thank you for the birthday present we'd sent. He caught us before we could call him—we expected he'd be busy with his birthday party until after dinner.

It appears "something came up" and his parents cancelled the party. So instead of swimming with his friends, Tucker is at home while his parents attend an event at the university.

I get it. Work emergencies come up, but damn those people. He'd already given up what he really wanted to do to please their biases, and now he gets nothing?

They have no idea how special their son is. With the bullshit he puts up with, he should be a rebellious tyrant instead of a level-headed young man. He's got such a good heart and so much potential. Every time he's around here I clearly see he means to take advantage of every good opportunity he's given.

There's a little of Walter in him, in fact, and I'm glad. Which means, along with being mad, I'm also in problem-solving mode. Walter and I already agreed—Tucker gets a birthday party when he arrives this summer. Not that we'll call it that, but still.

He deserves to have some fun. Plus, I'm pretty sure we can convince the rest of the horde to join in, official party or not.

Mischief-making and problem-solving seemed like similar tasks at the moment to Ginny. She was as determined as her mother had been.

Tucker needed a surprise birthday party.

"We could rent space at Rough Cut so the guys could play pool," Kelli suggested.

"They did some of that at Ashton's party," Ginny said grumpily. "I mean, it's a good idea, but what I'd really like is to make this something that's part of the past and celebrating the future."

"Hey. Kel, you never told me my sister was coming over." Luke sauntered into the kitchen and rested his elbows on the island, grinning maniacally at them both. He was supposed to be out picking up something for Ashton, so showing up in the kitchen unexpectedly like this meant he was trying to get in their way. "Hi, sis. What a surprise. Good to see you."

"You're such an ass," Ginny offered her brother dryly.

"Yeah, but he's my ass," Kelli countered. "So no poisoning him."

Ginny rested her fists on her hips. "It was one time, a *long* time ago. I don't know why you all keep bringing it up."

Luke slipped behind Kelli, sliding an arm around her waist. "We figure it's better to keep ahead of potential danger." He winked at Kelli. "I'm glad to be your ass. That means this one's mine, yes?"

A small squeak escaped Kelli, and she jumped as if Luke had goosed her butt. "Behave."

"No idea why you think I'd start now," he drawled.

Ginny rolled her eyes. "Since you have a good memory about some things, let's see how far back it goes. What did we do for your fourteenth birthday?"

Luke paused, blinking in surprise. "That's a strange question."

Ginny raised a brow.

He looked thoughtful. Frowned, then his eyes widened. "Oh, yeah. Pretty sure that's the year we went to the indoor amusement park. Foosball, indoor go karts, that sort of thing."

Inspiration struck in a rush. "Perfect."

Her brother's expression grew concerned. "What are you doing?"

"I have no idea what you're talking about." Ginny blinked innocently.

"Bullshit. I'll pretend you're not being annoying. Also, now that you've brought up birthdays," Luke said slyly, "I have a request."

Kelli leaned back against the counter and folded her arms over her chest. "Is that allowed?"

A cocky, confident grin flashed across his face. "You like it when I tell you what I want."

Oh, gag.

Ginny made a rude noise. "How come you're allowed to make borderline sex comments around me, but if I even so much as think the word sex, you get all squirmy?"

"You're delusional," Luke said. "I am a mature, un-squirmy adult male."

Oh really?

Ginny turned to Kelli. "If you want to plan a getaway, Tucker and I can recommend some great hotels within a two-hour radius. You know, the places we used to meet for our secret trysts so we could spend hours and hours—"

Luke stuck his fingers in his ears and began singing loudly. "La la la la la la la."

Kelli howled with laughter then pushed him toward the door. "You. Go entertain yourself, and that comment has no sexual connotations intended. Plus, I'm warning you now, if you want me to take Ginny up on that secret tryst information, you'd better be willing to help us with a surprise in a few days, got it?"

He used her own hand to pull their bodies together, kissing her deeply with a great deal of love before letting her go and winking at Ginny. "Always willing to help, and if the surprise is something that's going to make Tucker happy, even better."

Her brother left, whistling like a freaking bluebird.

Kelli shook her head even as she smiled at Ginny. "He's a jerk sometimes, but damn, I love him."

"He is a good guy," Ginny agreed. "Now, let me tell you what I'm thinking, then you tell me how we can make it even better. We start by turning Luke's party into a surprise party for two. Tucker will not be expecting that, but he will definitely be in attendance to celebrate with Luke."

Kelli's jaw dropped. "That's perfect. It's sneaky, and Luke won't mind, I'm sure of it. And the arcade idea?"

"I have a feeling I know what Tucker would have asked for at his party at age fourteen if he'd gotten a chance to really say what he wanted. Plus, I know just how to make it happen."

They spent the next hour planning, making shopping lists and phone calls. Nothing too complicated, but very doable and highly entertaining.

Tucker wasn't going to know what hit him.

Or more literally, he'd know exactly what hit him, and that would make him happy.

Ginny couldn't wait to make it happen.

TUCKER DEALT with some last-minute emergencies, including an error in the mess hall kitchen order that needed to be sent off first thing Monday morning.

Too few groceries delivered late to the mess hall was not a good idea. Tucker didn't know if he was more afraid of what the men would do, or the cook, JP. It was probably the surest way to have a riot on his hands.

Which meant by the time he headed up the stairs to Luke's

house, there was a healthy collection of trucks outside. Luke would get a kick out of having all his friends there to celebrate his birthday, and Tucker was damn glad he got to join in this year.

It was the one thing about having a birthday in the winter he'd grown to really dislike. All the kids who had summertime birthdays complained because they never got to have their school friends around. Having a summertime birthday would have meant Tucker celebrating with the Stones.

Truth came in many forms. Him being here in Silver Stone now was nearly the best almost-birthday present he could have asked for.

He took a deep breath of the crisp wintery air in satisfaction.

One step into the house, and happiness struck even harder as he breathed in the savory scent on the air, and the sound of laughter echoing through the room filled his ears.

"Finally." Luke came forward with a hand outstretched to welcome him in. He called over his shoulder into the kitchen. "Pull the food out. Tucker's here."

"You shouldn't have waited for me," Tucker scolded. But he pulled Luke into an embrace and patted him firmly on the back. "Happy birthday, old man."

"You're such a jerk," Luke muttered. "Old man, my ass."

Tucker let him go and handed him a wrapped package. "I hear old people start to lose their eyesight. All that squinting into the sun. Maybe this will help."

Walker stepped forward, greeting Tucker and laughing softly. "I always heard it was something else that made guys lose their eyesight."

"Not as much of *that* needed these days, for any of us," Luke quipped before groaning dramatically as he smacked a palm against his forehead. "Dear God, I just made a sex joke to the man involved with my sister."

"I told you, you have issues." Ginny's voice carried across the room along with a whole lot of feminine laughter.

Luke ignored her and unwrapped his present, whistling softly when he discovered a set of compact binoculars. "Very nice. Thanks."

"Leave them in your saddlebag. Then you won't have to keep asking me to identify our animals when we're more than twenty paces away," Tucker suggested with a drawl.

Luke patted him on the shoulder, then turned him into the crowded room.

There were a lot of familiar faces. People Tucker had gotten to know over the past months, including Tamara's three brothers-in-law.

Ginny came and tucked herself under his arm. "Glad you made it."

"No way on earth was I going to miss this." He pressed a kiss to her temple and spoke softly, for her ears only. "This is a milestone. Getting to be here, I mean."

She gave him a squeeze then pushed him toward the kitchen where everyone loaded up plates. It seemed the first order of the evening was to eat as much pizza, chicken wings, and other teenage menu items as possible. Dessert was individual-sized dirt cakes—chocolate pudding mixed with rich cake, with gummy worms and candy insects scattered on the surface of each cup.

It was only after they were sated that the rest of the presents came out.

Tucker paid barely any attention as Luke unwrapped his gifts, more interested in watching Ginny. She sat in his lap, speaking quietly to Tamara's youngest sister, Julia.

Tucker was warm and relaxed, belly full of food that could

only be considered high calorie treats. His woman leaned against his side as she chatted. Comfortable, as Tucker trailed his fingers up and down her thigh in a teasing caress.

Every time he stroked a little higher, until he slid his fingertips over her ass on every pass. Her cheeks slowly brightened with heat.

Oh, yeah, this was fun.

"Hey, Tucker."

Tucker glanced away from Ginny's flushed face to find Luke rolling his eyes. Annoying Luke was a bonus if anything. "Yeah?"

His friend thrust forward a package. "This one's got *your* name on it."

What? "Really?"

"Really." Luke shook it slightly, rising to close the distance between them. "Here. It's your name, see? *Tucker*. Plain as day."

Tucker eyed the box with confusion. "Yes, I understand it's got my name on it. But why?"

"Hell if I know, but I'm not opening it." Luke shoved the thing against Tucker's chest then let go, forcing him to grab it or let the box fall.

A small sound escaped Ginny.

Tucker glanced at her, suspicion rising. "What did you do?"

She pressed a hand to her chest, jaw dropping slightly to an O position. "Moi?"

"Yes, *toi*. Malicieux."

"Me, mischievous?" Ginny laughed out loud, scrambling off his lap and settling on the coffee table in front of him. "Well, maybe. Now open it."

Everyone had stopped what they were doing to come watch. Tucker shrugged and unwrapped the box.

Inside was a face mask with green light panels and a water pistol that was too heavy and shiny to be for water. "Oh my God, really?"

Luke clapped his hands and used an announcer voice to be heard over the chatting. "I challenge all of you, but especially Tucker, to the ultimate laser-tag birthday throw down."

"May the best birthday boy win," Ginny added.

"Or at least die with their boots on," Caleb offered.

Chaos reigned for the next few minutes as Luke explained the rules—three lives, hits would register on the gun or facemask, masks on at all times—then everyone who wanted a try with the laser guns reached into a bag to pull out a number with the order for play.

Julia's husband, Zach, did something to the TV, and suddenly there was a split screen showing three different views of a strangely lit place that looked vaguely familiar.

"Is that your *basement*?" Tucker asked.

Luke nodded, slipping head gear onto his forehead and pointing toward the stairs. "We stapled cardboard to the bare wall studs, so it's more of a maze than a basement right now. But don't lean too hard on anything or you'll break through, and that's not going to be pretty."

Tucker shook his head in disbelief. He had wanted to play laser tag forever. So damn awesome.

"You are going down," he said conversationally to Luke. "Just so you know."

Luke threw back his head and yowled evilly before offering Tucker a death stare. "Bring it."

Tucker raised one brow.

His friend snickered. "Okay, everyone not playing this round, sit and enjoy the show."

Round one began. In addition to Tucker and Luke, there

were four more players—Dustin, Josiah, Karen Coleman and Tansy Fields.

At the bottom of the stairs, Tucker paused to admire the amount of work that had gone into the set up. Three different sized openings led into the basement proper. Music rose around them to a hard, pounding beat that would cover any noises. On a microphone so he was clearly audible, Zach's voice carried on the air. "Team one—Karen, Tucker, Josiah. Face masks in place, then enter the maze now."

The three of them saluted each other, then slipped into the semi-darkness.

Tucker's heart pounded, and he was pretty damn sure his cheeks were going to hurt from grinning so hard. His laser gun had three bright green stripes along the barrel, and a green glow shone from his head.

So. No shooting green teammates. Got it.

He stepped carefully, turning corners and wiggling through narrow passages. He backed into a side alcove in the hopes it would allow him to hide.

Zach's voice sounded again. "Team two, face masks in place. There is a green ring and a red ring in the maze. Find your team's ring and return to base to win extra glory. Team two, enter the maze now."

Shit. Tucker hadn't been listening hard enough before. The 'find a thing and bring it back' was unexpected. It meant he couldn't simply sit there and wait for the enemy to come to him.

He inched out of his hiding spot reluctantly, desperately trying to separate out the sounds of music from the potential danger of—

His gun hand lit up, and a high-pitched *zap* sounded. He'd been hit from the left. Tucker spun and shot at the same time, accidentally aiming far too low to hit anything.

Except Luke was on his hands and knees, and Tucker's rapid fire hit him three times in a row and his red lights died instantly.

"Well, damn," Luke said with a laugh, then he sprawled dramatically and shook with mock death throes.

Tucker chuckled but saluted his friend before inching farther into the maze.

Three corners later he got caught in the crossfire between Josiah and Dustin, and Tansy and Karen. When the music went down and the lights went up, the only one still standing was Karen.

She lifted the gun to her lips and blew across the opening before grinning.

The entire thing had taken less than seven minutes.

For the next two hours they took turns, random groups going down at the start, and then in teams that were good-naturedly arranged ahead of time.

The best face off of the night, in Tucker's estimation, was when the women took over the maze. The four Coleman sisters —Tamara, Karen, Lisa, and Julia, grabbed Kelli and Ginny. Lisa switched allegiances and joined Ginny and Kelli on team two.

Tucker and his friends watched the action on the screen. The pace was wicked and fast, shouts and screams and feminine laughter loud enough to rise through the floorboards. By the time team two had finally eliminated team one—it took a lot of energy to get Karen out of commission—Lisa, Ginny and Kelli were each down to one life left. But they'd also found the bonus ring.

"Well done, guys." Lisa offered high fives then casually pulled out her gun and shot her two teammates where they stood.

The screams of laughter didn't stop for a long time,

especially since Lisa raced out of the basement twirling the ring around one finger.

Josiah shook his head, but he laughed as well. "You are never going to live that down," he warned as she happily presented him with her prize.

"Life is danger," she offered back with a smirk.

But she did try to run, unsuccessfully, when her sisters and teammates surrounded her, grabbed her, and threw her outside into a snowbank.

The entire night, Luke and Tucker put themselves on opposing teams. Once the dust settled, they'd played six rounds and the score between them was even, three-three.

By now, it was late enough that couples had slowly begun peeling off to head home until only a few stragglers remained. Dustin and Shim were battling with Fern and Tansy for the fourth time in a row.

Luke lifted a beer to his lips and sipped, watching the screens with amusement. "Those boys are gluttons for punishment."

"Completely," Tucker agreed. "Oh, look. Dustin's about to go down."

Fern was evil with her laser. She'd somehow attached it to her prosthetic arm, and she looked like a *Star Wars* hero while taking out Luke's brother, yet again.

In the kitchen, Kelli and Ginny were chatting. Heads nodding, laughter spilling free. Beside where Tucker and Luke sat, the fire crackled softly.

"It was a good party," Tucker said quietly. "Thanks for sharing it with me."

"It *was* a good party. Do we need to go one more round to find out who's the ultimate champion?" Even as he asked, Luke sipped his beer slowly, not moving a muscle otherwise. Obviously comfortable where he was.

Tucker watched the laser-tag screen out of one eye, but more of his attention remained focused there in the room. On his friend and Kelli. On Ginny, who radiated sunshine everywhere she went. "Nah. We'll call it even for today. But *next* time, you're going down."

"Deal." Luke stretched his legs out, turning his head just far enough to meet Tucker's gaze. "Happy birthday, bro."

Warmth like a summer day slipped in. Tucker offered a chin dip in agreement. "Happy birthday to us."

22

$\mathcal{I}$t had been another busy day, but a productive one. Ginny admired the rows of containers lined up on her kitchen table with satisfaction. The neat labels with the beautiful logo Fern Fields had designed for her shimmered in a pale, glittering green.

Goddess Gifts.

Over the past month, Ginny had received half a dozen responses to her requests for information regarding local artisan products, and while the possibility of putting together a local gift box was still out of reach, Ginny kept exploring. Kept thinking and kept dreaming.

Bonus, working from home meant never being far from relaxing. She stopped work at three o'clock, poured herself a cup of tea and took it and her notebook out onto the porch. She still had to curl up under a warm blanket, but the sunshine felt good. It had been an unusually warm March, and while they were still far from the time when green things would bloom outside instead of in the forced confines of the greenhouse, it felt as if magic whirled in the air. Deep breaths of the clean air refreshed her soul as well as her body.

Flipping pages in her mother's journal first, Ginny found a story that made her howl, because it was so her mother, and such a clear memory from when she would have been about thirteen, the journal entry triggering details from that summer night to return in glorious Technicolor.

Found a bunch of recipe cards from the 1930s - 1970s. Dear lord, I can't decide if the cooks who created these were sadists, or were simply fooling around and never thought they'd be taken seriously.

I decided I had to make one for the family, but the trouble came in deciding which one was off the wall enough to make them blink. Teenage boys will eat anything, after all.

I decided to try four of them all at once.

Poor Walter. When I put the food on the table, he looked as if he doubted my sanity. Still, he carefully scooped up one portion of each dish onto a plate and passed it around.

Caleb didn't seem to notice. Luke and Tucker gave each other looks but tucked in like everything was normal. Walker smirked but dug in resolutely. Dusty asked for a second bean-stuffed tomato.

Ginny stared at me for the longest time before a noise escaped her. I thought for a second she was choking, but it was giggles.

Do you know how hard it is to keep a straight face when your daughter is snickering like crazy even as the menfolk dig into miniature castle-shaped creamed-chicken-Jell-O? Or a very bold pink Salmon Shortcake Delight?

I think every year on Canada Day, I'll make one of these old-fashioned monstrosities.

Ginny wiped away the tears, because the meal really had been that bad. The tastes, the colours—all of it incredibly terrible. When she peeked into the pocket on that page and found the actual recipe cards, she laughed all over again.

The next time Dustin and Shim came for supper, she was totally making the creamed chicken recipe.

Still snickering, she put aside her mom's journal and picked up her own, flipping as usual to an open page about a third of the way in.

At the top of the page, words poked her.

My one regret.

Interesting how with every one of these prompts, she could come back again and again, and every time the answer might be slightly different. If she'd read this question a year ago during her travels, she might have regretted not having asked all the right questions before she'd even left.

But here and now, the answer rising up the clearest was how she felt deep inside, and how she hadn't shared it nearly enough.

How much she loved and appreciated Caleb for everything he'd ever done, not just for her, but Dare as well. How much she enjoyed Walker and Ivy's company, how much big brother Luke and live-wire Kelli meant. How Dustin made Ginny laugh and smile, and his wide-open future was something she couldn't wait to encourage him to explore. How Tamara was magically meeting Ginny's needs for a mother figure and a good friend at the same time.

How much she loved Tucker. Body, mind and soul.

That one was too huge to rush past.

The feeling inside wasn't something new. She'd probably loved Tucker in some way since she was a giddy youth. But the real moment of the change, she remembered so clearly.

Out on the dance floor. The end of January. In that moment, she'd known that everything he'd said before was absolutely true.

He'd claimed her. Straight up, no doubt about it, he'd made it plain that he wanted her. Damn the consequences; damn her trying to make his life easier.

I want you even if it's not easy.

She glanced in her notebook.

My one regret.

She was pretty sure Tucker knew she cared about him. He had it down pat that she liked having him around. But given his background, given his *parents*, how often in his life had he heard the actual words?

She'd been holding them back, and that was wrong.

Ginny dropped the journal onto the bench and shot to her feet.

Here's where the magic took place, because the prompt from her mom didn't feel like a chance to pour out her heart and set a solid foundation to build on.

This one felt like the encouragement to fix a mistake.

She pulled on her boots and coat, and headed into the sunshiny day.

Crossing the path between the cottage and the main ranch house was easily done. She knocked briefly then let herself in, happy to discover Tamara in the kitchen with Caleb by her side.

Ginny paused for a split second when she realized she'd

interrupted them kissing. But then again, who cared? "I need to tell you something," she announced.

Tamara's cheeks were rosy, but she stayed tucked up against Caleb's side. "Yes?"

Ginny marched up to Caleb and looked him straight in the eye. "You are amazing, and I am so glad you're my big brother." She turned to Tamara. "I think you're the coolest sister-in-law ever, and I'm so glad you're in this family. I love you both so much."

Then she threw her arms around their necks and squeezed tight for a moment.

A deep chuckle escaped Caleb. "Well, that's good."

"It is," Ginny said happily even as she wiggled free and headed back to the door. She regally waved a hand in the air as she left. "Sorry to interrupt. Carry on with your fooling around."

Laughter danced behind her as she closed the ranch house door.

The next couple of confessions took place over the phone. Ginny caught Ivy and Walker at home, and brought them up to speed by all but shouting it at them after Walker obediently opened up to speaker phone.

"I love you. You guys are the best, and you're going to be super parents. But right now, you're a super brother and sister, and I can't wait to enjoy more time with you going forward."

Walker's deep rumble of amusement trickled over the line. "A little early for drinking, isn't it, kiddo?"

Ginny blew a raspberry. "Gotta run. Chat soon."

"We love you, too," Ivy said softly before hanging up, the sound of laughter once again echoing in Ginny's ears.

Luke was working, and so was Kelli, which meant she'd share with them later.

But Tucker? She knew where he was. As if he was the

north pole and she was tuned in on him, tracking him down took only minutes.

A crowd had gathered at the railing to watch Luke work one of the new rides. Tucker stood in the middle of the men, the hands around him a mix between nonchalance and sheer hero worship.

She didn't blame them. Tucker was everything thirteen-year-old her had dreamed of in a man. The tall, dark-haired, and broad-shouldered parts were very nice, but it was the rest that she'd truly come to appreciate. Confident as he pointed out Luke's actions, explaining the training method patiently to the young man beside him.

Tucker must've caught a glimpse of her motion, because of course he did. The man was aware of everything that went on around him, including her unsteady half stride, half run approach.

He straightened, turning toward her. "Ginny? Everything okay?"

She all but threw herself at him. Forget looking calm or sophisticated, the words burst free. "I love you."

Masculine snickers sounded, and suddenly the crowd of men at the railing all seemed to have urgent tasks, sliding farther away to give them privacy.

Tucker's jaw hung toward the ground. "Goddess?"

Ginny shook her head. "No. You're usually really good at doing the right response at the right time. So when I say I love you, you say it back, okay?"

His lips twitched. "What was I thinking?"

"I have no idea," she shouted, amusement rising as laughter welled inside. "Tucker Stewart, I love you."

His expression had gone absolutely unreadable. "You have no idea how tempted I am to simply repeat back what you said, word for word."

She smacked him gently on the shoulder. "Don't be a turkey, say *my* name."

"Ginny Stone," he said obediently.

"You're going to make me pull it out of you one word at a time, aren't you?" she demanded.

"Okay."

He was the most frustrating and most wonderful man on the entire planet. "Repeat after me. Ginny Stone, I love you."

He turned her in his arms and pressed her against the nearest fence post. "With everything in me. Now and forever. Until there's no breath left in my body, and if it's possible, even longer than that."

Oh damn, he was good, because how could a girl possibly get pissed after her man had said something so incredible?

Ginny cupped his face in her hands. "I should've said it sooner. I should've said it years ago, because something inside me has always loved you."

"One step at a time," he reminded her with a wink. "I do love you, Ginny."

Then he kissed her.

They'd had so many kisses over the years. Sweet and innocent. Wickedly hot, nearly spontaneous combustion. They'd had lazy kisses that rolled along until an energy-consuming spark ignited them.

But this kiss was about forever. About love and about being together for all the right reasons.

No regrets.

A shot of hot air blasted past her ear, and Tucker chuckled, his lips curling into a smile even as they stayed pressed to hers. "I think we're being told to move along."

Ginny glanced over her shoulder to discover one of the horses had come over to investigate what they were doing, sticking its nose past her cheek and between her and Tucker.

"I didn't request a horse chaperone," she said, glancing around to discover Luke grinning at them.

"Hey, you interrupted our foreman in the middle of a task. I can't help it if you get interrupted when you're in the middle of something as well."

Tucker straightened, curling Ginny against his side. "I'd apologize, but after all these years, Ginny *finally* came to her senses and told me she loves me, so it was kind of important."

Ginny pinched the bridge of her nose. "I do not believe you just said that."

"She has this thing about privacy. I simply don't get it," Tucker said. "Very shy and retiring, our Ginny."

"I noticed," Luke said dryly. He waved a hand toward where the rest of the ranch hands had begun whistling and cheering. "We all noticed."

Laughter floated up from somewhere around her toes and rose skyward. It was the contagious type, because Luke laughed as well, and Tucker stared at the ground and shook his head as if the two of them had lost their minds, but she knew he was amused.

He didn't need to grin from ear to ear for her to know how he felt, what he thought.

How much he loved her.

~

SPRING ARRIVED. Tucker hovered between exhaustion and bliss, each day starting with early chores and often dragging late into the night.

But no matter what time he was done, his days also finished with him at the cottage with Ginny by his side, and he woke up wrapped around her. And that made it all worthwhile.

Alex came rushing into the office one morning. "It's time."

Tucker blinked for a second. "Damn, the way you're buzzing, I'd have guessed you had a baby on the way."

His friend grinned. "Nah, that's Ryan and Madison."

"Damn, they do not fool around—" Tucker stopped as Alex outright guffawed. "Okay, bad phrasing."

"Sorry to laugh and run, but Dad is up for preliminary tests in two days. And Mom just messaged that her doctor says he suspects her appointment will be within the week."

Wow. "Good news, although we'll miss you while you're gone," Tucker shared honestly.

Alex held out his hand and shook Tucker's firmly. "I'll be back. There's a lot I still need to accomplish."

"Need me to look after anything while you're gone?"

The other man's smile turned sheepish. "Don't think it's a good idea to ask you to run interference if Yvette starts dating any of the hands, but I'm still tempted."

Tucker patted him on the shoulder as he walked Alex to the door. "Sorry, can't make any promises in that direction. But I will try to sing your praises as often as I can."

"More than I could hope for." Alex tipped his hat and left.

Changes were happening, although still not all the ones Tucker hoped for. His uncle, for example, was still tight-lipped and uncooperative when it came to his relationship situation. Or the seeming lack of it.

At least the woman had stopped making macramé before his rooms were buried in them.

But convincing a sixty-something to get his butt in gear was low on Tucker's list when it came down to it. Since he appreciated not having his love life meddled with, he gave Ashton the same consideration.

The last weekend in April, the Stones held a joint birthday party for Caleb and Tamara, who happened to have birthdays only one day apart from each other. The entire family was invited, which included Tucker, a fact that tickled him silly.

Crossing the short distance between the cottage he now shared pretty much full time with Ginny and the main ranch house, he caught himself one second away from damn near skipping. Walking hand in hand with Ginny felt so right Tucker couldn't believe he'd lasted so long without her being his.

The chaos of the meal and party were sheer joy.

After dinner, Ginny tugged him into the laundry room for some privacy. She tangled her arms around his waist and grinned up at him. "You're smiling an awful lot there, superman. You'll lose your fearsome reputation if you don't watch out."

He raised a brow. "Superman?"

Ginny covered her mouth and snickered harder. "You look so perturbed right now."

Shrieks of laughter rang out from the main room, and Tucker leaned back to see what was going on.

Dustin sat on the couch in the living room, a niece on either side as he pointed out things in the old photo album in his lap. Sasha made all the noise.

Dustin offered her a mock-glare. "You take that back."

"What are you tormenting your uncle about now?" Tamara demanded.

Everyone peered at Sasha who continued to grin hugely. "He's a total write-off as a fashion statement, Mom. Look. He's wearing a fuzzy sweatsuit. Uncle Luke looks terrible as well. I want to know if he kept any of his vests or acid-washed jeans, because I could wear them to school now and win all the retro-awards."

"Ha, ha," Dustin pretended to be grumbly, but he winked

at Tamara. "I guess you're right. I haven't always been the hottest fashion plate in the family."

"What's acid wash?" Emma asked. Sasha reached over the album to point them out.

Meanwhile, Dustin continued to stare at the page, confusion twisting to outright glee. "Hey, Ginny. I think I have another clue to add to your puzzle."

That got everyone's attention.

Ginny rushed forward, Tucker following hard on her heels. "There's something in the album?"

"Sort of," Dustin said. "I thought about it the other day. Why didn't *I* have a present in the box? You know, the one Tamara found that had things for everyone else, all wrapped in the same paper."

Ginny paused. "Not sure."

Her little brother grinned. "Because I'd already opened it."

The room went silent.

His shoulders lifted in a gentle shrug. "Correct me if I'm wrong, but I don't think Mom was the type to do anything without a reason. If she gave Ginny a puzzle that involved gifts for all her kids, and they were all wrapped up at the same time, and we were supposed to *work together* to solve the puzzle, it makes sense that I should have gotten a gift as well."

They all looked down at the photo album. "That's your birthday party, yes?" Ginny asked.

Dustin nodded. "December, which means I opened one extra gift that was actually part of Ginny's mystery package. Then Luke would open his in February, Walker in March, Caleb in April, and Ginny in June."

There'd been so many disappointments before, Tucker didn't want Ginny to get her hopes up only to have them dashed again. Yet maybe, just maybe, this was going to actually happen. "So what did you get?"

Dustin pointed to the page, then lifted the entire album in the air so everyone could see.

Cute as anything, eight-year-old Dusty showed off a gap-filled smile made of a mix of baby and adult teeth. Against his cheek he held a stuffed calico cat.

"That is eerily lifelike," Tucker said.

"I remember that thing," Ginny said. "You hauled it everywhere forever."

"I still have it," Dustin confessed, quieter now. "I put it in the box along with the rest of my baby stuff Mom had saved."

Caleb laid a hand on Dustin's shoulder, but didn't say anything.

Luke held up fingers. "Okay, *work together* was the clue. Caleb got straw bales and I got a horse. Add in Dustin's cat, and the first place I think of is the barn."

"God, I hope not. I don't see how anything could still be hidden in there after all these years." Ginny leaned harder into Tucker's side.

He curled an arm around her and squeezed. "Keep going. Walker—how does your treasure box fit into the barn theme?"

Her brother shook his head slowly. "It's not made of barn wood, it's not even a real box." He frowned. "Why does it feel as if I'm missing something? Like something teasing at the edge of my memories."

Tucker turned to Ginny. "And your present. Don't forget to include it."

She blinked. "Mine? How do the journals possibly mix in?"

He tapped her on the nose. "No, goddess. The journals were part two. You got the puzzle page *and* a necklace."

Her jaw dropped. "I totally forgot."

"You didn't tell us you got something else," Kelli said.

Ginny reached into her shirt and pulled out the wooden

piece she'd started wearing constantly. "I didn't think of it as a present."

The instant she held it up in her palm, a loud whoop echoed through the room.

"Holy cow, that's it," Walker shouted. "I think I know the answer. To all of it." He turned on his heel and headed toward the door.

"Walker?" Ginny asked.

"Come on," he insisted. "We're headed to the barn for a trip down memory lane."

They must have looked quite the sight. The entire Stone family, all eleven of them, plus Tucker, marching across to the main barn and climbing into the old, old hay loft. The place where Tucker had so many memories from summers filled with love and laughter.

Surprisingly, Walker led them straight to the Operation *Prove It* headquarters.

He grinned as he glanced at his sister. "Seems Caleb isn't the only one good at making hay forts."

Ginny tilted her head toward him. "Tucker's got skills."

Kelli snorted.

Tamara gave her a look, but her lips were curved at the corners. She let Tyler down to play in the pen-like area formed by the bales. "You plan on letting the rest of us in on the big mystery, Walker?"

"Hold on." He leaned toward the window, examining the boards closely. "Ginny, this is your discovery to make. Come here."

Ginny squeezed Tucker's fingers before letting go and joining her brother at the window. "Time for the big reveal, Houdini."

Walker glanced around at his siblings. "Confession first. When I was little, Mom caught me digging holes in her garden to bury treasure. Which she said was creative, but a poor way to get a carrot crop. So she gave me a treasure box and told me to find places to hide it that didn't involve her garden. It was a magic box, so if someone did discover it, they couldn't open it without having the secret key."

Ginny frowned, placing a hand on the wooden sill at the right edge of the window. "A magic treasure box?"

"Made of wood. I stopped using it at one point and gave it back, but I had told her some of my favourite hiding spots. I think she used it for your present."

The entire group of them leaned forward with Ginny as she examined the vertical wall closer. And when she wrapped her fingers around what looked like part of the windowsill and pulled, Tucker held his breath.

In her fingers, she held a brick-sized box.

"Oh my word." She lifted her gaze to Tucker. "We found it."

"Now use your magic and open it," he said softly.

Everyone settled on the bales. Luke and Kelli cuddled together, Ivy and Walker doing the same. Tamara and Caleb were surrounded by their children, all wide eyes and eager smiles.

Dustin sat to one side, feet up, elbows on knees. "Is it a trick box? Walker, you know how it works."

Walker shook his head. "This is her moment. I know Ginny can figure it out," he said quietly.

Ginny took off her coat and spread it on the bale that was usually their footrest. She placed the box in the middle, turning it slowly as she examined it.

Her eyes lit up as she figured something out. "That's wonderful."

She slipped the necklace over her head and tucked the

strangely-shaped wooden piece into a small slot on one side of the box.

The top of the box pivoted. The side slid open, and a brightly coloured bag fell to her coat.

"Treasure," Emma said excitedly.

Ginny's eyes had filled with moisture. Tucker couldn't stop himself; he dropped next to her and slipped an arm around her waist, supporting her the best he could. "Emma's right. It's treasure from your mom."

A collective inhale echoed through the space as Ginny opened the bag and tipped the contents into her palm.

Coloured stones flashed in the light from the window.

"Oh." Ginny glanced up at them all. "It's Mom's family ring."

She slipped it on her finger and held her hand in the air.

Tucker thought it was Luke who started the slow clap of approval. But whoever it was, the rest of them picked it up. Laughter rose as well, and the next minutes were filled with a happiness Tucker was so grateful to be a part of.

When the hugs and back pats of congratulations were done, Tucker was amused to discover the four sets of couples had remained settled in place, while Uncle Dustin did his duty and took the girls and Tyler to say good night to the kittens.

Tamara held Ginny's hand and admired the ring. "It's very pretty, but do you know why there are eight stones? There are five of you, plus your parents."

"Mom got the ring when I was about ten. I just remember thinking it was wonderful because it sparkled." Ginny shook her head. "Caleb? Do you know?"

He looked thoughtful for a moment. "Don't remember them telling us anything more than Dad bought it for Mom to represent all of us. I didn't really understand what the ring was about, so I didn't know it was slightly off."

"I thought maybe they had a baby they lost somewhere in there, but they never explained. And we never asked," Walker admitted.

"Well, it's beautiful," Tamara said. "And a very wonderful sweet-sixteen present."

"Plus the journal," Ginny reminded her. "Maybe I'll find an explanation for the ring in one of her entries."

Then she turned her bright eyes to Tucker's, leaning hard into his side and wrapping her arms around him, silent but happy.

He leaned in close, ignoring the fact that all her family were right there, watching closely, because this moment was too important to let pass by. "Love you, goddess. I'm very happy for you right now."

"I love you, too," she whispered, lifting her lips for a kiss before resting her head on his chest and letting a huge sigh escape. "Happy birthday to me."

23

June 18, Ginny's 30th birthday

The birds were singing, calling back and forth to each other. One on a nearby tree would say *hey you*, and a second later, one farther in the bush would respond *hey you* back.

Tucker sat a little straighter in the saddle to stretch his back, breathing deep and truly enjoying where he was.

"Need any help later today getting things set up?" Luke swayed comfortably as he rode at Tucker's side, lazily covering a yawn. "Damn, I need a nap before the party."

"Of course you do. Old people like you should always have a nap in the afternoon."

A snicker greeted him. "You're the same age as me," Luke pointed out.

"It's the extra five days you've been alive. Makes a man tire far more easily," Tucker deadpanned. "Don't worry. I'll make sure you don't get caught drooling in your sleep."

Luke eased his horse close enough to offer a brotherly punch to Tucker's shoulder. "Ass."

"Jerk."

His friend turned his horse toward his house. "On that note—call if you need help."

"Will do."

Tucker headed back to the cottage—back *home*—and wasn't that an outright thrill to acknowledge? Ginny had thrown down and demanded he give up the pretense of living anywhere but with her.

Moving in had not been a hardship, although Tucker now eyed the small cottage with ideas for improvements that would fit their new future.

A future together.

A future he'd like to define a little more clearly, and today seemed as good a day as any.

Ginny stood outside at the picnic table he'd built, wooden spoon moving through a massive bowl as she mixed up enough potato salad to feed the horde of people expected to descend for her birthday barbeque.

"Need a hand?" he asked.

She paused and offered her lips for a kiss. Then smiling contentedly, she considered. "Food is under control for now. Kelli and Tamara are making the rest of the salads, the steaks are marinating, so until the barbeques need heating up, you are off the hook."

Exactly where he didn't want to be—off the hook. He wanted hooks, and strings, not to mention promises of forever.

Tucker glanced around, but for once, miracle of miracles, there were no Stone nieces or Silver Stone ranch hands in sight.

He pulled the spoon from her fingers and dropped it in the bowl. Then he went down on one knee beside her, holding her hands in his.

Their fingers slipped, mayonnaise from the salad coating them in a slippery, mustardy layer with bits of thyme thrown in for good measure. He made a second grab, holding tighter this time even as amusement rose.

Of course they'd end up slathered with food with Ginny involved.

"Goddess."

Ginny frowned for a second, then snickered. "Really?"

"You love me, I love you. It makes sense."

She brayed out a laugh. "Points for the least romantic proposal ever."

Tucker raised a brow. "What makes you think I'm proposing? I just wanted to know if I could have your potato salad recipe."

She plopped onto the picnic bench, snickering so hard she gasped for air. Her cheeks shot to rosy red, and she smiled with her heart in her eyes. "I do love you, superman."

"I know, which means it would be a really smart move if you were to marry me."

She tilted her head to the side. Adorable, sexy. Everything he'd ever wanted. "What if I want you as a boyfriend for a little longer?"

He gave up kneeling and sat beside her on the bench. "Nothing can be simple with you, can it?"

"Probably not. Yet you seem willing to sign on for more of this delectable torture." Ginny wiped her palms carelessly on her shirt then cupped his face. "Do I want to be with you? Absolutely."

"Then marry me."

"I thought we'd get engaged a year after the night Tamara gave me your naked booty as a Christmas present." Ginny suggested. "Although we won't mention that part to her, okay?"

"Christmas Eve? No, that's unacceptable." Arguing wasn't

part of today's agenda, but neither would he stop until he had her agreement. One way or another this was happening sooner than six months from now. "I'm yours," he said simply.

"Darn tootin', you are," she agreed.

"If you don't want to do it today because it's your birthday —although I'd remind you it's a wonderful chance for everyone to find out quick—we can officially get engaged in a week or so and then get married next Christmas."

She turned thoughtful. "Does it sound morbid if I kind of want to get married in February?"

Tucker brushed his knuckles over her cheek. "Not morbid at all. You want a new, happier memory to balance the sad."

Ginny popped easily into his lap and proceeded to kiss him senseless. Turning him on and turning him inside out, so that his ears were ringing when they finally came up for air.

He reached into his pocket and pulled out the box he'd hidden away for today. "Marry me, Ginny. Next week, next month, next February. Those details don't matter, but I want my ring on your finger."

"Let me see," she said, popping the box open and inhaling appreciatively. "Oh my God, Tucker, it's beautiful."

"Just like you." He pulled the diamond ring from its pillowy perch and slipped it on her finger.

Ginny held out her hand and the diamond sparkled in the sunlight. Then she faced him again. "Just to make it official, yes. *Yes*, I'll marry you, because you're exactly who I need. Past, present, and future."

"I love you." He whispered it this time, so many years of memories built up between them coming together in this moment. "I'm yours," he said again.

It was the utter truth.

~

THE YARD between the main ranch house and Ginny's little cottage was full of friends who had come to celebrate her birthday and to spend time in the beautiful June sunshine.

And, unexpectedly, to celebrate her and Tucker's engagement.

The last-minute addition to the agenda had been received with everything from shouts of approval and a massive back pounding for Tucker from Luke, to adorable kisses as Emma and Sasha welcomed their new uncle-to-be into the fold.

Everywhere she looked, Ginny saw happy faces and people close to her heart. But one thing was still missing.

Which was why, when her sister's truck pulled into the yard, Ginny all but vibrated with excitement.

Jesse and Dare had made the drive from Rocky Mountain House for the birthday party. They'd brought their three boys, and Ginny couldn't wait to not only get caught up, but to sniff a few toddler cheeks.

Babies were on the someday list. Which meant using her sister's children to stave off the craving that had begun to simmer deep inside.

Getting engaged was enough excitement for right now.

"Don't get run over," Tucker warned with a chuckle when she shot to her feet and went to rush forward.

Ginny held herself back long enough for Jesse to put the truck into park, and then she hauled open Dare's door and swamped her sister with a massive bear hug. "You're finally here. Oh God, it's so good to see you."

"Can you see anything but my backside?" Dare teased, but she squeezed just as hard. "Welcome to your thirties, babe. The water's fine."

"Tucker," Jesse called. He walked from around the truck carrying one of the twins in his arms while three-and-a half-year-old Joey blasted forward out from under his feet and headed at a toddler sprint toward his cousins up the hill. "Come and shake my hand then buy me the drink you owe me."

Ginny frowned at Tucker. "Why do you owe him a drink?"

Her brother-in-law adjusted the infant he held. "It's a permanent debt. I plan to collect from now to eternity."

Tucker raised a brow but turned to answer Ginny. "You told Dare about us fooling around. She told *him*, which means for the past three plus years, he's had to keep it secret."

"You know how hard it's been to know such a juicy tidbit and not spill the beans every time I saw your brothers? You totally owe me." Jesse wrapped an arm around Ginny's shoulders and squeezed. "Hey. How's my favourite poisoner doing?"

"Peachy," she said with a smile.

"That's a fine flavour. Distracts from the convulsions and paralysis that follow." Jesse held out a hand to Tucker. "About time you proposed."

"I didn't know you were waiting," Tucker deadpanned. "Sorry, sweetheart, I'm taken."

Laughter welled around them as always. The four of them, carrying the nearly year-old twins, moved up the hill to join the party. Tamara came forward, hugged her cousin and Dare, then handed toddler Royce to Kelli before stealing little Ryan for herself.

Ginny and Dare ended up sitting outside the cottage minutes later, babies safely off in the arms of their sisters-in-law. Joey played with Tyler under Sasha's watchful eye.

Tucker and Jesse stood on the lawn halfway between the party and the cottage, as if ready to move at a moment's notice whichever way they were needed.

Which—pretty much summed it up, Ginny realized. Their guys and what they stood for. Ready to do what was right.

Dare glanced behind them at the cottage where she'd lived while growing up. "I'm glad she's yours now. Yours and Tucker's."

"It's a sweet sadness to be here without you, but I swear I can still feel love radiating from the walls," Ginny said softly.

Dare nodded. Then she thrust out her hand. "Show me."

Placing her fingers with the shiny new engagement ring in her sister's hand made bubbles dance in Ginny's belly. "I really had no idea he'd already gotten me a ring."

"You happy?" Dare waved off the question. "What am I saying? Of course, you're happy. You're so perfectly happy you're glowing."

No denying the truth.

Dare pointed at Ginny's other hand. "Now the treasure ring." Ginny switched hands, and Dare let out a hum of happiness. "It's beautiful. Eight stones and all."

Ginny tilted her hand as the sunlight caught the stones, sparkles flashing bright. "I really love it, but it's not just the ring. It's how every time I see it, I'm reminded of everything connected to it. The puzzle, and Mom's planning, and her journal, and the one she made me." She lifted her gaze to Dare's. "Reading Mom's thoughts has reminded me over and over how lucky I really have been. I had good roots. I've been surrounded by people who truly love me. I have a forever friend and sister in you—that makes me so happy."

Dare wrapped her arms around Ginny's neck and squeezed tight. "I love you, too. I love that you're my sister."

The sweet joy of hearing that was a rush like the river in the spring.

A mischievous expression slid onto Dare's face. "You have one hell of a sexy man at your side. Add that to your list."

That was a funny part of the past six months. "I actually *have* lists these days. I guess Tucker's been wearing off on me."

"Ha, try again. You've *always* had a list when it came to that man," Dare said. "And he's always thrown his lists to the wind to make you happy. It's part of what makes you perfect for each other."

Another sweet thought.

"Even after all the frustrations involved in solving the puzzle, I don't wish any of it away," Ginny confessed. "In fact, I'm a little sad I don't have more boxes to open. More things from Mom and Dad. They really did give us good roots."

"They did, and I'm grateful too, but mostly, thank *God*." Dare let her head fall back and let out a groan that hung on the air. "I thought you'd never say it."

What was going on? Ginny mentally repeated her words, but had no idea what Dare was talking about. "What did I say?"

"Jesse." Dare leaned forward and shouted at her husband. "A miracle just happened. Get it out of the truck and bring it here. Please?"

Jesse hooted, then motioned to Tucker. "Come on. It'll be your responsibility to haul around from here on, so you may as well get in training."

Tucker glanced at Ginny, but all she could offer was a shrug. "No idea, but if he shoves you in the back and drives off, I promise I'll find you before he can hotwire a tractor to dig a hole and bury you."

"So bloodthirsty, that one," Jesse said with a wink at Ginny. "Nah, I'm not getting rid of the body. He seems well behaved. So far."

"Relatively," Tucker said.

Jesse was still laughing when he marched up and deposited a banker's box at Ginny's feet. "Right here, Tucker."

A second box landed on top of the first. "You pawning off financial records, Dare?" Tucker asked.

Dare cleared her throat and looked Ginny in the eye. "When I moved to Rocky, I cleaned out this cottage. Everything, including stuff my mom had tucked in the tiny attic area. These two boxes were up there."

Ginny eyed them, but still had no clue what was going on. "And you brought them back because...?"

"She brought them back because I said it was okay to cheat a little," Jesse said quietly. "If she had to."

"Didn't come down to that." Dare grinned widely. "There's a tag on the side that says *Do not open. Give to Ginny or Deb when they ask for them.* Until now, you didn't ask. When your mysterious present showed up at Christmas, I wondered if the two things were connected. Which is why I kept pestering you to solve the puzzle page."

Tucker settled beside her, and Ginny felt another pulse of excitement. "Do you think?"

"That this is your missing *number three* gift?" Tucker shrugged. "Only one way to find out."

The edge of the cardboard box was taped down. She broke the seal and lifted the lid.

A dozen red journals were lined up neatly inside. "Oh my God."

Dare peeked in and gasped. "More journals?"

"Wow." Tucker laid a hand on Ginny's thigh and held on. Centering her. Keeping her grounded while her heart took flight.

A quick check confirmed it—both boxes held journals. Ginny lifted a book from the pile and opened it at random. Her mother's familiar handwriting once again covered the page with stories, and memories, and tales of love.

She stared at the ordinary bit of magic in her hands before turning to her sister. "It's a treasure I never knew I needed. Thank you for guarding it for me all these years."

"I love you, Truth," Dare said softly.

"I love you, Dare," Ginny said back before lifting her gaze to Tucker's.

She couldn't say another word, not even to tell him how much she loved him. How grateful she was that he was there, and that he'd promised to always be there. Her throat closed up with too much joy and sadness and full-on contentment.

It seemed she didn't need words.

"I know, goddess," Tucker said with a wink. "I know."

Three months later.

THE WOODEN STAIRS CREAKED A WARNING, and Tucker gave up on the idea of surprising her. He paced slowly to the small area still tucked to the side of the loft and discovered Ginny right where he expected her, doing what he expected.

She glanced up from the journal she'd been reading, wiping uselessly at the tears on her cheeks. "Hey, you."

"Hey." He noticed the tears, but also the sweet smile. He noticed everything about this woman who was his heart and soul. He settled beside her and leaned in for a quick kiss. "You okay?"

"Yup." She glanced at the Operation *Prove It* headquarters. "I guess I need to accept this will vanish soon."

"I don't know. I think I have some pull with the powers that be. It's important to have spots for...cats...to play."

A laugh escaped her then, dancing away the sadness. "That's good."

"Face it. Hay lofts are multi-purpose at the best of times. The Stone family takes that to the extreme."

Ginny nodded. "Secret forts when we were little.

Operation *Prove It* headquarters this past year. Mysterious birthday treasure hideaways. It's a bittersweet thought that so many years ago, my Mom crawled up here and hid my gift, all the while thinking about our family. She probably laughed over the tangled confusion she was about to cause, but I know she planned on clapping extra hard when the mystery was finally unraveled."

"She would be proud that you solved it."

"We solved it together." She linked her fingers with his. "I love you."

Getting to say it back was everything. "I love you, too."

He leaned in, intending on offering a kiss, but she leaned away and held up the book in her other hand. "I've been reading the most fascinating entry in Mom's journal. This one, you need to hear."

Kisses temporarily put on hold—very temporary if he had any say in it—Tucker stretched back and pulled Ginny's feet into his lap as he offered his full attention. "Go for it."

She cleared her throat, glanced up at him with a shine in her eyes, then read out loud.

Walter gave me a family ring for Christmas. I didn't say anything in front of the kids because thankfully none of them noticed, but I had to tease him.

The ring has eight stones, not seven.

I asked if he had someone on the side I didn't know about, and for a minute or two, he clearly had no idea what I was talking about. The man is adorable when he's flustered.

Then he told me he'd screwed up, but in the end decided it wasn't really a mistake. See, he'd made a list of the kids and all our birthdays then sent it to the store. All our kids—as in he'd automatically included Tucker's name and birthday.

We both sat there for a moment after he told me that, and I realized he was right. The boy might not be my flesh and blood, but he's mine as much as if I birthed him. I'm proud to have Tucker as part of this family, and I hope in the future, we can find a way to make it not just a summertime thing, but an all-the-time thing.

He deserves a big happy family around him, and he's already part of Silver Stone. When it's appropriate, we'll make sure it happens.

The longer Ginny read, the more Tucker's throat closed as emotion swamped in. Having Deb and Walter's approval and love stated so clearly meant...

Meant *everything*.

He took a deep breath and focused to control himself.

Ginny rearranged herself, wrapping her arms around him and holding him tight. Her cheek pressed to his, their torsos meshed. Not sexual, but intimate and connected. One soul, one heart.

He held her and let the tears come. Just now. Just once.

In the end, they both needed tissues to clean up and be ready for the next thing.

"You happy?" she asked, climbing back into his lap.

"Very," he confessed.

"Good." Mischief danced into her eyes. "Tucker? I want you. Today, tomorrow. Forever. I love you so much."

Then she kissed him until he couldn't think straight. Ginny, generous and warm, teasing until there was nothing to do and nowhere to go but right here and now. Slipping together intimately in another way. Bodies heating, kisses and panting breaths until she covered her mouth with her hand and her face twisted with pleasure. Coming hard around him. Taking him over the edge.

Together. Always.

Forever.

EPILOGUE

June, two years later, Silver Stone ranch

Contented as only a man can be with a fishing rod in his hand and an afternoon off from work stretching before him, Dustin Stone laid back on the shore and covered his face with his cowboy hat.

Sunshine had warmed the grass, and the scent of early summer filled his senses. Peacefulness wrapped him up in an embrace as he half-dozed, half-daydreamed, the sound of songbirds filling his ears.

The peace was interrupted by an incoming message from his best friend, Shim. Another ping sounded, and Dustin lazily pulled the phone from his pocket.

Shim: *you never told me. Holy crap, seriously?*
Shim: *in case you need it. Here:* [link]

Dustin stared at the message, confused. He clicked through the link Shim had included, only to end up on one of those scroll-through-the-bullshit clickbait articles. The title alone made him blink.

Ten billionaire cowboy bachelors you need to meet!

His phone pinged, and again. This time one was the tone he'd assigned a different friend as well as a third message from Shim. Dustin ignored them both and kept reading, not sure what the hell kind of joke Shim was playing.

The fourth clicked-through page made the hair on the back of Dustin's neck stand up.

There were pictures of him. One at a horse auction with Luke and Kelli, and one of him by himself, looking all serious. That someone had decided to plaster these shots all over social media? Dustin rolled his eyes. Stupid what people wanted to waste their time on.

His gaze leapt to the words of the article, wondering how much worse it could get.

Plenty.

Set your sights on this #SilverStoneStud

He might be young, but as part of the newly minted Silver Stone success story, twenty-four-year-old Dustin Stone is one very eligible bachelor. The ranch seems to have found the pot of gold at the end of the rainbow after a tragic beginning. This second-generation family operation is gaining ground in a huge way in the horse breeding community. Plus—we've heard there's now oil rights added to the story, and well, there's only one unmarried Stone who still needs to find his perfect match. You can all see that in the physical area, he's got what it takes to make anyone sit up and take notice.

Who's going to be the lucky woman to strike Silver?

Dustin flopped back on the ground, hands flung to the sides as he stared into the sky and groaned. His friends and brothers were never going to let him hear the end of this.

New York Times Bestselling Author Vivian Arend invites you to Heart Falls. These contemporary ranchers live in a tiny town in central Alberta, tucked into the rolling foothills. Enjoy the ride as they each find their happily-ever-afters.

The Stones of Heart Falls
A Rancher's Heart
A Rancher's Song
A Rancher's Bride
A Rancher's Love
A Rancher's Vow

Holidays in Heart Falls
A Firefighter's Christmas Gift
A Soldier's Christmas Wish
A Hero's Christmas Hope
A Cowboy's Christmas List
A Rancher's Christmas Kiss

The Coleman's of Heart Falls
The Cowgirl's Forever Love
The Cowgirl's Secret Love
The Cowgirl's Chosen Love

ABOUT THE AUTHOR

New York Times and *USA Today* bestselling author Vivian Arend loves to share the products of her over-active imagination with her readers. She writes contemporary, western, and light-hearted paranormal romances. The stories are humorous yet emotional, usually with a large cast of family or friends, and a guaranteed happily-ever-after. Vivian lives in British Columbia, Canada, with her husband of many years— her inspiration for every hero and a willing companion for all sorts of adventures.

www.vivianarend.com